"How do you do?"

Lila Rose's voice sounded a little shaky.

Had Drew made a mistake to bring her down to meet the cowhands?

"Howdy, Miss Lila Rose." The men all spoke at the same time, jostling each other and reaching out dust-covered hands.

"Um..." Lila Rose stepped back.

"Now, boys, you know better than that." A protective feeling welled up inside him. "Maybe you can shake hands later after you clean up." He set down the hamper. "Now, y'all go ahead and eat." He offered her his arm again. "Miss Lila Rose, may I escort you back to the house?"

She blinked her eyes in surprise. "Why...why, yes, thank you."

This time she gripped his arm like a lifeline. Even gave him a little smile.

Warmth flooded his chest. He needed to keep a barrier between them, but somehow he couldn't hold back those nice feelings any more than he could hold back the flooding of the Rio Grande.

Only a simpleminded cowboy let himself fall for a city gal...because it would only lead to a broken heart.

Florida author **Louise M. Gouge** writes historical fiction for Harlequin's Love Inspired Historical line. She received the prestigious Inspirational Readers' Choice Award in 2005 and placed in 2011 and 2015; she also placed in the Laurel Wreath contest in 2012. In addition to writing, she enjoys copyediting for her fellow authors of Christian historical romance novels. Please visit her at louisemgougeauthor.blogspot.com, www.Facebook.com/louisemgougeauthor and www.bookbub.com/profile/louise-m-gouge.

Books by Louise M. Gouge

Love Inspired Historical

Finding Her Frontier Family
Finding Her Frontier Home

Four Stones Ranch

Cowboy to the Rescue
Cowboy Seeks a Bride
Cowgirl for Keeps
Cowgirl Under the Mistletoe
Cowboy Homecoming
Cowboy Lawman's Christmas Reunion

Visit the Author Profile page
at LoveInspired.com for more titles.

Finding Her Frontier Home

LOUISE M. GOUGE

LOVE INSPIRED
INSPIRATIONAL ROMANCE

LOVE INSPIRED®
INSPIRATIONAL ROMANCE

Recycling programs
for this product may
not exist in your area.

ISBN-13: 978-1-335-49849-6

Finding Her Frontier Home

Love Inspired
22 Adelaide St. West, 41st Floor
Toronto, Ontario M5H 4E3, Canada
www.LoveInspired.com

Printed in U.S.A.

Whoso findeth a wife findeth a good thing,
and obtaineth favour of the Lord.
—*Proverbs* 18:22

This book is dedicated to my beloved husband, David, my one and only love, who encouraged me to write the stories of my heart and continued to encourage me throughout my writing career. David, I will always love you and miss you.

Thanks also to my granddaughter, Savannah Reese, a champion horsemanship and ranch rider, who read my manuscript to be sure I got all my horse information right.

Special thanks go to my wonderful agent, Tamela Hancock Murray, and my fabulous editor, Shana Asaro. Thank you both for all you do.

Chapter One

Charleston, South Carolina
April 1888

"I am sorry, sir." Her pretty face marred by a condescending sneer, the young gal seemed determined to shut the front door on Drew. "As I've already told you, Mrs. Mattson is not receiving visitors."

His stomach chose that moment to growl. He should have eaten at the train station, but his eagerness to accomplish his mission won out over his hunger.

To her credit, the gal's expression softened. "If you're hungry, you can go to the back door, and our housekeeper will give you a sandwich." Again, she tried to shut the door.

Angry at himself *and* this obstinate woman, Drew slammed his hand against the wooden edge of the portal. Blue eyes widened with alarm, she jumped back, sending regret spiraling through him. As usual, his temper had got the best of him. Most times he managed to hide it from others, but today the stakes were too high for him to surrender so easily to a stubborn female.

"Do you mind?" Her alarmed expression dissolved into a glare as she tried again to shut him out. As if this little slip of a gal had any chance of that.

He held fast to the edge of the door but wouldn't force his way in. Better to tell her what was what.

"Ma'am… Miss… I'm Andrew Mattson. Don't you think Mrs. Mattson would like to see one of her sons for the first time in close to nine years?"

Her jaw dropped, and she seemed unable to move or comprehend his words.

"Lila Rose, who is it?" Mother's soft but unmistakable voice came from beyond the wall to the left of the foyer. She sounded older, of course, and tired.

Drew's pulse kicked up as he anticipated a reunion with his parent. Maybe he should just charge right past this vexing woman.

"Please," she whispered, suddenly agreeable. And a whole lot prettier. "You must let me prepare her."

"Uh, well…" He'd only been thinking about his own feelings. No doubt his unexpected appearance would shock Mother. "Sure. Go ahead." He still held onto the door.

The blond-headed gal beckoned him inside. "Wait here."

As she disappeared into the hallway on the left, Drew stepped over the threshold and set his suitcase down, then removed his wide-brimmed hat and hung it on the oak hall tree. Soon her soft, cheerful voice reached him, but he couldn't make out the words.

Subduing his anxiety, he gazed around the foyer.

It was smaller than he remembered. But then, the last time he'd been here over ten years ago, he'd been four-teen and more than a few inches shy of his full-grown height. As he recalled, down the long hallway in front of him were the doorways to the formal dining room and kitchen. The curved staircase to his right led up to the bedroom where he'd been born, and to three more bedrooms, where he and his four brothers had spent their early years. Set in a genteel neighborhood, this two-story house had been home for the Mattson family long before the war, and through hard work, Pop had managed to hold on to it after the Confederacy's defeat. When the family moved to New Mexico Territory, Mother wouldn't let him sell it. Maybe she'd always known she'd come back.

A twinge of homesickness swept through him, but he didn't give it place. For him, *home* now meant the wide-open spaces of the West, the Double Bar M Cattle Ranch, three married brothers and their growing families, another brother who was unmarried, and, of course, Pop.

Pop, whose approval Drew had never been able to earn, no matter how hard he tried. The middle son in a family of five boys, Drew did keep on trying, and would at least this one final time. Maybe it was a harebrained idea to return to Charleston to talk Mother into going back with him. If this didn't work, if Pop didn't finally notice all his efforts for the family—well, Drew would pack up and move to Colorado. Or someplace.

Depression began to creep into his mind. He shook it off. Now was not the time for self-doubts. Instead, he must think about his strategy for persuading Mother that life would be different from how it had been in 1880, when she'd despised the hardships of the frontier life enough to leave them.

"Mr. Mattson."

Deep in his thoughts, Drew started at the girl's sudden appearance. With her expression now welcoming, she was downright attractive. Her pert little nose had a cute upturn at its tip, and her smooth ivory cheeks displayed a natural pink blush while the pleasant scent of her rose-perfume fragrance swept over him.

"Yes?" To his annoyance, his voice cracked like an adolescent boy's. *No, no, no.* This was not the time for admiring pretty young females.

"Mrs. Mattson—I mean, your mother will see you now." She set a hand on his forearm. "Please, be gentle."

Did he seem rough to her? Probably. He should have dressed up. Should have…but never mind. "Yes, ma'am."

He followed her down the hall to the small parlor, a room he'd never been allowed to enter as a boy. Sometimes he and his brothers would stand in the doorway and wonder what was so special about it. Now he could appreciate that it was a woman's room, all pink curtains and delicate furniture, designed for women's tea parties. Mother sat in her same old pink velvet chair, a replica of which now graced the ranch's drawing room. She looked thinner and younger than he'd expected. He figured she was about fifty, but unlike Pop at sixty-one, no gray shaded her dark brown hair, and her blue eyes exuded the intelligence he remembered.

"Andrew." She stood and walked toward him, reaching out to shake his hand. "How good to see you."

So stiff and formal, while his own knees felt as though they might buckle. He gently squeezed her offered hand, fighting the urge to pull her into his arms.

Instead, he bent to kiss her cheek. "Mother."

"You have met my companion, Miss Duval." She nodded toward the pretty blonde.

"Not really." Drew turned to the younger woman, who hovered protectively beside Mother. "How do you do, Miss Duval."

"Mr. Mattson." She gave him a genuine smile. "Please call me Lila Rose."

A flicker of disapproval crossed Mother's eyes, but she said nothing.

"You can call me Drew." He shuffled his feet like a schoolboy. "That's what everyone calls me."

"Not everyone."

Mother's frosty tone chilled him, bringing back memories of Pop's coldness toward him. Did she hate— *dislike* him, too? Maybe coming here had been a mistake.

"Sit down." Mother waved toward the flowery brocade settee that looked like no one had ever sat on it. "Lila Rose, please have Ingrid bring tea."

"Yes, ma'am." As graceful as a swan, the young woman swept from the room.

Drew forced his focus back to Mother. Time to get on with his plan. "You look well, ma'am. I wish the rest of the family could see you."

"If they want to see me, they can follow your example and come back home."

Drew subdued the anger that was always so close to the surface. He'd expected her response and planned his own. "Ah, well, as you probably remember, ranching is how we earn our living, and it takes all hands all year round. And you may have heard about the blizzards out west this past winter that wiped out many cattle ranches. The Lord sure was looking out for us, because Pop and Rob thinned our herd last fall and sold off most of it before the first snowfall. Rob brought in a new bull and is planning to breed—"

"Do not speak to me of such things! Ladies do not discuss—"

"Here's our tea." Lila Rose led another woman into the room. "Set the tray here, Ingrid." She waved a hand toward the coffee table as she sat on the other end of the settee and went about pouring cups of tea. The plate of cookies beside the teapot made Drew's mouth water.

She prepared a cup and handed it to Mother, then smiled at him. "Cream and sugar?"

Her soft tone said more than her words, and Mother settled down right away. Nice to see this little gal was a peacemaker, just as Drew was trying to be. Maybe she would help him win Mother over. Only now, he knew not to bring up the rougher parts of ranch life.

"Yes, ma'am. Both. Just one lump of sugar."

"How was your trip, Drew? Did you come by train?" Lila Rose laughed as she handed him a delicate china cup and saucer. "How silly of me to ask that. Of course you took the train. You wouldn't ride a horse all the way across the country." She held out the plate of cookies, and he helped himself to two.

He grinned. "No, ma'am. That'd take a mite too long, and I'll be needing to get back soon." He took a bite of one cookie. "Mmm. Tastes good." He proceeded to devour it.

"So, tell us, sir…" Lila Rose glanced at Mother, whose fond gaze toward the gal bespoke maternal affection he couldn't recall ever experiencing. "What brings you here?"

He'd planned to ease into the topic, but now that she'd opened the gate, he might as well go in. "Very simply, I'm hoping Mother will go back with me for a visit." He took a sip of tea. Too used to coffee, he should have asked for more sugar to liven up the weak beverage. "Mother, there's been lots of changes since you were there. The railroad came the very year you left, so now we can get all sorts of modern goods and conveniences shipped in. The ranch is doing real well, as Pop's probably told you in his letters. So we're doing great financially. 'Course, best of all, you have three fine, hardworking daughters-in-law, so you won't have any work to do while you visit other than bask in the high regard all us Mattsons enjoy in the community."

Mother seemed a bit overwhelmed by his rehearsed speech. Maybe it was time to go for her heart. "Ma'am, you must miss Lavinia since she came to live with us last year. That sweet little gal is the darlin' of the ranch. And 'course you know about Robbie. He's not a baby anymore. No, sir. He's growing like a weed and doing his share of the work around the ranch. And now you have two more grandkids to get acquainted with. Maybe Pop wrote to you about Cal and Jared gettin' married and havin' young'uns, Rob gettin' married again. Even Will has a gal—"

"Your father has never written to me. Furthermore,

I have never met my granddaughter." Her last words held a hint of sadness.

Drew swallowed hard to keep from choking on his tea. "What—"

Lila Rose bent forward slightly to catch his eye. "Your mother once asked Maybelle to bring the child for a visit, but she refused." She spoke casually, probably to soothe Mother's obvious pain. "We didn't learn about Maybelle's death until Lavinia's governess had already taken the little girl to New Mexico Territory. We learned about it from Mr. Mattson's lawyer." She gave a little shrug and sighed.

"I'm sorry to hear that. I guess Maybelle had her own heartaches." Drew couldn't help but be peeved by his late sister-in-law's behavior. Like Mother, she'd abandoned her husband—Drew's brother Rob—*and* her young son and had come back to Charleston with their baby girl. But Drew wouldn't speak ill of the dead. "Well, you'll love Lavinia. She's five years old now, and Robbie's ten. And those two babies are growing like weeds. Just wait till you see 'em."

With practiced skill, Lila Rose concealed her alarm over Drew's reason for coming here. As Rebecca's companion these past four years, she had learned about much of the drama and unhappiness in this dear woman's life. She never dreamed one of those "unruly ruffians"—as Rebecca described them—would come to fetch her back to a family from which she had fled almost nine years ago. Nor had Lila Rose ever considered that *unruly ruffians* might be a misnomer. Drew Mattson might look a bit shabby around the edges, but despite his show of temper at the front door, he clearly possessed good manners and a kind heart.

Of course, that didn't mean Lila Rose would permit him to drag Rebecca back to the life she feared and hated. Many Southerners had gone west after the war, and this lady had obediently packed up her five sons, one daughter-in-law and one grandson and followed her husband to New Mexico Territory. It had taken her just over a year to realize she wasn't made for that life. And no wonder. The very idea of forcing this genteel lady to help create a segment of civilization in the midst of a savage wilderness was beyond the thinking of any decent woman. Who could fault Rebecca for returning to the home where her marriage had begun, where her sons had been born?

Lila Rose's late mother had been acquainted with Rebecca as a young woman, so when Rebecca had advertised for a companion, Lila Rose applied. She found in Rebecca a replacement for the mother she missed so terribly. Together they formed their own little family, along with Ingrid and Eric, the couple who took care of their house and grounds.

Lila Rose forced her thoughts away from the past. "We would have been so happy to have Lavinia live with us." She smiled at Rebecca, dismayed to see the tears in the dear woman's eyes. Time to offer words of cheer. "But we have enjoyed sewing for the orphans through our church and seeing their sweet, bright faces in Sunday school."

Drew cleared his throat, clearly as filled with emotion as she was. "You like children, do you, Lila Rose?"

"Yes, indeed." Why did his words stir her feelings

again? Easy answer. Yes, she loved children and longed to have her own. But with Rebecca to care for and no money of her own, she was unlikely ever to marry.

A new sense of alarm struck her. What if Drew persuaded Rebecca to go with him? That would leave Lila Rose alone. Again. She'd felt no grief when her abusive father died, even though it had left Mama and her with very little to live on. But Mama's death had devastated her. She would have to do everything in her power to keep Rebecca in Charleston.

"Well, Andrew," Rebecca said, "I suppose you'll have to stay here tonight. Ingrid." She addressed their housekeeper, who stood just inside the doorway. "Please prepare the east bedroom for our guest." To her son, she said, "How long will you be here?"

He grinned, showing one slight dimple on his left cheek, and Lila Rose's heart skipped. My, what a handsome man he was. Oh, mercy. She must not be attracted to him. Not only did she want no part of a cowboy's life, but the last time she'd cared for a young man, he wouldn't marry her because her father had lost the family horse farm through gambling and drinking. Having believed he loved her, she'd suffered a broken heart. She wouldn't let that happen again, especially not with a man who had a temper.

"As long as it takes me to talk you into going back to New Mexico Territory with me." He quirked an eyebrow in a mischievous way. "As I said, just for a visit, mind you. I'll bring you back whenever you're ready."

Humph. Lila Rose added *manipulative* to her list of qualities in Drew that were becoming reasons not to approve of him.

Rebecca's eyes took on a steely glint. "Explain to me why your father suddenly wants to see me after all these years. And if he's so eager to do so, why did he send you instead of coming himself?"

Indeed. Exactly what Lila Rose was thinking. She looked expectantly at Drew. To her surprise, he stared down at his now-empty teacup and chewed his lip.

"Weelll…" He drew the word out slowly. "He doesn't actually know I'm here. I, uh, wanted to surprise him."

The three of them must have sat in silence for a full minute, with the ticktock of the mantel clock the only sound in the room. Four years with Rebecca had taught Lila Rose when to speak and when to let the lady digest shocking information. For Drew's part, he glanced between his mother and Lila Rose, a pleased grin lighting his entire face, clearly oblivious to the fact that his announcement had stunned them.

At last Rebecca stirred, staring down her nose at her son as she would one of the unruly boys at church. "I am certain Ingrid has your room prepared by now. You should rest from your journey." Her tone made her words a clear command.

Confusion crossed Drew's eyes, and his shoulders dropped. "Yes, ma'am." He rose to leave.

Still uncertain about how to manage this situation, Lila Rose stood as well. "Would you like something more to eat before you go up? I mean, were the cookies enough to hold you until six o'clock, when we have supper?"

"No, thank you, ma'am." He took a step toward the door. "I don't need anything more."

"Shall I show you to your room?"

He gave her a lopsided grin. "No, ma'am. I remember where it is."

She laughed softly. "Yes. Of course."

After he left, Lila Rose turned her attention to Rebecca. Usually when something shocking happened, she needed to calm her employer. Today, however, a strange serenity softened Rebecca's face.

Lila Rose knelt beside her employer's chair and took her hands. "Are you all right?"

Rebecca gazed at her fondly, clearly understanding the depth of her question. "Yes, my dear." A tear still glistened in the corner of her eye. "I should have known Ralph would not have sent Andrew, that his coming was his own idea. Of all my sons, he was always the peacemaker." Her forehead wrinkled briefly. "Perhaps a trip isn't out of the question." She exhaled a long sigh. "I would so love to see my grandchildren."

The yearning in her voice touched a chord deep within Lila Rose. With no family—not so much as an aunt or uncle or even a cousin twice removed—she was alone in the world. If Rebecca went with Drew to join their large and growing family, perhaps even staying in New Mexico Territory, where would that leave Lila Rose?

"But shouldn't they come to see you?" Guilt smote Lila Rose's heart. She should be thinking of Rebecca's best interests, not her own.

"Humph. You're right." Rebecca tapped her chin thoughtfully. "Perhaps I should send an invitation…" She sighed again. "No. Not after all these years."

"Why not? Invite them for a summer holiday. Or Christmas."

"You don't understand." Tears now slid down Rebecca's cheeks. "All these years, although Ralph has never written a word to me, he has been sending money for me to live on. Yet I have never so much as written one thank-you letter."

"Ah. I see." Prepared for a long discussion, Lila Rose moved to a nearby chair. "I thought you inherited from a relative."

Rebecca nodded. "I did. But it isn't enough to support myself indefinitely, much less to pay you and Ingrid and Eric. Without Ralph's money—"

"Yes, well, we're doing fine, don't you think?" Panic crept into Lila Rose's chest. If she could just keep Rebecca thinking of the members of this household as her family, maybe she wouldn't go west with her son. "The trains may make the trip easier than the prairie schooner in which your family made the trip in '78, but once you get there, you'll still be required to ride in buggies over rough roads instead of our smoother streets. I can't imagine you would enjoy that. Nor would it be good for your sciatica. And think of how you would miss your church family, our ladies' reading circle and our dear little orphans who depend upon you to teach their Sunday school class."

Rebecca released a long, weary sigh. "Yes, you're right. The trip would be more than I could manage." She patted Lila Rose's hand. "Thank you, my dear. You always speak such good sense when I must make a difficult decision."

Lila Rose stood and bent to kiss Rebecca's cheek. "I'm just glad to help in any way I can."

But if she truly wanted the best for her employer,

why did she feel such guilt at the thought of keeping this dear lady from her husband and sons—and especially those grandchildren?

Carrying his baggage, Drew trudged up the front staircase, weary from his trip but glad he'd stayed in the hallway before going to his room. He knew it was wrong to eavesdrop, but he couldn't be bothered with manners right now. And a good thing, too. Just as he'd feared, that young female was all sweetness to his face, but behind his back, she was doing all she could to thwart his plans. He might be seeking Pop's approval, but in truth, his parents' reconciliation was a far more important matter, and he mustn't let a deceitful, two-faced gal interfere.

As for Mother, her tears revealed to Drew what he'd always believed: She did have a heart. She did care for her family. And somehow, he must use that love to entice her to come with him before Pop's health got any worse. Surely she would spend the rest of her life burdened with regret if her husband of thirty-one years died before they had a chance to reconcile. He didn't want to use that reason to persuade Mother, though if push came to shove, he'd do it. But should he?

Lord, what do I do now?

Before his prayer was finished, he had a new idea. And he would start tonight at supper.

In the bedroom he'd once shared with Will, he found several boyhood books and toys they'd left behind. How interesting that Mother hadn't disposed of them. This evening he would suggest she give them to the orphans in her Sunday school class.

After unpacking, he lay on the bed for a rest, not intending to sleep. Before he knew it, however, a knock on the door awakened him.

At his invitation, Ingrid brought in a pitcher of hot water, soap and a towel. "Will there be anything else, Mr. Andrew?"

"No, thanks." He glanced at the bedside table. "Say, there's not a speck of dust in here. You sure did get this room fixed up fast."

"Not at all, sir." She smiled. "Miss Rebecca wants me to keep the house in order all the time, just in case..." She stopped and shrugged. "Well, she just does."

Just in case someone came for a visit? Say, maybe family? Drew's heart kicked up a bit. That she would still have hope of reuniting the family after almost nine years was more evidence that she loved them and longed for them to come back here. That wasn't going to happen, but maybe he could convince her that traveling to see them was a worthy substitution.

After washing up and shaving, he donned a clean shirt and the Sunday frock coat he'd decided to bring at the last minute. Mother probably still dressed for supper, as she had when he was a boy—an important memory if he wanted to convince her that civilization had come to New Mexico Territory. In fact, Viola, his newest sister-in-law, came from Virginia society and had taught the whole household, the young ladies of the town and even a few of the cowhands some of the finer points of etiquette.

He glanced at his watch. Not quite five o'clock. He had time to tour the house and grounds before supper, maybe meet the groundskeeper. Drew was glad Mother could afford servants. He'd often wondered how she managed to live on the money Pop sent her every month. He sure didn't keep much for himself. Drew doubted Pop would begrudge her that inheritance, but she sure did live in fine style here. For their first few years in New Mexico Territory, before their cattle business became successful, the Mattson men had scratched out a mighty slim existence. Now they each shared the income from cattle sales and selling their extra hay. Drew had scrimped and saved for five years now, planning this trip at his own expense. He prayed the Lord would bless it, and so far, He had.

He started his tour by going out the front door. Like everything inside, the wide wraparound porch had been swept clean, and the hanging swing outside the parlor window looked freshly painted. Every spring, that had been Drew's job when he was a boy. Who did it now?

Down the front steps and around to the right side of the house, he found the arched white trellis, the gateway to the backyard, in need of repair. He could do that in a few hours, maybe earn some approval from Mother. In the back garden, lilac, rose and gardenia bushes held a profusion of buds ready to bloom in the next few weeks. Mother might balk at leaving her flowers, but he was ready for that, too.

He headed for the back door and barely avoided tripping over Lila Rose, who was kneeling by a bed of blooming daffodils.

"Oh!" She looked up, her pretty blue eyes round with surprise.

Drew swallowed the sudden lump in his throat. "Excuse me, ma'am." He reached out to help her up.

"Thank you." She accepted his hand and stood gracefully. "Mr. Mattson—Drew—what brings you out here?"

"Well…" He chuckled. "We cowboys spend most of our lives outside, don'tcha know?" He gently nudged a rock on the gravel pathway with the toe of his boot.

"Yes, I suppose you do." As though trying to hide a smile, she turned away and studied the flowers in her hands.

The girls at church back home liked it when he acted bashful. Maybe that would charm Lila Rose, too. And maybe he needed to win her over just as much as Mother. That would be far better than defeating her contrary plans.

"Say, do you think you could dig up a few of those bulbs for me to take back with me? I know my sisters-in-law would love to have them."

She blinked those blue eyes at him, and a funny little hitch occurred in his chest. *No, no, no.* Until she agreed to help him talk Mother into going west, she was the adversary he needed to persuade, not an appealing female he should give a different kind of attention. That wouldn't do any good, anyway. She was as prissy as a female could be—hardly the type for a rancher to pursue.

As she looked up at Drew's charming smile, Lila Rose did her best to shake off the odd little tremors near her heart. My, this man's height was impressive. He appeared about six feet tall. But then, only five feet tall herself, she found most men's heights a bit intimidat-

ing. She must not let this cowboy captivate her thoughts
or her emotions.

"Yes, of course. We can wrap the bulbs so they can
safely travel." She brushed past him. "If you'll excuse
me, I must get these flowers in a vase for our supper
table."

"That'll be nice. My sister-in-law Viola likes flowers on the table, too." He followed close on Lila Rose's
heels. "Say, do you suppose rose and lilac stems would
travel well?"

"Yes." She stopped to face him, and he jumped back,
barely avoiding a collision. "The plants will survive the
journey much better than your mother would."

"You think so?" One dark eyebrow arched. "You
keep telling her that, and I'm sure she'll believe it. I, for
one, think she's hardier than you give her credit for."
He grunted. "'Course, it's to your advantage for her to
doubt her own strength."

Heat rushed up Lila Rose's neck, and she had to bite
her lips to keep from lashing out at him. Instead, she
turned back toward the house. Once again, he followed
her. But when she reached the back stoop, she realized
he was no longer in pursuit. A quick glance revealed
he had stopped to speak with Eric.

"Ja, ja." The groundskeeper spoke with his musical
Norwegian accent. "Dey travel good, dem plants. I fix
dem up good for you. Cold und warm weather I know,
und how to make tings grow either way."

Not caring to hear the rest of the conversation, Lila
Rose hurried into the kitchen to find a vase for the daffodils. The aroma of roast beef and onion gravy made

her mouth water. On the counter, a freshly baked chocolate cake sent out its own inviting smell.

"I can see you went all out for our guest, Ingrid." Lila Rose filled Rebecca's favorite crystal vase with water from the tap, then poured in a few inches of white pebbles before finally arranging the daffodils and baby's breath in a nice display.

"Yes, ma'am." Ingrid concentrated on mashing potatoes into a creamy mound. "You think he'll like peas and carrots for the side dishes? That's all I had close to ready."

"Humph. Anyone who shows up unexpectedly and uninvited can eat what they're served." Even as the words came out, Lila Rose felt shame. She knew better than that.

"Yes, ma'am." Ingrid spooned the potatoes into Rebecca's fine-china serving bowl, covered it with a lid and set it near the stove. She walked over to admire the flowers. "Oh, I do love our daffodils." She eyed Lila Rose. "You're worried about Miss Rebecca going with her son, aren't you?"

Lila Rose's eyes stung with sudden tears. "Well, I—"

Ingrid set a hand on Lila Rose's forearm. "We may not have expected Mr. Drew to come visiting his mama, but God knew. Scripture says He knew everything from before the foundation of the world. And if He knew all that, who are we to worry about tomorrow? Trust in Him, *kjære lille jente.*" She chuckled in her deep, throaty way, as she often did after calling Lila Rose *dear little girl.* "I already been thinkin' about what Eric and I will do if she goes out west with her son. Not worryin', mind, but just making plans. We'll be all right, and you will be, too." She moved back to the stove and checked the rolls baking in the oven. That was Ingrid. Always dispensing wisdom and encouraging others in their faith.

Later, as Lila Rose took the seat adjacent to Rebecca's at the formal dining room table, she tried to embrace the truth Ingrid had spoken. Hadn't the Lord provided this job for her when she'd been close to destitution? If Rebecca left, He would provide for her again. But this was more than a job to her. She truly loved Rebecca. She might not be blood family, but the bond they had formed transcended familial ties.

After seating his mother, Drew pulled out the chair across from Lila Rose…and immediately moved the vase of daffodils that stood like a wall between them. Then he winked at her. Not a flirtatious wink but a victorious gesture, as though he'd already won the battle.

The very idea!

"Everything smells mighty fine, Mother. My compliments to the cook."

Looking rested from her afternoon nap, Rebecca gave him a maternal smile. "Thank you, Andrew. Will you say grace, please?"

"Yes, ma'am." As they all bowed their heads, he prayed, "Father, we thank You for this fine meal before us and pray You will use it for the nourishment of our bodies. And may the words of our mouths and meditations of our hearts be acceptable in Your sight. In Jesus's name, amen."

Lila Rose hardly knew what to think. Drew's words sounded so sincere, so truly spiritual. Did she stand a chance against his prayers? What Ingrid had told her came to mind. God knew he would come here, and Lila Rose should trust Him to work things out. Oh, if only she *could* trust Him.

As they passed the serving bowls, she glanced at Rebecca to see if she would begin the dinnertime conversation. The lady was busy ladling gravy onto her potatoes.

"Drew, please start the meat." Lila Rose waved a hand toward the platter of sliced roast beef. "Now, tell me about your family. How interesting that you are one of five brothers." Seeing Drew help himself to a large serving of meat, she had no doubt Rebecca had been overwhelmed by cooking and caring for all of them. "And not one sister to help your mother."

"Yes, ma'am. I'm the middle brother." He chuckled softly. "But that's all different now. When Viola—that's Rob's new wife—when she brought Lavinia out to the ranch, she started whipping us all into shape. She runs that house like a well-oiled machine, and she teaches Robbie and Lavinia all their lessons. Even started a school of etiquette for the local gals. It didn't take Rob long to fall for her."

"Well, what man wouldn't appreciate a woman who works so hard?" Lila Rose did her best not to scoff. She could just imagine a lowly governess eager to snare the widowed oldest son of a wealthy rancher.

Drew frowned. "It's not like that…"

"Tell me, dear." Rebecca sent Lila Rose a warning glance before focusing on her son. "What about Cal and Jared and their families?"

He turned his attention to her. "Aw, Mother, you'll be so surprised. Those young'uns have grown up as tall and strong as the rest of us, and they're hard workers.

'Course, they don't live at the ranch anymore. Like I said earlier, they married sisters and moved over to the Sharp-family sheep ranch. And oh my, those babies are beauties. Strong and healthy like all us Mattsons. Just wait till you see them... That is, if you come out with me."

"So..." Rebecca dabbed her lips with her linen napkin. "That still leaves Viola with tending to the needs of four men and two growing children."

Frowning again, Drew looked at his mother as if searching for something. "As I said, it's not like that. We're all working together to build a life that suits all of us. Viola has two ladies who come in and help as needed. You know—laundry, spring-cleaning and such."

Rebecca sniffed. "That's all well and good if the life you're building is the life each of you wants."

Lila Rose concentrated on eating her supper. Rebecca was handling the situation very well without her help.

"Yes, ma'am." Drew didn't actually back down, but his expression softened. "Viola is always humming or singing around the house, so I think she's pretty happy. She laughs with the young'uns and teaches them games. Robbie spent most of his first nine years with just us menfolk. He was a serious little cowboy and growing up way too soon. Having his sister come to live with us helps him enjoy his childhood a bit more. Not that he doesn't do his share of chores. Milking, gathering eggs, that sort of thing to help Viola." He stopped talking and started eating again. "Mmm-mmm. This sure is tasty."

Lila Rose caught on to his tactic right away. He was painting an appealing picture of the family's ranch life—a picture that left out Rebecca, as though saying she wasn't even missed. But if that were so, why would he have come to fetch her? What was missing in his happy story?

"Drew, how is your father?" Lila Rose knew it wasn't her place to ask, but she doubted Rebecca would.

He blinked. "What do you mean?" He took another bite of meat.

"Is he enjoying the same robust health as all of you Mattson men?" To her shame, she could hear the sarcasm in her own voice.

He didn't answer right away. Instead, he gazed fondly at Rebecca and reached out to take her hand. "Mother, truth be told, Pop's health isn't the best." He cleared his throat as if chasing away some deep emotion. "In fact, Doc Warren has warned him to either slow down or get his affairs in order."

Rebecca gasped, then stared in silence at Drew for a few moments. "I can't imagine that man ever slowing down. He came back from the war wounded but determined to build a new life. And he's done it. But at what cost? His health? His life?" The sorrow in her eyes gave way to determination. "Well, we can't let that happen, can we, Andrew?"

Lila Rose tried to swallow a bite of potatoes, but it sat like a lump in her throat. She was forced to wash it down with coffee. She had no right to stop Rebecca from leaving. Maybe she could offer to stay here and take care of the house or—

"Lila Rose!"

She jumped. "Yes, Rebecca?"

"Didn't you hear me? We must get packed. We're going to New Mexico Territory."

"We?" Lila Rose heard Drew's snicker at her weak response.

"Yes, *we*, my dear. Do you think I could go out to that wild country without you as my companion?"

Stunned—no, *beyond* stunned—Lila Rose couldn't speak. While Rebecca and Drew continued their conversation, seemingly unaware of her, a faint glimmer of hope began to grow in her hollow chest. Yes. Yes, she could go out west. She could be the best companion any lady ever could hope for. And when Rebecca once again tired of the harsh rustic life in New Mexico Territory, Lila Rose would be right there beside her to bring her home safely.

As he prepared for bed, Drew could hardly believe how well the conversation had gone at supper. And he hadn't even needed to bring up Pop's failing health. While Lila Rose's question may have been asked out of curiosity—with a hint of sarcasm thrown in—it had opened the door for him to reveal his actual purpose for coming to fetch Mother without clearly stating it. This way, she wouldn't think he was trying to manipulate her.

And Mother's reaction had been just what he'd hoped for. She was worried about Pop's health enough to make the difficult journey to see him...maybe even restore their marriage, if Drew wasn't inferring too much from her response. *Thank You, Lord.*

The only thing he wasn't thankful for was Mother's insistence that Lila Rose go with them. The little gal herself seemed shocked by the idea. Now, what would he do with a pesky female who would probably complain all the way? Then Mother might change her mind and hurry back to the ease and familiarity of Charleston.

He wished they could leave tomorrow, but women always needed to buy new clothes and pack and finish a whole list of other things before they could get on with the matter at hand. He did understand Mother's desire to say goodbye to her church family. He'd go with them on Sunday and take the toys and books he and his brothers had left behind all those years ago.

Even then, they couldn't leave yet. He'd spoken to Eric about doing some repairs to the house, jobs one man couldn't do alone. The groundskeeper had expressed his gratitude for the help in advance, so Drew needed to keep that promise.

He found it interesting that the kindly Norwegian couple had come south like missionaries after the war to see how they could help folks mend their lives. Now they offered to stay here and manage the house until Mother returned. *If* she returned. But Drew was careful not to say *if* to any of them, or Miss Lila Rose Duval might get her nose out of joint. Cute little nose that it was.

Uh-oh. Better stop that sort of thinking before he cut off his own nose to spite his face.

Chapter Two

"Oh, look, Rebecca." Lila Rose could hardly contain her excitement as their train chugged across the massive bridge spanning the Mississippi River. "You can see so far up and down the river." As much as she'd tried to dissuade Rebecca from making this trip, she'd finally decided to enjoy herself. After all, if not for this trip at Rebecca's expense, she never would have had the opportunity to see such sights. The scenery from Charleston to Missouri had given her an appreciation for the wider United States beyond the far different world of her seaside hometown. "Just look at those trees. Everything's coming alive with spring colors."

In the three weeks since Rebecca had decided to go with Drew, Lila Rose had been happier than she'd been since Mama died. Once they began their travels, she'd kept a journal about these new wonders and experiences so she could recall them in detail later—perhaps even write a travelogue to sell, should she ever need to find independent employment.

"Humph." Rebecca studied her knitting, counting

stitches before adding more. "Just you wait until we get farther west. Nothing but brown and red dirt everywhere. And danger around every turn."

"Mother, things have changed since you first came out here." Drew pulled their bags from the rack above his seat across the aisle, preparing for their imminent arrival in St. Louis. "There's lots of ranches and farms all across Missouri and Kansas—even Texas—and lots of green things growing. Civilization is moving west at a pretty fast pace. Has been since before the war."

"Humph." Rebecca seemed determined not to enjoy their travels. She'd paid for their comfortable seats in the Pullman car, but even that amenity didn't seem to please her.

Lila Rose guessed her employer was bracing herself against disappointment. Perhaps she feared her husband had already died. Lila Rose prayed that wasn't so. When she asked Drew about it, he shrugged it off, but she could see he was worried about the same thing. How she prayed Mr. Mattson would be there to greet them.

The train pulled into the station in St. Louis just after noon, and with their next train not leaving until morning, Rebecca insisted they go shopping.

"Not that I expect anything like our shops at home, but I want to buy some gifts for my grandchildren."

Drew obliged them by hiring a buggy and driving them to the center of town, where they found nicer shops than expected. With his suggestions, Rebecca found appropriate gifts for the four grandchildren and the one he admitted would be born later in the summer to Rob and Viola. To his credit, his face turned red when he mentioned it.

The cowboy was starting to grow on Lila Rose but only as a friend. She knew the two of them would never suit as a couple. Although she came from a once-prosperous Southern family, her subsequent loss of wealth had reduced her status too far for a wealthy rancher's son to choose her as his bride. Not that she wanted him, anyway. While his temper had cooled since that first day—probably because he was getting his way—his life still held no appeal for her. She could enjoy this tour of the Wild West, but she would no doubt grow tired of it and long for a more civilized life back in Charleston.

Why was she even thinking such things? Wasn't she content with her life as Rebecca's companion, no matter where they were? After her fears of her employer leaving her behind had been allayed, she had revised her entire view of the matter. She had embraced the idea of making this trip as enjoyable for Rebecca as possible. In the process, she was enjoying it as well. And that wasn't difficult, because so far, the trip had been more than enjoyable. Drew was right: civilization had moved westward, at least as far as St. Louis.

In addition to gifts for the children, Rebecca bought both herself and Lila Rose new parasols just as stylish as any sold in Charleston. When that hadn't satisfied Rebecca sufficiently, she went on to purchase various presents for each member of the large family they would soon be meeting. Distributing them would be a grand event and would undoubtedly help to improve Mr. Mattson's health.

At least, Lila Rose prayed it would.

As the train sped south along the Santa Fe and San Francisco tracks, Drew stretched his legs out contentedly. The Pullman car sure was more comfortable than the hard benches he'd sat on as he headed east. The onboard Delmonico Restaurant and the stops at Harvey House restaurants served far more satisfying meals than the inexpensive sandwiches he'd quickly purchased at various train stations on the journey here. No wonder Lila Rose had offered to feed him that first day. He must have been a sight to behold—and not a good one. He sure had been tired. Now he just felt excitement. If all went well, they would reach home in about four days, and he could watch his parents reconcile.

Mother seemed to enjoy spending her own money, for which he was grateful. His own stash, which he'd saved over the years while planning this trip, had dwindled to a few dollars, most of which he needed to send a telegram to Will to meet them at the train station in Riverton when the time came. Will had always been good at keeping secrets, so Drew trusted he'd kept with the plan to tell everyone that Drew had gone up into the Sangre de Cristo Mountains to check the pasture and line shack before summer grazing.

The most dangerous part of the trip, however, was yet to come. He'd been careful to avoid any talk of train robbers, but the possibility of being attacked was always there. To be prepared, tomorrow he'd have to strap on his gun, then wear his frock coat all the time, hoping Mother and Lila Rose wouldn't notice he was armed.

Traveling through Indian Territory, Lila Rose enjoyed the passing scenery of the vast grass-covered plains. That is, until she saw a group of men on horseback in the distance, all of them appearing to carry guns. Swallowing her alarm, she said, "Are those Indians?" *And are they about to attack the train?*

Rebecca glanced up from her knitting. "Yes, dear. Don't be alarmed. It's a hunting party."

"Oh." Lila Rose shot a look at Drew, who now sat on the seat across from them. The newspaper he was reading didn't quite hide his grin. Was he smiling because his mother had shown no alarm or because Lila Rose had? "I'm glad to know that."

"When we came across these prairies in '78—" still no alarm colored Rebecca's tone "—our wagon train was protected by hired guards. We still had encounters that were less than pleasant."

Lila Rose's already-high esteem for her employer rose significantly. After enduring all those frights and deprivations, no wonder she had fled back to her comfortable life in Charleston.

At last the train crossed the border between Texas and New Mexico Territory. As Rebecca had said, the colors of the scenery included very little green. The soil was red—much like the red clay of the Piedmont region of South Carolina, where Lila Rose had been born and raised—but lacking the abundance of thick forests and rushing rivers and streams.

Like the Indians she had seen the day before, five men appeared on horseback, all wearing handguns strapped to their sides, and fell in beside the train at a full gallop.

"Look, Rebecca." Lila Rose waved a hand toward the cowboys. "Maybe it's a welcoming party."

"Uh...no."

Drew spoke just as two of the riders swung dangerously from their horses and jumped onto the stairs at the front of the car and disappeared. In seconds, they opened the door and entered the car, brandishing their pistols.

"Nobody move," the first man growled, pointing his gun at the well-dressed gentleman across the aisle.

Rebecca looked up, alarmed at last. Lila Rose felt a scream rising in her own throat but managed to stifle it. A woman several rows back had no such compunctions and shrieked in a high voice that would make a professional soprano proud.

"Shut up." The outlaw—for that was surely what these men were—fired his gun over the woman's head. She fell over in a dead faint. "Now, all of you better co-operate, or the next time, I won't miss."

Numbness overtook Lila Rose. What would happen now?

Terrified for the ladies he'd brought to this danger-ous place, Drew threw himself over Mother and pulled Lila Rose close to his side. "Don't move," he whispered.

"Stop it." Mother shoved him away. "They wouldn't dare rob a lady."

Before the words left her mouth, the first outlaw shoved Drew farther to the side.

"Put your valuables in the bag." He pointed to the brown leather satchel his cohort was holding, put his gun to Drew's head and glared at Mother. "That brooch will do just fine." He reached across Drew for the ruby pin she wore at her neck.

"How dare you?" Eyes blazing, she stabbed her knit-ting needle deep into his hand.

"Ow!" He jumped back with a yelp and a curse, dropped his gun in the aisle and clutched his wound.

The businessman in the opposite seat grabbed the gun, pushing his half-retrieved wallet back into his jacket at the same time. Lifting the weapon, he fired at the man with the bleeding hand. The outlaw went down, clutching his side, and his companion aimed his gun at the businessman.

Drew whipped out his Colt. "Don't try it." He swallowed hard, unwilling to kill the man even though the outlaw would have killed them all without a smidgeon of regret.

With two men aiming firearms at him, the outlaw dropped the satchel and fled out the door. The wounded man rolled on the floor and groaned.

"Anybody hurt in here?" The uniformed conductor hurried into the car carrying a Winchester Model 1873.

"The lady back there might need some help," Drew said.

"I'll go." Lila Rose made her way back toward the woman. Drew's admiration for her kicked up a notch.

The conductor eyed the outlaw and growled, "Get on your feet."

"I can't," the man whined pitifully. "I'm shot."

"Oh yes, you can." The businessman who'd shot him grasped his shirt and pulled him to his feet, then shoved him toward the conductor. "Here's his gun." He handed the weapon to the railroad employee.

"Many thanks." The conductor took it and shoved it in his belt. "You folks did a good job back here. The other three scalawags made a fatal mistake trying to rob the mail car. We never travel without armed guards."

Mother harrumphed. "If this one had bled on my granddaughter's blanket—" She wiped the bloodstained needle with one of her dainty handkerchiefs. "Well, I don't believe in making threats, but he would certainly have been sorry."

The car erupted into laughter.

Drew gazed at her with amazement…and pride. After all these years, she would do fine at the ranch.

Then he glanced at Lila Rose, who was comforting the weeping woman in the back of the car. Another kick of admiration hit his chest. Yep, she'd do fine at the ranch, too.

"I certainly hope we don't encounter any further difficulties," Mother said as she packed away her knitting in preparation for their imminent arrival in Riverton.

This was the first time she'd mentioned yesterday's attempted robbery. Drew wanted to reassure her but knew better than to make promises he couldn't keep.

"Me too." Maybe he should redirect the conversation. "I sure hope Will got my telegram and can get to the train station before our arrival so we can be on our way to the ranch immediately. I'm sure you're eager to see…everyone." Especially Pop? He could only hope.

Mother released a long, deep sigh. "Yes. Well. That's why I came. I just hope no one is too shocked to see me." She scolded him with a look. "You really should have told your father what you were up to. Let's pray the shock doesn't kill him."

He grimaced. That thought had never occurred to him. "Yes, ma'am."

"Oh, my. How gloomy we are." Lila Rose tucked her

journal into her bag. "Won't it be nice to be out walking around instead of rumbling down these railroad tracks day and night?" She added her musical laugh, which never failed to cheer both Mother and Drew.

But this time, Mother just sighed again.

"Married!" Drew could hardly believe his ears…or his eyes as he gaped at the wedding band on Suzette's left hand.

"Yep." Will grinned broadly, clearly proud of himself. "Hello, Mother." He approached her carefully and set a quick peck on her cheek. "Welcome to New Mexico Territory—or should I say, welcome back?"

"Thank you, William." Tears rimmed Mother's eyes. "My, how you've grown, both you and Andrew. Suzette, I'm so pleased to meet you."

"Thank you, Mama. Is it all right if I call you *Mama*? I was so excited when Will told me you'd be coming." Suzette hugged Mother, and surprisingly, Mother let her.

In fact, she gripped Suzette's hands as though to keep her close. "You may call me Mother, as my sons do." Her tone was pleasant but brooked no contradiction.

"Oh. Sure. Glad to." Suzette shrugged, clearly not bothered by the correction. "I'm sorry you missed our wedding, but with my pa selling the mercantile so he could go out to San Francisco, we decided to go ahead. And we had another reason…"

"Your pa's sold the mercantile?" Drew looked between his brother and new sister-in-law. "But I though you two were going to run it."

The newlyweds shared a mischievous look.

"Change of plans." Will gave a sheepish shrug.

"After Suzette was—" He glanced at Mother. "I mean, we just want the whole family living together at the ranch. We moved into the little house Viola uses for her school. With her and Rob's family growing, she may have to stop teaching."

Suzette nudged him. "Aw, come on, sweetie. We can tell them the other reason." She laughed. "They'll find out sooner or later."

"Find out what?" Mother still held one of Suzette's hands, which was an odd gesture on her part.

Will shuffled his feet. "Suzette was kidnapped by those outlaws who robbed the store last fall."

Mother and Lila Rose gasped.

Drew took a slower, deep breath. "Go on."

"They were mad," Will said, "'cause she saw that one fella's face, and they were scared she'd identify them. Turns out their hideout's in a canyon near town and... Well, you can figure out the rest."

"No, I cannot." Mother touched Suzette's cheek, already the caring mother-in-law. Drew's heart skipped a beat. "You must have been so frightened."

"No, ma'am." Suzette wrinkled her nose. "Mostly mad at myself for not having my gun handy that afternoon. Anyway, Will and Rob and some of the ranch hands, even Señor Martinez and his vaqueros, came after me and made short work of those varmints." She laughed again, as though the whole thing had been an adventure. "But enough of that. Let's get you home." She waved a hand toward the surrey awaiting them near the train depot.

"Hang on a minute." Drew beckoned to Lila Rose, who had hung back for the family reunion. "This pretty little gal is Mother's companion and good friend." He was shocked by his own words. Should he have called her *pretty*? The blush on her cheeks and shy smile on her lips hinted that she didn't mind. "Lila Rose Duval, meet my brother Will and his new wife, Suzette."

"How do you do?" She reached out to Will and shook his hand, then repeated the gesture with Suzette.

"Howdy, Lila Rose," Suzette said. "What a pretty name for a pretty lady. Welcome to New Mexico Territory."

"Thank you." She backed away and looked to Mother as though awaiting instructions.

Drew didn't like seeing her act like a servant. She was a guest. His guest.

"Lila Rose is enjoying her tour of the Wild West." He winked at her. "We're so glad she was free to come along with Mother."

She blinked those pretty blue eyes. Then understanding filled her expression, and she smiled at him…a smile he felt clear down to his toes.

No, no, no. He would not feel anything for her other than friendship. She was a Southern lady and a city gal who would never want to live on a ranch. Falling for her would be a serious mistake, one he couldn't afford to make.

Besides, he had a more important matter to concentrate on—the upcoming reunion between Mother and Pop. He would know within two hours whether this whole years-in-planning trip was a success…or the worst mistake he'd made in his twenty-four years.

The surrey made its way along the road beside the fast-flowing Rio Grande with fewer bumpy spots than

Lila Rose had expected. Seated with Rebecca and Suzette behind Drew and his brother, she breathed in the clean, clear air and permitted herself to enjoy the scenery. Distant mountains still sported white peaks, flocks of geese flew overhead on their way north and cattle grazed in distant fields. A few yellow wildflowers bloomed along the way, adding a surprising splash of color to the redundant reddish-brown landscape. Even the adobe houses they passed were the same reddish-brown, although most had colorful gardens outside their front doors.

She saw children playing in the yards, not minding the dirt. No mother or governess in Charleston would permit their charges to revel in such scruffiness, yet these children clearly enjoyed their playtime.

All the way from Charleston, Lila Rose had schooled herself to accept a servant's position among the Mattson clan. But Drew had quickly dispelled that mindset by suggesting she was a lady on a holiday of her own choosing, not a paid companion. At every turn, he surprised her—from his manners toward her and his mother, to his courage when facing the outlaws, to the very way he carried himself with strength and an air of authority…a man who seemed to know his own worth. She supposed that came from being the favored son of a successful rancher.

They traveled from the train depot through the small town of Riverton, then on toward the Mattson ranch, the brothers chatting easily as they caught up on ranch business. Suzette spoke with Rebecca, telling her more about her abduction and assuring her mother-in-law she'd escaped unscathed.

Rebecca shared a troubled look with Lila Rose. "Let us pray that's the last encounter we have with outlaws. Mercy, such a fright." She patted Suzette's hand. "And you were so brave."

While the story had also alarmed Lila Rose, she'd managed not to show it. The assurances Drew had given them in Charleston that this territory was safe for decent people to travel was turning out not to be accurate. First, their lives had been threatened by the would-be train robbers. Now this brave young woman had actually been abducted by outlaws. Yet she recounted the horrifying incident with lighthearted humor. It seemed to her these people were ignoring the life-threatening dangers that surrounded them.

Whatever the situation, one thing was clear to Lila Rose: Drew might be handsome, mannerly and brave, but she had no intention of falling for a man who failed to see danger for what it was. No, she and Rebecca certainly did not belong here, and Lila Rose looked forward to their return to civilization.

"What do you think, Mother?" Drew glanced over his shoulder to see her reaction to the ranch's entrance. He'd always thought the iron Double Bar M sign perched over the archway gave the ranch an air of respectability and prosperity—but would she be impressed?

"Hmm." Not so much as a flicker of an eyebrow changed her blank expression. In fact, the closer they got to the ranch, the more she seemed to withdraw into herself. Not a good sign for a reconciliation. He reminded himself she'd come for the grandchildren. Still, he couldn't help but hope and pray she and Pop would reconcile.

"It's quite impressive." Lila Rose offered him a benign smile, maybe trying to make up for Mother's indifference. "Oh, my. Look at the house, Rebecca." She nodded toward the two-story white clapboard structure set on a rocky bluff above the river. Pop had built the antebellum mansion especially for Mother. "How beautiful. Was it complete before you left?"

Now Mother's eyes did flicker. "Not entirely."

Drew glanced at Will, who shrugged and mouthed the words, *What did you expect?* His brother had warned him this scheme might not work, but he'd had to try.

Will drove the surrey into the circular front drive and up to the house, and Drew jumped down. "Let me go in first."

Despite the local custom of folks using the back entrance, he entered through the front door. In the drawing room, he found Viola working at her sewing machine. He gave her a peck on the cheek. "Howdy, sis. You sure do look pretty, as usual."

"Now, Drew." She laughed in her older-sister way. "How's everything up at summer pasture?" She studied him up and down and brushed lint from the sleeve of his frock coat. "You don't look like you've been traveling in the mountains."

"Well, it's a long story. I'll tell everybody at supper."

Mother chose that moment to enter the house, her mood still guarded, as though not sure if she'd be welcomed. The others entered close behind.

Drew gently ushered Mother over to his sister-in-law. "Mother, this is Rob's wife, Viola. Viola, this is my—*our* mother."

"Mrs. Mattson, what a lovely surprise." Viola's voice caught, and her eyes welled up with tears as she stood and kissed Mother's cheek. As with Suzette, Mother permitted the familiar gesture and returned a smile. "I know Robert and the children will be so glad to see you."

After introducing Lila Rose, Drew glanced toward the interior door. "Is Pop in his office?" A harsh cough came from that direction. "Guess that answers that." He grasped Mother's hand. "Ready?"

She tugged away from him. "I'm ready to get acquainted with another of my daughters-in-law."

"Please sit down. I'll bring coffee." Viola left the room, and Mother settled into the pink velvet rocking chair as if she'd never left.

"Go on, then." Looking at Drew, she waved a hand toward the hallway.

Heart in his throat, Drew had no choice but to go it alone. Otherwise, Pop would emerge from his office to find out what all the noise was about, and Drew would lose any semblance of control over the situation. But now he had to face Pop and explain why he'd been gone for nearly five weeks without even saying goodbye.

The office door was open, but Drew still knocked. "Hey, Pop. I'm back."

He barely glanced up from his ledger. "You were gone?"

Drew slumped and turned away without another word. If he thought Pop was joshing, he would have laughed. But he had no doubt whatsoever his father hadn't even missed him. Hadn't even asked Will or Rob where he was.

The full weight of his terrible mistake in bringing Mother here hit him in the chest like the kick of an angry mule.

Chapter Three

Lila Rose sat on the brocade settee, enjoying the fresh coffee and shortbread Viola had served. She tried to stifle the dull, irrational ache in her heart as she watched her employer bond so quickly with her two daughters-in-law. In fact, Lila Rose found them both charming in their vastly different ways, one with the manners of a society lady and the other…well, a cowgirl—sweet but undeniably rough around the edges. To her credit, Rebecca showed no partiality toward either of them.

Perhaps now was the time for Lila Rose to admit to herself once and for all how precarious her own situation was. What if Rebecca decided to stay here? She certainly had that right. But Lila Rose would never agree this place would be good for the older lady's health and well-being. Hadn't that been well proven almost nine years ago? And again only yesterday, with the attempted train robbery?

Drew returned from the other room, his posture drooping and depression written across his handsome face.

Where had the brave, self-assured cowboy gone? Lila Rose shook off her own concerns and focused on him.

"Mother, I…"

Rebecca stood and approached him. "What is it?" She sent a cross look toward the door. "What's he done now?"

"He ignored me. Wouldn't even let me tell him you're here."

"Oh, man." William jammed his hands into his pockets and shook his head. "I was afraid of this."

Viola and Suzette traded a worried glance.

Drew looked so defeated that Lila Rose's heart ached with sympathy. Whatever Mr. Mattson had said to his kind, thoughtful son, shame on him. She didn't often dislike people, but she could generate no good feelings toward this man she had yet to meet.

"What's going on out here?" A graying, older version of Drew and Will stalked into the room. "What's all this noise? What—" His jaw dropped. "Rebecca!" He glared at Drew. "Is this your doing?"

Instead of wilting, as Drew was doing, Rebecca marched over to her husband. "Hello to you, too, Ralph." Her face like flint, she grabbed his arm and tried to shove him back toward the doorway. "We're going to have a talk."

"No, we're not. You can just get back on your high horse and ride out of here."

Drew stepped closer to his parents. "Pop, won't you just listen—"

"You stay out of this." Rebecca shook a finger at him. To her husband, she said, "March. Now."

This time, Mr. Mattson obeyed, although his eyes

blazed, and his jaw jutted out in a defiant expression. A door slammed, and soon muted angry voices emanated from the back room while silence reigned in the parlor.

At last, Will clapped Drew on the shoulder. "Never mind, brother. You had to try."

"Oh, yes." Suzette squeezed Drew's hand. "You were very brave to—"

"Now, now." Viola set her coffee cup down with a clink. "I'm sure once Pop and Mrs. Mattson... *Mother...* have had a chance to sort matters out..." She trailed off, seeming unconvinced by her own hopeful words. Turning to Lila Rose, she said, "I'm so glad you came with Mother." She tapped her chin thoughtfully. "Hmm. We have five bedrooms. With Will and Suzette now living in the little house, I'll put Drew with Robbie, and you with Lavinia for the night. That way, Mother can have a room to herself." She did not mention that of course she and Rob shared a room. Or that Rebecca and Mr. Mattson would not.

"Thank you." Lila Rose had not thought about accommodations, nor had Drew mentioned anything about where she and Rebecca would sleep. "I'm sure that will be fine."

"Thanks, sis." Drew dropped down onto the settee. "Lila Rose, I'm sorry you got dragged into this mess."

"Not at all." Lila Rose sipped her coffee. She had no doubt Rebecca would need to rest after their long trip once her discussion with Mr. Mattson was over. And despite that man's inhospitable behavior, Viola clearly was the lady of the house, so her invitation for them to stay overrode his orders to leave. At least, Lila Rose hoped so. "Rebecca will need my companionship for her return trip to Charleston."

Drew's frown deepened. "Um, yeah, I guess so."

His defeat seemed so thorough that her heart ached, and she longed to comfort him. But he was among his own people, so it wasn't her place.

"Uncle Drew!" An adorable little brown-haired girl of perhaps five years dashed into the room and threw herself into his arms. "Where you been? I've missed you soooo much!"

His expression brightened as he returned the child's hug. "Hey, sweet pea. How ya doing?"

"I'm doing real good."

Viola cleared her throat.

The little girl giggled. "I'm doing very well, thank you." She turned her attention to Lila Rose. "Who are you?"

At her sweet brown-eyed gaze, Lila Rose's heart melted. What an adorable child.

"This is Miss Lila Rose Duval." Drew nodded to her. "Miss Lila Rose, this is my niece, Lavinia. She's Rob and Viola's daughter."

"How do you do—"

"And I got a brother, Robbie, and we're gonna have a new—" She looked at Viola, whose well-rounded middle told the rest of the story.

"Well," Lila Rose interrupted. "It's nice to meet a growing family."

Soft chuckles came from the other adults.

"Drew, while you and Will bring in the ladies' luggage, I'll start supper." Viola pulled herself to her feet and, hand pressed against her lower back, straightened.

Although the arrival of her child did not appear imminent, she did seem to require adjusting to her ungainly
posture as she stood.

"Yes, ma'am," the brothers answered together and
walked toward the front door.

How alike they were, yet not as close as twins. To
Lila Rose, Drew's slightly younger face was more appealing, possibly due to that dimple in his left cheek.

Oh, my. She truly must stop these musings.

"Come along, Lavinia." Viola moved toward the
hallway on the left. "Lila Rose, please make yourself
comfortable. We have books and newspapers for your
reading pleasure." She indicated a bookcase set against
the inner wall. "Suzette, will you help me with supper, please?"

"Sure thing."

"Let me help, too." Lila Rose had no idea how to
cook, but she relished the idea of getting better acquainted with these young women so close to her own
age, no matter how short her and Rebecca's visit was
sure to be.

In the somewhat rustic kitchen—at least rustic in
comparison to the one in Rebecca's Charleston house—
an oval table and chairs took up much of the room. A
fairly new cast-iron stove radiated warmth without causing stifling heat. A large icebox sat near the open back
door, which appeared to lead to a mudroom. Everything
in the kitchen looked well-used but clean, evidence of
Viola's housekeeping skills. How long would she be able
to keep it that way in her condition? And who would
help her as her time drew near? These weren't the sort

of questions one asked in polite society. Perhaps those ladies Drew mentioned would come to help.

Viola and Suzette busied themselves with various tasks, both seeming to know just what to do. Even Lavinia knew to begin setting the dining room table in the next room without being asked.

"How can I help?" Lila Rose shed her gloves and travel jacket, then accepted an apron from Suzette and tied it around her waist.

"You can peel those potatoes." Viola pointed to a bowl of round red potatoes that sat on the table. "You may need to sharpen the knife."

Lila Rose blinked. Sharpen the knife?

Suzette giggled. "I'll do it." She snatched a paring knife and whetstone from the sideboard and set about brushing the blade over the stone in a circular motion. After wiping it clean on her apron, she handed it, handle first, to Lila Rose. "Save the peeling for the pigs."

Pigs? "Very well." Lila Rose began her unfamiliar chore, trying her best not to dig too deeply into the potatoes. Still, more white flesh came off with the skins than should have. As she worked, she listened with interest to the other two ladies go on about their labors, chattering about this and that with such camaraderie it made her heart ache for friendship like theirs. She loved Rebecca, but she had often longed to have younger friends, too. Even the ladies in their reading circle back home were all Rebecca's age.

"Hmm." Viola stared at the platter full of cut-up chicken she'd just retrieved from the icebox. "I think we need more meat for supper. Suzette, will you go fetch another chicken? Get the brown hen that hasn't been laying."

"Sure thing." Suzette washed her hands under the pump in the sink, then went out the back door.

Lila Rose swallowed hard. Just like that, the young woman was going out to kill a hen for supper. Lila Rose could not imagine killing a chicken. Or removing its feathers. Or any other part of preparing it for cooking. In Charleston, Ingrid had managed all the grocery shopping and brought home meat that was already dressed.

Oh, my. Tonight she would write in her journal this additional reason for never wanting to live in this untamed land.

"Drew!" Rob strode up to the surrey and helped him pull Mother's trunk from the back. "When did you get home? And what are you doing with these trunks? And why are you in this getup?" He gently backhanded the shoulder of Drew's frock jacket. "Don't tell me you wore this up to summer pasture."

Unloading two of the smaller bags, Will chuckled. "See? I kept your secret even from him."

"What secret?" Rob scowled at him. "What have you been up to, Drew?"

"Let's talk before we go in." After Pop's angry reaction, Drew dreaded this encounter. With Pop not doing so well, Rob had been running the ranch for over a year, and he didn't like anybody taking bold initiatives without clearing it with him first.

"All right."

They carried the trunk to the front porch and set it down, then sat on the steps.

"I went to Charleston and brought Mother back home." There, he said it. Now came the storm.

Rob gaped at him for several moments. "Mother? Here?" He glanced toward the front door. "Huh." He scratched his jaw. "And you got her to come?"

Not the reaction Drew had expected. "Yeah. That's something, isn't it?"

"What did Pop think?" Concern crossed Rob's brow.

"Well, he wasn't too happy. He and Mother are in the office now, hashing things out." At least, that's what Drew hoped.

"Huh," Rob repeated. "Well, I'll be switched, little brother. That's really something. I'll go check on them." He chuckled. "Sure will be good to see Mother after all these years." He stood and went into the house.

Drew let out a long breath. As the oldest son, Rob had always acted like a bossy parent to his four younger brothers. "Marriage sure has mellowed him."

Will chuckled. "Yep. Marriage has been good for me, too. I didn't know what I had in Suzette until I almost lost her." He gave Drew a sidelong look. "Now that four of us brothers are married, when are you gonna take the plunge? That pretty little Lila Rose seems like a perfect match."

Drew scoffed. "A city gal like her? Not for me, brother. Not for me."

Even as he said the words, he felt a gentle tug on his heart. Sure, he'd like to be married to a sweet gal similar to any of his sisters-in-law. Which sure didn't include a prissy lady like Lila Rose Duval. No, sir. Not at all. No matter how his heart skipped a beat whenever he was around her.

The aroma of frying chicken made his stomach growl. It sure would be good to have Viola's home cooking again.

He and Will moved the trunks up to the bedrooms, as Viola had ordered, and Drew shed his frock coat.

"I'm gonna find Robbie," Will said as they came back downstairs. "We'll get the milking done before supper. You want to come?"

"No, not now. I'm gonna see if I can help with supper."

"Suit yourself."

With Pop and Mother still behind the closed office doors, Drew wandered out to the kitchen.

"Drew, will you help Lavinia put the leaves in the table?" Viola pointed to the closet where the leaves were stored. "She didn't realize we would have ten people for supper tonight, did you, sweetheart?" She brushed her hand over Lavinia's brown braids.

"No, ma'am." Lavinia gazed at her stepmother with adoration. As the child's governess, Viola had brought Lavinia from Charleston last year, and with her had brought a lot of joy to this household as well. Lavinia's welcome home hug had been the one bright spot in this dismal afternoon. Well, Rob's benign acceptance of Drew's surprise had been nice, too.

"Glad to help, Viola." He retrieved the two wide leaves for the table, then helped his niece fold back the tablecloth. "Watch your fingers, sweet pea." He tugged the table apart and inserted the extensions, then shoved them all together. "Now, let's finish the job." He smoothed the long tablecloth back into place and began resetting the cutlery and plates.

"Let me do that." Lila Rose appeared beside him and reached for the silverware he was holding, seemingly unaware that she had bumped his arm. Which, to his annoyance, sent a pleasant shiver up to his neck. "I didn't do so well on peeling the potatoes, but I do think I can set a table."

Her lighthearted self-deprecation gave him a chuckle. "I don't know, Lila Rose. Are you sure you can manage?" He winked at Lavinia, who giggled.

"Humph. Just watch me." She set a knife and spoon on the right side of a plate and a fork on the left side, then used two finger widths to measure the equal distance each lay from the table's edge. "Perfect." She looked up at him, blinked and quickly looked away. "And that's how you do it."

Did she sound a little breathless? Was he having the same effect on her that she had on him? He'd best put some distance between them before they both got into trouble...*heart* trouble.

"So, did you learn how to set a table in some fancy boarding school?" Drew had finished eighth grade, like all his brothers—like most everybody around here. That was all the formal education a cowboy needed. They got the rest of their schooling doing hard work on the ranch, learning how to raise prime beef. Learning tough and realistic life lessons, not vague philosophies and ancient histories.

"Why, yes. I graduated from a ladies' seminary in Charleston." She spoke lightly but then frowned and ducked her head. "Well, I'd better get back to the kitchen to see if there's anything else I can do."

He wanted to ask why her mood had changed, what

had saddened her. But he let her go. Caring too much about her life before she worked for Mother was dangerous.

Besides, his family had to be his focus. Right now, he could hear Rob talking with Mother in the hallway.

"I'll get him to come to supper."

"I really don't care whether he does or not. I'm here to see my grandchildren. Where are they?"

They entered the dining room, Rob's arm around Mother's waist. Drew was glad to see it. They all needed to forgive Mother for leaving them so long ago, and it seemed they were well on their way to achieving that goal.

An hour later, Lila Rose, Suzette and Viola each carried a serving bowl to the table.

"Is everyone washed up?" Viola set the mashed potatoes in the center of the table. "Shall we be seated before everything gets cold?"

After a few awkward moments of folks shuffling about, Drew found himself sitting beside Lila Rose. He introduced her to Robbie, who'd just come in from milking and plunked himself down across the table. The little rascal winked at her, but Drew couldn't fault him. It's what he saw his uncles doing to pretty gals. Might have to have a talk with that boy. And quit winking at the lady himself.

"Mother, you sit here." Viola pulled out the chair at the foot of the table, the family's traditional place for the lady of the house.

"Oh, no, dear. I'm not going to take your place."

"Nonsense." Viola took her hand and led her to the chair. "This is *your* place."

Drew had to suck in a breath. His sister-in-law had wholeheartedly embraced Mother as the family matriarch, even surrendering her own place at the table.

Pop entered reluctantly, tugging against Rob's grip on his upper arm. "I'm not hungry."

"Well, then, just sit with us." Rob pulled out the captain's chair at the head of the table.

Pop's eyes found Drew, and he speared him with an angry look. "You did this," he muttered as he lowered himself into the armed chair.

Drew's heart dropped, and he swallowed hard.

Viola came in with a platter piled high with fried chicken and set it in front of Pop. "Here you go. Just the way you like it."

"Smells mighty fine, sweetheart." Rob sat to Pop's left. "Now, Pop, please say grace *like you always do*."

While everyone else reached for the hand of the person next to them, Pop glared down the table at Mother. "I will never forgive you for abandoning us…"

"And I will never forgive you for…you know what!"

"That… That…" Pop gripped his chest and gasped. "I can't…"

Rob jumped up and loosened Pop's bolo tie and top shirt button. "Will, help me get him upstairs. Drew, go get Doc Warren. Now!"

After shoving back from the table, Drew ran from the house to the barn. To his relief, Ranse Cable had just saddled up, maybe to go to town. "Ranse, I gotta use your horse. Emergency."

"Sure, boss." The amiable cowhand moved back and offered Drew the reins.

Drew snagged them from his grasp and jumped into

the saddle. All the way to town, the drum of the horse's hoofbeats seemed to say, *"You killed your father. You killed your father."*

And Drew had no argument against the accusation.

Chapter Four

"Now, Ralph, I've told you to take it easy." Doc Warren tucked his stethoscope into his black medical bag, removed his spectacles and scowled at Mr. Mattson. "You have five sons who can keep this ranch running— well, *three* who live here, plus a passel of ranch hands. You need to stick to quiet activities, like your wood-working, until your heart heals. This one was mild, but I can't promise the next one will be. For now, I want you to stay in this bed until I come back in three days, unless I'm needed sooner."

Lila Rose stood beside Rebecca just inside the door of Mr. Mattson's bedroom. Clearly, the good doctor had no idea that family drama had brought on his patient's heart attack. At that dreadful moment, Rob had taken charge, sending poor Drew scrambling to fetch Dr. Warren. Now Rebecca wouldn't permit her middle son to enter this room, lest his father have another episode. Even now, the old gentleman barely tolerated his wife's presence. And Lila Rose stuck close to Rebecca in case she needed support.

Mr. Mattson peeked around the doctor and glared at Rebecca.

"I don't need you," he growled—if his weak, guttural voice could even be called a growl. He gave her a dismissive wave of his hand.

"Now, Ralph," Dr. Warren said, "you need a nurse and—"

"Rob and Viola can take care of anything I need."

Dr. Warren clicked his tongue. "You leave that young couple alone. Rob's running this ranch, and Viola's running this house. And she's expecting your grandchild, so you are not to add to her work." He cast a glance toward Rebecca, but his eyes also took in Lila Rose.

Oh, no. I can't be his nurse!

To her relief, the doctor's gaze settled on Rebecca. "You up to this?"

Rebecca straightened to her full five feet two inches. "I most certainly am." Lila Rose had never heard such steel in her genteel employer's voice.

"Good." The good doctor gathered his coat and medical bag. "Let's go downstairs, and I'll give you a treatment plan."

Lila Rose stood to one side so Rebecca and the doctor could leave the room. Before she could follow them, Mr. Mattson called out from his bed, "Who are you?" He sounded more curious than cross.

Good manners said she should smile, but her lips quivered as she spoke. "I'm Lila Rose Duval, sir. I'm Mrs. Mattson's companion."

She expected a cross reply, much like her father would have given her.

"Companion? Huh." He sat back against his pillow.

"Well, how do you do, Miss Duval. Forgive me if I don't get up and greet you properly, but you're welcome to make yourself at home for however long you're here."

She scrambled to recover from her shock at his good manners. Where was the ogre who had shouted at Rebecca at the dinner table not two hours ago? "Thank you, sir. That's very kind of you. Please excuse me."

She hurried after Rebecca. Whatever the doctor prescribed for Mr. Mattson, Lila Rose must memorize everything in case Rebecca had a lapse of memory. Not that she'd ever shown a hint of senility, but anyone could forget details during times of stress.

Seated at the dining room table, Rebecca was writing the doctor's instructions on a tablet. One at a time, he held up small medicine bottles and told her what dosages to administer and when to do so. Her eyes bright with understanding and determination, Rebecca seemed like a general out to conquer this illness that had struck down her husband.

So much for her needing Lila Rose to memorize instructions. Perhaps she could find another way to help. Surely it was time to prepare supper.

Drew, his brothers and Suzette stood nearby, their faces filled with concern. From the kitchen came the sounds of Viola and the children chatting as though nothing was amiss. In the few hours Lila Rose had been in Viola's presence, she had been impressed by the lady's serene disposition amid the chaos of this family.

"Well, I'd better get that fencing finished before dark," Rob said. "And those cows won't get milked with us just standing around." He stared at his broth-

ers one at a time, as if deciding whom to send out to
do the chore.

"I'll do it." Will bent to kiss Suzette's cheek. "You
all right?"

"Yep." She looked up at Will with love shining in
her eyes. "I'll go help Viola with supper."

Lila Rose took a step to follow her, for surely another pair of hands, however inexperienced, could make
lighter work for Viola. "I can peel potatoes again."

"No, no." Suzette waggled a finger at her in a
friendly way. "You're company, so you just go sit in
the parlor and read." She giggled. "Besides, the pigs
had plenty of peelings from your last go at it."

Lila Rose laughed. "Very well." She couldn't take
offense to the sweet girl's comment. She had indeed
butchered those potatoes.

With Rebecca and the doctor still conferring and
Rob and Will gone to do chores, only Drew remained.
He leaned against the doorjamb, hands in his pockets,
shoulders slumped, expression crestfallen. He looked
like one of the orphan boys in Rebecca's Sunday school
class when scolded for misbehavior, so very different
from the confident young man who had knocked on
Rebecca's door only three weeks ago. So much for her
assumption that he was a favored son. Yet he'd had a
noble purpose in seeking to reconcile his parents, only
to have his hopes dashed. What could Lila Rose say to
encourage him? She stepped over and patted his arm.

"None of this is your fault." The impulsive words
seemed to pop out before she could stop them. What
did she know of this family's history, gathered in vague
bits and pieces from Rebecca over the years?

He gave her a rueful smile. "You're kind to say so, but it *is* my fault."

"Nonsense." Had she lost control of her tongue? "From what the doctor said to your father, I gather he's had heart trouble for some time."

"Yeah, but I didn't have to make it worse."

"Drew, you—"

"Just leave it, Lila Rose." He pulled away from her and took a step toward the front of the house, then turned back. "I know you mean well, but somebody who comes from a perfect family doesn't have any idea what I'm going through."

A perfect family? Where had he gotten that idea about hers? Before she could contradict him, he stormed away, and soon she heard the front door slamming.

How rude! All this time she had thought him reasonable, thoughtful, sensitive to others. He was none of those things. Which gave her just one more reason not to open her heart to this ruffian cowboy.

Drew wanted to kick himself for speaking to Lila Rose so rudely. Sure, she didn't have any idea how hard family life could be. She'd lived like a princess—first as an only child, then as Mother's companion. No responsibilities but to pour Mother's tea and add cream and sugar. He could imagine her growing up spoiled by her parents on the horse farm she'd mentioned as they traveled west.

But that didn't give him the right to snap at her when she was trying to be nice to him. In fact, she seemed— much like him—to want everyone to get along. Now he could add being a lousy host to his failure in bringing Mother home.

Home. No, she didn't consider the Double Bar M her home.

Striding across the barnyard, he kicked a rock and nearly hit Robbie's dog, who yelped and scooted away.

"Sorry, Sport. Didn't mean to scare you." He knelt and beckoned to the black-and-white sheepdog. "Come here, boy."

The year-old pup ducked his head and cautiously approached. Drew ruffled his fur and talked affectionate nonsense, and soon Sport was wiggling all over with forgiveness. If only Drew's father were so forgiving.

In the barn, he found Will busy milking one of the two milk cows. "I'll take care of Clara." He snagged a clean bucket from the peg on the wall and settled on a stool beside the brindle-gray cow.

"Thanks." Will kept his attention on black-and-white Mildred, who sometimes decided to kick while being milked. At least she gave warning with a particular twitch of her tail. They'd all learned to read the signs after painful encounters with the beast or a bucket of spilled milk.

They worked in silence for several minutes until Will finished with Mildred. Full bucket in hand, he came over to Clara's stall. "You know, I had no idea Pop would blow up that way or that it would cause him to have a heart attack. Maybe I should have told him what you were doing."

"Yeah, I guess my idea of surprising him was pretty stupid." Drew swallowed a lump in his throat. Most of his ideas were stupid, and none of them brought out the recognition from Pop that he desperately longed for.

Will released a sigh. "Not stupid. I think all five of us have had an idea from time to time about getting Mother and Pop back together but never did anything. At least you tried." He clapped Drew on the shoulder.

"Is Rob mad at me?"

Rob appeared around the corner of the stall. "No, I'm not mad. Just wish you'd warned me so I could have warned Pop. Say, on another topic, how about that pretty little gal you brought with Mother? Is she really just sightseeing, or is she out to lasso herself a cowboy?" He gave Drew a teasing grin.

Drew finished his chore and stood. "Guess I deserve that after the way we hassled you about falling for Viola. But no. She's actually Mother's companion, and she's well and truly a city gal. Can't wait to get back to Charleston. In fact, I think after Pop gets better, she'll be trying to get Mother to go with her."

"*If* he gets better," Will said.

"Aw, now…" Rob began to herd the two of them toward the house. "Let's stay positive about this." He grunted. "Not that I think he's in the clear, but I get the idea from Doc's attitude that this wasn't as bad as Pop made it out to be. Doc may scold, but he doesn't seem worried."

Rob's words lifted Drew's spirits. "You think not?"

Will clicked his tongue. "Maybe there's hope for Mother and Pop after all. What say we all work together and help Mother change her mind about living out here?"

"I'm game." Rob clapped Drew on the shoulder. "You?"

"Sure. That's why I brought her here." Drew gave his brothers the best grin he could muster. But deep inside, he doubted it would work. Especially not with Lila Rose pulling from the other direction.

After preparing for bed, Lila Rose rubbed hand cream into her reddened hands, soothing away the chafing from washing dishes in such hot water. It was a simple task, but one she'd never attempted before. Yet she'd insisted on helping Viola and Suzette after supper, if for no other reason than to avoid Drew. During supper, she'd studiously kept from looking at him across the table. Not that she'd needed to worry. He hadn't seemed interested in seeking her out, either. Was he embarrassed by his earlier rudeness, or still annoyed with her for trying to console him after his father's tirade? Ungrateful man! She wouldn't try that again.

During supper, the children had provided a convenient reason for all the adults to keep their conversation light and mainly centered on ranch business. Rebecca had taken supper to Mr. Mattson and remained upstairs in his room. If not for Viola and Suzette including Lila Rose in the conversation, she would have been more than a little uncomfortable at the dining table.

"Suzette." From his place at the head of the table, Rob had focused on his newest sister-in-law. "Would you skin my hide if I sent Will to ramrod the operation up at summer pasture?"

She'd given him a saucy grin. "Not at all, if you let me go with him."

"You don't have to do that." Drew had set down his fork and given her a long look. "I'm planning to go…"

"And deprive me of my honeymoon?"

Herding cattle on her honeymoon? Lila Rose had given Suzette a long look of her own—a rather unlady-like gesture, but she couldn't stop herself. Thankfully, no one had noticed, as all the attention was on Suzette.

"Well, if you feel that way," Rob had said, "I'm all for it. The way you managed those outlaws who kidnapped you, I know you'll be fine. Just let Old Fuzzy do the cooking. Feeding a passel of cowpokes isn't much of a honeymoon."

She had laughed. "And let my poor husband suffer from eating prairie dog stew? No, sirree. Our men will be the best-fed cowpokes on the mountainside."

As the quips had continued to fly around the table, Lila Rose counted another reason to flee this savage land: What kind of man—however nice Will might be—agreed to take his new wife on a cattle drive? And what kind of woman considered three or four months in a mountain wilderness a honeymoon?

After supper, she had checked on Rebecca in Mr. Mattson's room. "What can I do to help you?"

Rebecca had given her a serene smile. "You go on to bed, Lila Rose. I'll be fine."

"Yes, ma'am. Call if you need me."

Now, in Lavinia's bedroom, with the child fast asleep, Lila Rose sat on the trundle bed, nursing her chafed hands and trying to devise some way to get Rebecca and herself back home. If her employer wouldn't go, what would Lila Rose do? While writing of today's happenings in her journal, she'd sniffed back unwelcomed tears, then scolded herself for such a self-pitying thought. The Lord had taken care of her after Mama's death, and He would see to her future.

Sleep eluded her as the day's events crowded into her mind. In the end, one stood out—how cruel it was of Drew to assume she'd come from a happy family. She brushed her right hand down her left arm. If only he knew...

Enough of that. After Father died, she'd decided not to let her past weigh her down. Losing Mama had been terribly difficult to recover from, but even so, she'd found strength in the Lord, especially when Rebecca hired her. In the serene atmosphere of her home in Charleston and the warm, welcoming church they attended, Lila Rose had found peace at last...until Drew showed up.

Surely by now, Rebecca could see her trip had been useless. Mr. Mattson might have been polite to Lila Rose, as Father had always been to strangers while treating his wife and daughter abominably. But her host had shown his true colors in his angry tirade that brought on his heart attack. Oh, she must get Rebecca away from that man and back home—the sooner, the better.

Seated on the front porch swing, Drew stared out into the darkened landscape, pondering his predicament. Suzette sure had spoiled his plans to get away from the ranch for a few months, but he couldn't fault her. Land, she was a spunky gal. Hardworking and unafraid, not at all prissy like Lila Rose. And look at the way Mother had commandeered the management of

Pop's care, showing her own gumption. In Drew's mind, that didn't square with what he knew of her.

She'd gone back to Charleston because of the hard life for women out here, yet she'd managed the return trip with barely a complaint, even risking her life by stabbing her knitting needle into that train robber's hand. For the first time in almost nine years, he wondered if there was some other reason she'd left. Pop worked hard, provided for her, never gave another woman a first glance, much less a second one. Drew tried to sort it out, but some distant memory remained just out of reach. He'd have to leave it for now. With his big plan to win Pop's approval ruined, all he could do at the moment was dig into ranch work beside his brothers. Once Will left for the mountains, Drew would start working with the new horses Rob had bought while Drew was back East.

Horse training. Now that was a job he could get lost in, spending hours upon hours working green yearlings and two-year-olds, training them for ranch work, sometimes forgetting to eat.

"Meow." Lavinia's calico cat jumped out of the darkness and onto the dimly lit porch, then wound around his pant leg.

"Hey, there, Puff." Drew bent to pet her. Being a housecat, she was plumper than the barn cats.

She accepted one brush of his hand before scurrying to the door and looking up at him expectantly.

"Yep, it's time to go in." Standing, he yawned and stretched. It had been a long, eventful day. He opened the door, and Puff scooted past him, making a silent dash up the front staircase. Chuckling to himself over the way the whole family spoiled that silly feline for Lavinia's sake, he removed his boots and tiptoed upstairs after her. He'd be sharing a bedroom with Robbie now and would have to be careful not to wake the boy.

Tired though he was, he peeked into Pop's bedroom. The old man lay propped up against his pillows, a soft wheeze replacing his usual loud snoring. In a wingback chair beside him, Mother sat fast asleep, her head resting on one arm. Sure as shootin', she'd have a crick in her neck come morning.

Drew tiptoed in and knelt beside her. "Mom... Mother, let's get you to bed."

"Lila Rose?" She slowly lifted her head and, hand to her neck, groaned. "Oh, Drew. Thank you."

"Yes, ma'am." He helped her up and gently guided her down the hallway toward the bedroom Viola had assigned to her. But it wouldn't be proper for him to prepare her for bed. Where was that Miss Lila Rose Duval, neglecting her employer at a time like this?

Lavinia's bedroom door stood slightly open, as it always did at night for Puff's convenience. Lila Rose peered out, gasped and withdrew, only to emerge a moment later in a woolen dressing gown.

"I'm so sorry, Rebecca." She practically shoved Drew aside and took Mother's arm. "I'll have you in bed in two shakes." She glanced over her shoulder. "You may go now. I can manage."

And just like that, she and Mother disappeared behind the now-closed door.

The nerve of that city gal, dismissing him that way in his own house. At least she'd be holed up in the house while he was working his horses, keeping out of *his* way. He couldn't wait to see the last of her.

But even as the thought flew through his mind, his heart dropped as he admitted the truth to himself. He liked Miss Lila Rose Duval. Once she convinced Mother to return to Charleston, he'd be sad to see her go.

Chapter Five

After breakfast the next morning, Lila Rose accompanied Viola and Suzette as they took their morning constitutional around the ranch. At Suzette and Will's pretty little clapboard cottage, which was nicely landscaped and surrounded by a white picket fence, recently planted marigolds flourished along the front stoop, sparking a memory for Lila Rose.

"Ladies, I almost forgot. Rebecca and I brought you some rose and lilac cuttings and some daffodil bulbs. We should probably get them planted before they dry out."

"How lovely." Viola's blue eyes sparkled with interest. "We can plant them tomorrow after church. Perhaps some here by the cottage and the rest by the house."

"I don't know, sis." Suzette shook her head. "We get a lot of cold and wind over here. Maybe Will can build a hothouse alongside the big house, especially for the roses."

Continuing their walk, they discussed various ideas for the plants. A hothouse would be nice, especially if it could be uncovered in the warmer weather. If it was built by the kitchen, the menfolk could install a pipe so that dishwater would drain out onto the plants. But that location didn't have enough sunlight. Other ideas were presented, but none seemed perfect for a flower garden. When Viola suggested Rebecca should have the final say in the matter, Lila Rose didn't argue. Surely Rebecca wouldn't be here long enough to care where the flowers bloomed—or even whether they did at all.

Across the barnyard, near where Robbie and Lavinia now played with two black-and-white dogs, a corral filled with perhaps eight young horses caught Lila Rose's attention. "Tell me about them."

"That's the new ranch stock Rob bought last week," Viola said. "After the main herd of cattle goes up to summer pasture, the men staying here will train these for future work. It's one of those ongoing jobs for ranchers."

In spite of herself, Lila Rose had a longing to join those men in training the horses. Would she remember all that her father's groom had taught her? She rubbed her right hand down her left arm, recalling one of her many unpleasant memories from those times. As always, when these memories assaulted her, she shoved the past to the back of her mind. But oh, how she would enjoy working with horses again. No sense in wondering, though. She wouldn't have a chance to put any of it into practice.

They meandered across the hill on which the big house sat. Below, a large herd of cattle grazed on the grassy pasture beside the Rio Grande. The scene was idyllic and inviting, at least for viewing.

"I think I'll just sit here awhile and enjoy the view." Lila Rose pointed to a fallen tree in their path and lifted her skirt a few inches to step over it.

"Wait!" Suzette grabbed her left arm with surprising force.

"What? Why?" Lila Rose resisted the temptation to pull away. She hadn't been wrenched about in that manner since Father died, so Suzette's aggressiveness alarmed her.

Suzette traded a look with Viola. "Sure can tell you're a greenhorn. Listen, you never step over a log without checking to see what's on the other side."

Lila Rose laughed. "Is this some of that cowboy—cow*girl* teasing I've heard about?"

"Not at all, dear." Viola couldn't be more than three years older than Lila Rose, but she had a maternal way about her. "Listen to Suzette."

"You never know whether there's a snake sunning itself alongside the log."

"Snake?" Heart in her throat, Lila Rose squeaked out the word as another horrifying memory came to mind.

"Sure thing." Suzette took the walking stick Viola had brought with her and gently poked the log, causing it to wobble. A black snake surely ten feet long slithered away in a hurry. "See? Just like I said. Now that little fella's a black racer, and he's harmless. But if it'd been a rattlesnake—well, enough said."

Little *fellow?* Lila Rose shuddered so violently she could barely take a step. How did these women so casually live with snakes hiding behind every log, poisonous or otherwise?

The reasons for returning to Charleston as soon as

possible were rapidly adding up. But without Rebecca—
without her job—she had no way of going anywhere.

Drew and Will rode their horses alongside the surrey driven by Rob and carrying the ladies and children.
Even though Mother loved attending church, she'd insisted on staying home to care for Pop. Probably a good
thing because the old man kept getting out of bed and
trying to do things Doc Warren had warned him not
to do.

And thinking of Doc, here he came, driving his phaeton in the opposite direction. Rob stopped the surrey
and hailed him.

"Morning, Doc. You headed out to see Pop?"

Doc doffed his hat. "Good morning, folks. Yep, I
thought I'd check up on Ralph and bring him some
more medicine. Rob, you know my sister came to work
with me last year. Cassandra trained with Clara Barton. She's willing to come out and stay for a while, if
that will help."

For a moment, Drew feared his older brother would
accept the offer. That would free Mother to leave at
any time.

"Thank you kindly, Doc." Rob glanced at Viola, who
sat beside him. She gave a little shake of her head. "And
thank Miss Cassandra. But I think our mother plans to
stay at least long enough to get Pop back on his feet."

"And maybe stay for good." Bless Suzette's heart.
She always piped up with her opinions.

Will grinned at his bride, and Drew felt an odd little pang in his chest. Rob and Viola, Will and Suzette,
Jared and Cal and their sweet wives. Only two years

ago, hadn't all five of them agreed never to marry? Yet here he was, the only Mattson man left without a wife. And he wouldn't think of marrying until his parents were reconciled. Not that he had anyone in mind…

Against his will, his eyes strayed to prim and proper Lila Rose, who sat with Suzette and the children on the surrey's second bench. Nope. Not her. She was the last person Drew would think of courting, much less marrying.

"All right, then. Ladies." Doc doffed his hat again. "You folks enjoy church. I may get back there before the final hymn. You tell the pastor I hate to miss his fine sermon, but Cassandra will take notes." He slapped the reins on his horse's haunches and drove away.

At the edge of town, Rob pulled the horses into the churchyard and parked under a tree. As usual, folks stood around chatting before the service. As the family climbed down from the surrey, several younger folks— mostly females—bustled over to welcome Drew back from his trip. After dismounting, he tied his horse to the surrey, smiled at the group and touched the brim of his hat.

"Mornin', ladies."

"You sure did a good thing bringing your mother home, Drew." Iris Blake, the banker's daughter, gave him a winsome smile. Her smallpox scars from last year's epidemic had faded, leaving only a few permanent ones. Once prideful about her beauty, she now seemed a more genuine, thoughtful person and not at all bitter about the change in her appearance. "I'll be praying for everything to go well."

"Oh, yes," Alice Arrington said breathlessly, batting her eyes at Drew as she spoke. "Me too."

Dolores Gentry practically pushed the other two aside to stand in front of Drew. "And for your father to get well soon."

He heard some snickering behind him. His brothers, of course. Now that he was the only "available" Mattson, he'd be the main target of these girls and their mothers. When he'd shared that honor with his brothers, it hadn't been so bad—but now…

He glanced over at Lila Rose, who was studying his situation with a bemused expression. Remembering how these same gals had snubbed Viola when she first came out here, Drew decided to head off that same treatment of Mother's companion.

"Ladies, I'd like you to meet our houseguest, Miss Lila Rose Duval from Charleston. Lila Rose, come on over and meet these sweet gals."

The "sweet gals" seemed to like his referring to them that way, if their soft giggles and sighs were any indication.

"Lila Rose. What a pretty name."

"Welcome, Miss Duval."

"What a darling gown you're wearing. Did you make it?"

They crowded around her and shook hands, and right away they started asking for the latest fashion news from back East.

Women! Drew shook his head and backed away.

Rob clapped him on the shoulder. "Good job, brother. But I doubt you'll be able to dodge getting shackled any better than the rest of us did."

"Getting shackled?" Viola sniffed indignantly. "Is that what you think of our marriage? The very idea!" The teasing smirk on her pretty face brought out a laugh from Rob and Will.

Suzette smacked Will's arm. "Yeah. The very idea!" Then she giggled.

This family camaraderie went a long way to soothe Drew's grief over his failure to reunite his parents. Mother might be sticking around because of a sense of duty, but he had no doubt she would leave once Pop was past his latest heart trouble. And Pop had made it clear he would be glad to see the back of her.

Once inside the church, he settled down to enjoy the service. He always appreciated Pastor Daniel's good words. Today he preached about marriage—which was interesting because Drew had been thinking so much about the subject. The preacher emphasized scriptures about husbands loving their wives and wives being helpful to their husbands. His parents had failed on both counts—but could Drew do any better, with all the mistakes he'd made? Another reason not to think about getting married.

On the other hand, his four brothers had found loving wives and seemed genuinely happy in their marriages. So maybe Drew should start praying that he would find a good wife, too.

Once again, his eyes were drawn to Lila Rose, who sat at the other end of the pew, her expression thoughtful as she listened to Pastor Daniel.

Nope. Not her, Lord. If for no other reason than she was a city gal and he a rancher. But then, Viola had also been a city gal, and look how happy she was on the ranch now. Drew figured her love for Rob gave her reason enough to adjust to such a different life from the one she'd been used to.

The preacher's voice broke into his thoughts. "Proverbs 18:22 tells us, 'Whoso findeth a wife findeth a good thing, and obtaineth favour of the Lord.'"

Favor of the Lord. Those last few words pierced Drew's heart. He knew the Lord loved him, maybe even favored him in some ways, because the Bible said God loved everybody. Now if only he could obtain his *earthly* father's favor...

When they arrived home after church, Doc Warren's buggy was still sitting outside the big house, to everybody's shock. Rob helped Viola down from the surrey, then quickly ushered her toward the back door, calling over his shoulder, "Will, help Suzette with the children. Drew, take care of the horses."

Drew huffed out a cross breath. Sometimes Rob gave orders like an army sergeant, drawing resentment from his younger brothers. This time, with everybody anxious to know why Doc was still there, Drew hated being sent to do a chore that could wait a bit. But then, good sense told him that no matter what, the horses needed to be tended to rather than left standing in the sun. Handing his frock coat to Robbie to take inside, he drove the surrey to the barn, where he brushed and fed the two geldings, then let them loose in the corral. He hurried from the barn to the house and cleaned himself up in the mudroom.

"Uncle Drew." Robbie peered around the door, a worried expression on his young face. "Pop broke his leg."

Drew's heart sank. Then lifted. At least it wasn't

another heart attack. He dried his hands and face and made his way to the kitchen. As always, Viola had matters well in hand. The meal she'd prepared early this morning sent mouthwatering aromas throughout the house. As Suzette, Lila Rose and Lavinia carried steaming bowls of food to the dining room table, their easy chatter hinted that Pop's condition wasn't too dire. Drew dashed upstairs to make sure.

He found Mother, Doc and his brothers around Pop's bed, where the old man lay, wearing an angry scowl as usual. His left leg, bound up in a wooden splint, stuck out from beneath the quilt.

Will sidled up to Drew and whispered, "He was trying to go downstairs and lost his balance."

Drew winced, imagining his old man's accident.

"I'm telling you, I'm fine. I don't need to take that laudanum." Waving away the spoonful of liquid Doc offered, Pop grimaced painfully. "Now, you all go on downstairs and eat your dinner."

As Drew filed out of the room with the rest of the family, he couldn't stop an odd, giddy feeling in his chest. Yes, he was real sorry Pop had a broken leg. But that would keep him laid up awhile and unable to get into any more trouble. And from the way Mother had hovered over him, albeit wearing a scowl similar to Pop's, maybe she would stay on the ranch to take care of him instead of going back to Charleston. Then *maybe* they'd have time to work out their differences, and she would decide to stay for good.

So whether or not Pop ever forgave him for interfering in their marriage by bringing her home, Drew knew without a doubt he'd done the right thing.

* * *

Used to a quiet life with only Rebecca and their two servants, Lila Rose could hardly keep track of the busyness of this huge family. After helping with cleanup after dinner, she had wanted to escape the hubbub. But with Lavinia napping in the room they shared and snakes slithering all over the ranch grounds outside, she had no alternative but to stay inside.

Although the dinner dishes had just been dried and put away, Viola and Suzette were already preparing the evening's supper. Viola had invited the younger Mattson brothers and their wives to join the rest of the family. Lila Rose had met them at church and had been deeply touched by Cal's and Jared's delight at the news about their mother's visit. Nothing would do but that they and their wives' parents would come see her as soon as possible, so Viola—ever the gracious hostess despite her condition—invited them to come that very afternoon. Lila Rose could hardly imagine the chaos more people would bring to this household.

Her failures in the kitchen notwithstanding, she joined the other two ladies to see if she could help. "Do let me try peeling the potatoes again."

"Sure thing." Her hands busy with bread dough, Suzette nodded toward the bowl of freshly washed potatoes and the paring knife on the table. "Why don't you just dig out the eyes, and we can cook them with the skins on."

"Very well." Lila Rose settled in a chair at the kitchen table and began the task slowly and carefully.

"Say, Viola," Suzette said, kneading the bread dough like an experienced baker, "are you going to keep on teaching your etiquette classes? Will said he doesn't mind you using the cottage while he and I are away for the summer, so long as nobody touches his stuff."

Placing a hand on her lower back, Viola stretched. "Well, I hate to disappoint the girls, but in truth, it does seem to be one of those things I'll have to give up pretty soon."

"You do what you have to do, sis. You and that baby come first." Suzette slid her gaze from Viola to Lila Rose. "Didn't Mother mention you attended finishing school?"

Lila Rose hesitated. "Yes. A ladies' seminary. Why do you ask?"

"That's it!" Suzette gave the mound of bread dough a final pat, then scraped the remnants of sticky flour from her fingers. "You can teach our Monday morning classes."

"Oh, no. I'm no teacher." Helping Rebecca with her Sunday school classes didn't count, did it? Besides, she didn't want to be obligated to stay here.

Viola focused on Lila Rose. "I had never taught before last year. I'm sure you could do it."

"It'll keep you occupied." Suzette greased a bowl, plopped the dough into it and covered it with a damp tea towel. "I mean, if you *want* to be occupied."

"Yes, of course." Goodness. Did she think Lila Rose was lazy? Hadn't she proved herself by volunteering to wash dishes and deal with these slippery potatoes? "But teaching? I—I don't know."

"It would just be the gals you met this morning, plus a few others." Suzette washed her hands in a bowl of sudsy water in the sink. "They're all real sweet, like

Drew said. I know they'd love to take etiquette lessons from you."

Viola seemed to be hiding a smile as she beat cake batter in a large bowl. Which left Lila Rose to wonder whether these ladies were just being kind or scheming to keep her here. But why? Oh, that was nonsense. All the family members had jobs to do here on the ranch, and maybe they just wanted to make her feel useful. These past four years, she and Rebecca had socialized only with older ladies, so spending a few hours once a week with those nice girls from church might be a pleasant pastime.

"Very well. Let me observe your class tomorrow." After all, if she decided not to continue, she could always beg off, saying she needed to stay near Rebecca in case she required assistance.

But Rebecca seemed to be doing very well in caring for her husband by herself, even carrying her meals upstairs and eating with him. After all these years, had she decided to reconcile with the irascible man? Lila Rose had always assumed their marriage was too broken to be repaired, and nothing she had seen so far indicated otherwise. Recalling her own parents' unhappy marriage, she'd even approved of Rebecca's stance.

But after hearing this morning's sermon, Lila Rose knew the Lord didn't approve of the behavior of any of them. Father had been abusive, and Mama had submitted to him…even made excuses for him. Yet the minister made it clear that God didn't approve of cruel husbands *or* broken marriages. What was the answer for Rebecca? And how could Lila Rose advise her, if asked?

One thing was certain. She herself would never

marry. Only then could she be sure never to suffer as her mother and Rebecca had.

Yet later that afternoon, when the younger brothers showed up with their wives and in-laws, Cal and Julia's laughing son and Jared and Emma's winsome daughter caused a stirring in Lila Rose she'd never before experienced. If it wasn't enough that she already adored Lavinia and found Robbie to be an exceptionally pleasant little boy to chat with, these eight-month-old infants made her long for a baby of her own. Without marriage, that longing would never be fulfilled. And marriage, which might or might not turn out well, wasn't worth the risk…was it?

When Rebecca told Emma and Julia about the rose and lilac cuttings they'd brought from Charleston, nothing would do for the sisters but to plant them that very day. Drew brought out the prepared plants and leaned against the picket fence while the sisters, Suzette and Lila Rose planted the roses along the back fence and the lilacs at a front corner of the house. The daffodil bulbs couldn't be planted until the fall, so they were put in storage in the root cellar beneath the kitchen.

As the afternoon wore on, the family camaraderie warmed Lila Rose's heart. These generous ladies included her in everything they did. Although she had only been here less than a week, she could happily bask in these blooming friendships…if only they lived in the safety of a town.

Chapter Six

If Lila Rose had thought yesterday's household hub-bub to be the height of ranch pandemonium, she would now have to revise her opinion. Early Monday morning, she was awakened by the thunderous, ground-shaking noise of stampeding cattle…or so it seemed. Through the bedroom window, she could see cowboys on horse-back, whistling and yelling as they drove bawling cattle up from the lower pasture toward the corrals near the barn. She feared the stampede would shake the house to pieces.

Should she grab Lavinia, who was still sleeping peace-fully, and dash downstairs? After throwing on her dress-ing gown, she opened the door and hastened down the hall to Rebecca's room. Her employer sat on her bed, brushing her long, dark brown hair. Her face showed no alarm, which instantly calmed Lila Rose.

"What's all that noise?" She took over brushing Re-becca's hair and began to fashion it into its customary chignon.

"Robert said they would be branding this morning."

Hand to her lips, Rebecca yawned. "They must brand the cattle before taking them to summer pasture. Herds from other ranches will be there as well, and at the end of summer, the only way to know who owns each steer is by the brand."

"Ah, I see." Lila Rose had never heard Rebecca speak of any specific ranch work, yet now she spoke about it casually. "Shall I help you dress?"

"No, dear. I can manage. You get dressed and see if Viola needs you downstairs. I'm going to Ralph's room to see how he managed the night."

In the kitchen, Lila Rose found Viola standing at the stove, making pancakes.

"Sit down and have some coffee." Viola handed her a steaming cup. "After we eat, we can go over the lesson for our class."

Our *class?* Lila Rose had a sinking feeling she'd made a mistake in saying she'd attend. Before she could correct Viola, a banging noise erupted in the yard outside the kitchen door. She peered out and saw a woman starting a fire over a pit and another pumping water into a cauldron.

"Laundry day?"

"Yes. Do you have anything you need to put in?"

"Indeed we do. Thank you. I wondered how I would manage Rebecca's and my laundry."

"Good. You can fetch it after breakfast." Viola lifted a platter of pancakes. "Will you bring the coffee?" She nodded toward two filled cups. Outside, she greeted the two women and urged Lila Rose forward. "May I present Agnes and Rosa." Viola set the platter on a stump.

"I don't know what I'd do without them. Ladies, this is Lila Rose Duval. She's visiting us from Charleston."

They shared pleasantries like old friends, a surprise for Lila Rose. But then, Rebecca had always treated her servants as friends, too.

The noise from the barnyard intensified, but the other women didn't seem to notice. Viola gave a final word of instruction, then walked back toward the door.

Lila Rose scurried after her "So, the men have the branding all in hand? The cattle won't get loose, will they?"

"Oh, no. They won't get loose. The men know what they're doing."

By the noise coming from the barnyard, Lila Rose could only wonder if that was true. "How long does this go on?"

"They should be done within the week."

Once back inside, Lila Rose fetched the laundry from upstairs while Viola fed the children, who had managed very nicely to dress themselves. With breakfast finished and the dishes washed, Viola gave her orders for the day.

"Robbie, you may go help your father. Lavinia, you and I and Miss Lila Rose will be going over to Aunt Suzette's house for our class, so wash up quickly. Don't forget to put a clean handkerchief in your pocket." To Lila Rose, she said, "Are you ready to go? We can go over the lesson once we get to the cottage."

No, not ready in the least. "Yes, I think so."

Viola laughed, clearly seeing Lila Rose's trepidation. "You'll be fine. We have a good time in our class."

Her prediction turned out to be right. In addition to Dolores, Iris and Alice from church, several Mexican girls took part in the lessons. In addition, Elena, whose mother was one of the laundresses, spent a half hour teaching Spanish to the rest of them. Even though Viola gave some instructions, it quickly became clear to Lila Rose that this was not so much a class as a social gathering, with many a tangent to the discussions and much laughter.

The girls accepted the news about Lila Rose taking over the class with only a little hesitation. She could see it was more that they would miss Viola rather than not wanting her to assume the post.

"But we can continue as we are now for a while longer," Viola said.

"I am only disappointed that you won't be teaching us to ride sidesaddle." Iris sighed. "Mother says I must learn how to ride like a lady, or no society man will marry me."

"Aw, that's not true," said Alice. "Any man who would reject you based on your horsemanship isn't worth having."

They all laughed, including Lila Rose. She hadn't enjoyed such camaraderie with other girls her age since attending the ladies' seminary. And now, in addition to her etiquette lessons, she had something else to offer these new friends.

"Ladies, I can teach you."

All eyes focused on her.

Viola gave her an encouraging smile. "Tell us more."

"I was raised on a horse farm, and my father's groom taught me everything you need to know about the subject." Until that fateful day…but she wouldn't mention that.

As the girls gushed with approval and encouragement, Lila Rose felt her face warming. She wasn't used to attention like this, but she liked it. "Do we have enough sidesaddles?"

"We have one," Viola said.

"My brother will provide one for me," Isabella said.

"Say, Alice—" Suzette nudged her friend "—did your pa sell that one we had at the dry goods store? It's been there since we first opened seven years ago."

"It's still there," Alice said. "I'll ask Pa if we can use it."

"Wait a minute." Viola held up a cautioning hand. "Let's not put the saddles before the horses."

Again, the ladies laughed, this time at her variation on the idiom.

"We can each bring our own horse," Dolores said.

"Before we go too far, I must advise that not every horse is suitable for the task." Lila Rose loved the idea of being useful to these new friends, but she hesitated to get too excited, lest she find out it wouldn't work. "Viola, do you mind if I ask Rob if I can train a couple of those new horses to the sidesaddle? If we start them off with it, they'll do better than horses only used to being ridden astride."

"Well, fiddlesticks." Suzette blew out a breath. "I'm sure gonna miss out. Guess I'll have to wait until next fall to catch up with y'all."

"I wish I could go up to summer pasture with you." Alice sighed dreamily. "It's so beautiful in the mountains in the summer." She slid a sly look at Suzette. "Is Drew going?"

More laughter.

"If Drew's going," Dolores said, "I'm going, too."

"*Si*, as will I," Elena said.

The others chimed in with their agreement.

"No," Viola said. "Drew is staying behind to work here on the ranch."

That news was greeted with approving remarks.

"Even so," Iris said, "we should plan an outing for late June or early July. We could pack enough food for several days and surprise them. And maybe—" she gave a wistful sigh "—Drew would accompany us."

While the others continued to laugh and banter about the notion, Lila Rose stared in disbelief. Surely these girls were only joking about such an outing.

An odd little thought wedged itself into her mind. Would Drew even be interested in any of them? From his behavior on Sunday, she doubted it. But why did that please her so much? She wasn't the slightest bit interested in Drew. No, indeed, she was not.

And to prove it, if only to herself, she barely spoke to the man beyond common courtesies for the next few days.

After the last steer thundered past him, Drew waved to Suzette and Old Fuzzy in the chuck wagon rolling away beside the herd once the dust had settled, then closed the gate and slipped the rope loop over the fencepost. He would miss Suzette. With her spunky personality, his newest sister-in-law had provided a buffer between him and Lila Rose.

In the less than two weeks since they'd arrived, Mother's companion—despite being a city gal—seemed to have found her place on the ranch and in the community. Of course Mother loved her like a daughter. Viola got along with her real well. The children treated her like a well-loved aunt. Pop spoke kindly to her from his sickbed. And everyone at church liked her.

Not that Drew minded her fitting in as long as she stayed in the house. But Rob had given her leave to select a couple of the new horses to use for sidesaddle lessons with the gals in Viola's etiquette class. What riding sidesaddle had to do with etiquette, Drew couldn't figure out. But with Suzette gone and all the gals in the class the very ones Drew tried to avoid, he'd have to make himself scarce on Mondays.

With the herd thinned down to Charlemagne, their bull, and fifty or so breeding cows, all of which needed very little tending, work now turned to repairs around the ranch. Rob wanted to add another fifty feet to the levee before flood season, which would keep them all busy.

Despite the harshness of this past winter, the barn hadn't suffered any damage other than needing another coat of paint—a three-day job at most, if Drew and two of the ranch hands set their minds to it. Then again, their best hands, Ranse Cable and Patrick Ahern, were terrible flirts, so if the women held their lessons in the corral not far from the barn, the painting might take longer.

If Drew mentioned the problem to Rob, his brother would only say he should find a wife among all those lovely ladies. At least, with Will gone for the summer and his two younger brothers managing the Sharp sheep ranch, Drew had some respite from the usual annoying remarks.

What bothered him most was that the remarks always hit their target. He would like to be married. More accurately, he would like to find a woman to love, as his brothers had. At the least, he wanted to be attracted to the woman he married. But the only woman he felt drawn to—against his will—was Lila Rose, the very woman who annoyed him the most. Which was ridiculous, of course. That city gal was the last woman he'd marry.

On the following Saturday, Lila Rose sashayed out to the corral with Viola and Lavinia. Well, *sashayed* might not be the right word. Drew had noticed that every time Mother's companion walked around the ranch, she kept looking around at the ground ahead of her, like she was scared something was going to attack her. Didn't she realize the dogs who ambled along beside them would warn of any danger? But he and Lila Rose barely exchanged a word, so he'd be the last to tell her. Maybe her fear of wild critters would keep her in the house.

Viola took Lavinia by the hand and whispered to her. They disappeared into the barn, probably to feed Lavinia's pony.

"These are the horses, Miss Lila Rose." Rob waved a hand toward the eight newcomers to the Mattson herd. "They're all saddle broke, so you can take a look at them and see which four you think will take to the sidesaddle."

Well, if that didn't beat all. Drew huffed in disgust. Rob was giving *her* first choice instead of him. What was next? Letting her decide when to bring in the first hay cutting?

No snakes had appeared on their walk from the house to the corral, so Lila Rose took one look at the fine horses in front of her and relaxed. Teas and book clubs were all well and good, but this was her favorite world—and oh, how she had missed it.

"Thank you, Rob. Let me spend a while with them." She'd brought a handful of carrots and now reached through the fence and offered one to the curious two-year-old geldings. A bay beauty stepped forward and took the carrot from her hand. She caressed its forehead. "Good morning, my lovely. Rob, do any of them have names?"

"No, ma'am. We usually leave the naming to whoever chooses 'em." He reached over the fence and rubbed the white blaze on the forehead of a black horse. After sniffing his hand, the horse moved away and took a carrot from Lila Rose. He chuckled. "Humph. Guess he's making his preference known."

"Oh, well, a bribe goes a long way in winning favor with them."

Behind her, she could hear Drew's snort. What was his problem? She turned to see him staring at the horses, a possessive gleam in his eyes.

"Rob, you know once she trains these horses to the sidesaddle, they'll be useless for herding cattle. They won't know the proper leg signals. In fact, all the signals will be wrong. And after she leaves, what will we do with a bunch of ladies' horses?" His scowl came close to being aimed at her.

Leave? When Rebecca seemed to have settled in for the summer? Lila Rose took a deep breath. "I'm so sorry. I had no idea. Perhaps this is a bad idea." To her surprise, her eyes stung from unwanted tears.

"Not at all." Viola emerged from the barn leading a pony, with Lavinia proudly seated in the saddle. "It's a wonderful idea. But I do agree with Drew. We can get by with two of the horses for our lessons—can't we, Lila Rose? Then when Lavinia grows too big for Champy, she and I can ride them."

"There you have it," Rob said to Drew. "Problem solved." He gave Viola a loving smile, which warmed Lila Rose's heart. How good it was to see a happily married couple. "Sweetheart, you and Lila Rose choose the two horses you want, and Drew can start training the rest for herding."

"Works for me." Drew's cross expression softened but didn't entirely disappear. "Let me know when you've picked out the ones you want. I'll take the left-overs." He strode away, hands in his pockets, shoulders slumped.

For the second time since she'd arrived at the ranch, Lila Rose felt a pang of sympathy for him. She'd had no idea that her being granted this privilege would cause a problem for him.

Halfway to the barn, Drew stopped. What was he doing letting that gal run him off? Not that she'd actually said anything to that effect. In fact, she'd offered to forget her plan…until Viola stepped in to support her. So of course Rob would side with his wife. *Women!* Nothing but trouble. But he wasn't going to let Lila Rose push him aside when he still had plans to win Pop's respect by training those cow ponies to do their job.

He turned and sauntered back to the scene of her victory to watch in case she messed up. At the least, he needed to know what bad habits he'd have to train out of the horses she chose.

"How about I bring out one at a time?" Halter in hand, Rob opened the gate and approached the bay, speaking gently as he put the leather strap over its head.

The horse tossed its head but finally settled down so he could lead it out. Taking one look at Champy, the gelding pinned his ears back and snorted, clearly not interested in making friends with the gentle old pony.

"That answers that." Viola lifted Lavinia from the saddle and took her to a safe place beside the fence. "We need a friendlier fellow if we're going to ride together."

"Right." Rob led the horse back to the herd and brought out another.

The black horse who had snubbed him in favor of a carrot gave Champy a curious sniff and nickered softly. The pony returned both the sniff and the nicker. Friendship accepted. The ladies voiced their approval.

And so it went until four horses were chosen.

"Four?" Drew fisted his hands at his waist. "I thought you said two."

Rob shot him a cross look. "Aren't you supposed to be feeding chickens or something?"

Feeding chickens? A child's job?

"Now, Rob." Viola seemed to be hiding a grin. Drew could always count on her to smooth things over. Or was she laughing at him?

He released a breath and started to turn away.

"We aren't through choosing." Lila Rose gave him a slight smile and, in the process, caused his heart to hiccough. *Mercy, she is pretty.*

Now where had that useless thought come from? Drew stopped in his tracks to watch what she was going to do with the horses next. *It's all about the horses, dummy!*

Lila Rose approached each gelding like an old friend, speaking gently and rubbing them in all the right spots. He couldn't help but approve of her methods…so far. And with each horse, she drew its head down, took a deep breath and placed a kiss on its nose.

No, no, no, he would not envy those beasts! No way did he want her to kiss *him*.

"Rob, I'm afraid you should check this dear boy. His breath smells a little sour. Did you check it before you bought him?"

Now how did she know to take the measure of a horse's health that way? Drew's respect and appreciation for the city gal kicked up several notches. And his heart jumped with another one of those annoying hiccoughs.

He might as well admit it: Miss Lila Rose Duval was getting under his skin, and he had no way to stop it.

Chapter Seven

Lila Rose tried to focus on Pastor Daniel's sermon, but her thoughts kept going back to Mr. Mattson. He had woken everyone last night with a terrible cough that had reverberated throughout the upstairs hallway, despite his closed bedroom door. Viola had brought a steaming kettle into the room, and Rob had tented a sheet over his bed so he could breathe the moist air. Only in the early hours had he finally settled down to a fitful sleep.

Of course, while the rest of the family attended the Sunday-morning service, Rebecca had remained at the ranch to care for her husband. Should Lila Rose have ignored her employer's instructions and stayed behind in case she was needed? If she wasn't sure Doc Warren would be out to see the old gentleman this morning, she might have argued to stay. But when Rob and Viola showed no alarm over the elder Mattson's condition, she decided to accompany them to church.

Drew was another story. He'd worn a worried frown all morning. If he hadn't rejected her previous attempt at consoling him, she would have offered a kind word.

Was she the only person on the ranch he disliked? He adored the children, and they delighted in his teasing. From what she could see of the ranch work from the house, he had the respect of the ranch hands. Rob trusted him with many important tasks, and he never appeared to shirk his responsibilities—indeed, did them all very well. And when they'd arrived at church, he'd been surrounded once more by the young ladies who always vied for his attention.

Which caused Lila Rose to wonder how the etiquette class would go tomorrow. Would these unattached and giggling girls show any interest in their lessons? Or did they come to the ranch just to see Drew? Well, they were welcome to him. Lila Rose had no interest in a man who shunned her like the plague. She'd been rejected by a man before and survived it.

"How do you view God?" The preacher's melodious voice broke into her musings. How could a man sound so gentle in tone and yet so thunderous in message? "Do you see Him as an angry father whom you will never please or a loving Father who loves and accepts you despite your faults and failures?"

Ah, good. Just what Drew needed to hear. Lila Rose glanced surreptitiously at the far end of the row to see his reaction to the preacher's questions. To her surprise, he had slipped out of the pew and was walking quietly to the back of the sanctuary. Was he ill? Such a shame when the preacher seemed about to address the very problem…other than *her*…that Drew had. So far, she could see no reason for Mr. Mattson's harshness toward Drew while showing Rob respect as an equal partner in managing the ranch.

She sat back to enjoy the sermon. Although she had

once viewed the Lord as an angry tyrant who thundered from Mount Sinai, she had learned in Rebecca's church that God was nothing like her earthly father. Instead, He loved and accepted her, even approved of her—not because she was good, but because He was. She would make it a priority to pray that Drew would grasp that precious truth. But without hearing about it, how could he believe? Only the Lord could sort that out, so she prayed He would.

Drew studiously avoided Rob's scowl as he left his seat and made his way outside. The last thing he needed to hear was how to earn God's approval when he couldn't even earn his father's. It wasn't like he didn't try. He worked hard, took on extra responsibilities, tried to be a gentleman to everyone—even the pesky young ladies who sought his attention.

Huh! All except that one young lady who didn't seek him out. A dart of guilt struck his conscience. He hadn't exactly been nice to Lila Rose. What did he have against her? Nothing, really, except that she was there. Pop still treated Mother badly, but he was a gentleman to her companion, so it wasn't as though he or anyone in the family found Lila Rose unlikeable.

Stepping down the front steps, Drew gazed across the road at Mission de Santa María, where congregants were entering for worship. One man on horseback saw him and rode across the dusty, rutted street, waving as he came over.

"Andrew, *amigo!*" Alejandro Martinez wore his usual ornate, finely tailored leather suit and silver-and-turquoise-adorned sombrero.

Drew and his brothers had decided the Mexican

always dressed so grandly so he could show off his wealth—not a very charitable thought toward a man who had saved their herd last year by warning of the imminent flooding of the Rio Grande. More guilt smote his conscience.

"'Morning, Martinez." Drew waved back.

"You do not attend your church with the others?" Martinez quizzed him with one raised eyebrow.

Drew shrugged. "It was getting a little warm in there."

"Ah. Well, *mi amigo*, you must come with me. It is always cool inside our adobe church." He beckoned with a wave and a tilt of his head. "*Vamos.* It is always good to hear what *Dios* has to say to us, *si*?"

Drew chuckled. "Well, I'd have to understand Spanish to know what your preacher says."

"Ah, so now you must learn it, *si*?"

"Sure." Drew understood more Spanish than he let on. He just never tried to speak it. "I'll try to pick some up from our Mexican hands."

"Muy bien." Martinez grinned, then grew serious. "Now, you must tell me, how is your father?"

"As well as can be expected."

"Ah." Sympathy shone from Martinez's eyes. "We shall continue to pray for him." Then he grinned. "Now tell me about the beautiful young lady who is residing at your ranch."

Drew laughed out loud. "You never fail to notice a pretty gal, do you?"

"Never, *mi amigo*. So, is she…*prometida*, promised?"

"Uh…" An oddly possessive feeling wound through Drew's chest. Where did that come from? Why should he care if this wealthy man was interested in Lila Rose?

"Alejandro!" His sister, Isabella, called from across the way. "You must come."

"*Si*, Bella." Martinez touched the brim of his hat. "*Adios*, Andrew." He turned his horse away, then turned again and waved toward Riverton Community Church. "Go back inside, my friend. You may hear something important. And if you become *caliente*, maybe *Dios* wants to tell you something, as He often tells me, Juan Alejandro Martinez." He touched the brim of his sombrero and rode away.

Right. Just what he needed—more guilt. Drew trudged back toward the white clapboard building to listen to the rest of Pastor Daniel's sermon, only to hear the unmistakable whine of the pump organ as Lacy Neal warmed it up for the final hymn. As he entered and returned to his place at the end of the pew beside Robbie, he could hear Lila Rose's pleasant alto intertwine with Viola's soprano. These two gals harmonized quite nicely with their singing, and it seemed to mirror the way they worked so well in everything, from household chores to those horses they'd chosen to work with.

Against his better reasoning, Drew liked that thought.

Just as Lila Rose expected, when the three girls from church arrived for their Monday class, they lingered outside the little cottage and stared off toward the bunkhouse…because there stood Drew. He was talking to several ranch hands, probably giving them orders for the day. Iris, Dolores and Alice giggled and waved, but the men were too absorbed in their conversation to notice. The other girls—Elena, Isabella and Juanita—hurried inside, eager for their lessons. Viola poured tea for everyone and passed around the still-warm muffins she'd baked earlier.

Although Lila Rose had no experience being around *enceinte* ladies, she felt concerned for Viola and watched her new friend to be sure she didn't overdo it. She'd often noticed Viola putting a hand on her lower back and stretching, as though trying to find a more comfortable position in which to sit or stand. And yet she never complained as she went about her housework.

"Ladies, we have a surprise for you." Viola took her place at the front of the room. "We have two horses designated for our sidesaddle lessons."

The girls all voiced their delight.

"Of course we need to train them first, and Lila Rose has agreed to take on that task." Viola nodded toward her. "When do you think we'll be ready for our first lesson?"

"The horses we chose should be easy to train. We should have them ready in three weeks. A month at the latest." As Lila Rose took in the bright-eyed attention the girls gave her, pleasant memories of helping Rebecca teach Sunday school came flooding back. It felt good to have eager students listen to her. Perhaps she was meant to be a teacher. If so, she must pay attention to Viola's methods.

As it had been last week, the class was more of a social time than an actual student-teacher situation. And yet Lila Rose noticed Viola's subtle instructions regarding serving tea, eating a muffin without a fork and using a napkin properly. She read a short passage from her Hosmer's *The Young Lady's Book* and reinforced its instruction with a Bible verse.

"Now, ladies…" Viola set aside the books. "I have an

idea. Suzette has offered us the use of her stove." She
pointed through the kitchen doorway to a new cast-iron
stove sitting against an outer wall. "What would you
think of spending next Monday morning preparing our
favorite recipes together? That way, we can all learn to
cook something new. It will also give us something to
do until the horses are ready for our lessons."

Cook? While the others gushed over the idea and
chatted about their favorite recipes, Lila Rose felt her
heart sink. Try though she might each day to help Viola
prepare meals, she only created disaster. Eggs cooked
so hard they were inedible or too runny to be appetiz-
ing. Bread dough refusing to rise. Cream that would
not become butter no matter how hard she cranked the
churn. She hadn't even tried to make gravy.

And yet, as the girls filed out of the house late that
morning, each one expressed delight over their future
riding lessons—so she did have something to offer
them. Most had ridden astride since childhood, but Iris
and Elena had not ridden at all. Lila Rose felt confident
she could teach them to feel comfortable around horses.
If only she could learn to manage household duties as
well so she could actually help Viola.

She'd taken over the sweeping and dusting so Viola
could rest more often. Even there, she still had much to
learn. Dust hid in the most obscure places. And despite
Viola reminding Drew, Rob and Robbie to clean their
boots in the mudroom, they carried part of the barnyard
into the house every day.

With Lavinia skipping along beside them, Lila Rose
and Viola returned to the house.

"How'd yer class go, Miss Viola?" Agnes, one of the

laundry ladies, removed an already-dry white shirt from the clothesline, snapped it in the breeze and folded it.

"Very well, thank you," Viola said. "Lila Rose and I will have your lunch ready shortly."

"Gracias, señora." Rosa stood at the washtub, scrubbing Robbie's brown trousers against the washboard.

In the kitchen a few minutes later, Viola sliced roast beef and bread. Lila Rose assembled the sandwiches, then placed some in a small box for the laundry ladies and some in a hamper for the men who were building a levee down by the river. She set two sandwiches on a plate and brushed the crumbs from her hands.

"I'll take these up to Rebecca." She had spoken to her employer only briefly this morning and didn't want to neglect her.

"If you don't mind, I'd like to see how Pop is doing." Viola prepared a bowl of potato salad and placed the plate and bowl on a tray. "Would you please take lunch out to the others?"

A response stuck in Lila Rose's throat. She hadn't walked outside by herself since coming to the ranch and had no desire to do so again. Yet how could she say no to Viola after trying to think of ways to help her? Heart pounding, she delivered the small box to the ladies, then inhaled a bracing breath and began her trek down the hill to the river.

"It's about time." Patrick Ahern tossed down his shovel and wiped sweat from his brow. "Breakfast was a long time ago. Say, take a look at our new waitress." He whistled softly. "Drew, you gotta introduce us to that lady."

Drew glanced up the hill to see Lila Rose carrying

the lunch hamper Viola usually brought down when they worked on the levee. As usual, she was staring at the ground and gingerly taking one step at a time. Something inside his chest jumped like a frog.

Ahern whistled a little louder. "Maybe I should go help her."

A couple of the other men laughed.

"No, I'll go." Ranse Cable stepped in front of Ahern and started toward the hill. The two shoved each other jovially.

The jumping frog in his chest turned into a sitting granite boulder. "Stay where you are." Did he sound jealous? Best to cut that off at the pass. "She's a lady, so I'll introduce you properly."

Leaving their teasing and protests behind, he strode up the hill to meet Lila Rose. "Let me take that." He gripped the hamper's handle.

She looked up in surprise. "W-why, thank you." She released her hold on the wicker box and turned back toward the house.

"You don't have to go." Drew had no idea why he'd said that. Best to cover his mistake. "The cowhands have asked to meet you. If you don't mind, may I introduce you?"

"Oh." She frowned. "Why would they want to meet me?"

Because you're a beautiful lady, and...

"Um, well, it's just good for everybody on the ranch to know each other."

"I see." Her puzzled expression showed she didn't really "see."

Hamper in one hand, he offered her his opposite elbow. "Careful. The ground's pretty uneven."

She blinked those blue eyes, and her jaw dropped slightly. After a brief hesitation, she placed her hand on his forearm. Her light touch sent a pleasant shiver up his arm all the way to his neck. He managed to hide the subsequent tremor that swept over the rest him. What on earth was wrong with him? He saw this woman every day. Ate meals with her. Must be the heat of the day affecting him. He cleared his throat and led her to the worksite.

"Miss Lila Rose Duval, these are our ranch hands." Drew waved a hand toward the men. "Ranse Cable, Patrick Ahern—he's Agnes's son—Juan Garcia, Julio Mendez."

"How do you do?" Lila Rose's voice sounded a little shaky.

Had Drew made a mistake to bring her down here? Was this some breach of that etiquette she and Viola went on about so much of the time?

"Howdy, Miss Lila Rose." Ranse Cable gave her that grin that usually charmed the ladies.

"¿Cómo estás, senorita?" chorused Juan and Julio as they swept off their wide-brimmed hats.

"Top 'o the mornin', miss." Ahern had the audacity to wink, completing the picture of the proud Irishman.

The men all spoke at the same time, jostling each other and reaching out their dust-covered hands.

"Um…" Lila Rose released Drew's arm and stepped back.

"Now, boys, you know better than that." A protective feeling he usually reserved for little Lavinia welled up inside him. He stepped in front of her to cut off their advances. "Maybe you can shake hands later, after you clean up." He set down the hamper. "Now, y'all go ahead and eat." He offered her his arm again. "Miss Lila Rose, may I escort you back to the house?"

Again, she blinked her eyes in surprise. "Why…why, yes, thank you."

This time she gripped his arm like a lifeline. Even gave him a little smile.

Warmth flooded his chest. He needed to keep a barrier between them, but somehow he couldn't hold back those nice feelings any more than he could hold back the annual flooding of the Rio Grande. Only a simple-minded cowboy let himself fall for a city gal, because it would just lead to a broken heart.

Lila Rose couldn't imagine what had brought about this change in Drew, but she deeply appreciated it. Not only had he protected her from being overwhelmed by the charming but dust-covered ranch hands, but he also now walked beside her as she returned to the house. If a snake crossed their path, he would know how to deal with it.

"Did you have a nice class?" Drew broke into her thoughts, surprising her again with his interest.

"Yes." She wouldn't mention the plan to include cooking in the curriculum. Her disasters in the kitchen had remained her secret with Viola, and she didn't want Drew and Rob to have a reason to tease her, as they did Viola and the children. "The girls are looking forward to learning how to ride sidesaddle."

At his frown, she regretted her comment right away. When Rob had let Viola and her take their pick of the new horses, his displeasure had been obvious. Now she'd shattered his brief moment of friendliness toward her. What could she say to restore it?

"Of course, everyone misses Suzette. She's such an inspiration to us all."

"Yep." Drew's frown softened. "I sure was glad to see her hog-tie Will. With his ugly face, he didn't seem likely to get a gal as pretty as her."

At his unexpected remark, Lila Rose's inner tension fled, and she burst out laughing so hard she had to stop walking.

"Now, what did I say to cause such a ruckus?" Drew seemed to attempt a puzzled expression, but his lips formed a little smirk.

When she could speak, Lila Rose said, "First of all, from the way Will looks at his lovely bride, I doubt he considers himself *hog-tied*." Drew raised a finger as if to object, but she didn't give him that chance. "*Furthermore*, you Mattson brothers all look alike, and I doubt anyone would ever call any of you ugly." *Oh, no!* Why had she made such a forward remark? She began walking again, giving him a sidelong glance to see how it had affected him.

He caught up with her, still smirking. "So, you think I'm—*we're*—handsome, do you?"

"Humph. I said no such thing. But from the way the young ladies—the *other* young ladies—try to get your attention, I'm assuming they consider you at least tolerable looking."

"Ah. I see." His pleased-with-himself smile didn't fade until they reached the house. "I'll leave you here and hurry back before the boys eat all those sandwiches."

Standing in the back doorway, she watched him trot down the hill.

His teasing revealed that something had shifted in his feelings toward her. While she had no idea what it was, it certainly would make life here on the ranch more bearable for however long Rebecca decided to stay.

Maybe more than bearable. Maybe undeniably enjoyable.

Chapter Eight

Drew fidgeted at the breakfast table, eager to get on with his day. If he had his way, he'd already be out the door. But Rob had taken on Pop's habit of discussing everybody's duties before sending them off to do them. As if Drew didn't know what his responsibilities were.

Rob offered prayer, then heaped a half dozen of Viola's pancakes onto his plate and poured on syrup. He added three fried eggs on top of that. "Sweetheart, you sure do know how to give us a good start on the day." He said the same thing every morning, and from the look on Viola's pretty face, she didn't mind the repetition at all.

Drew supposed he'd compliment his wife's cooking that way when the day came. He'd noticed with all four brothers that good marriages seemed to be made even better when the wife got the recognition and praise she deserved. Drew did the same with their ranch hands.

And his horses. Which was why he was so eager to get out to the corral and start working with the six horses left to him after Lila Rose got her pick.

Thinking of that young lady, where was she? Most days since she'd arrived, she'd been here in the kitchen, helping Viola get the meal on the table. Not that he'd actually seen her prepare anything, but if she was anything like Viola, she'd be serving up some fine meals one of these days. Maybe when Viola welcomed her little one into the family and needed to rest up for a while.

"Good morning, everyone." Entering the room with her usual gracefulness, the lady of his thoughts wore a brown denim skirt and blue shirtwaist, like she was ready to do some chore. Maybe the ladies had planned to start spring-cleaning today.

Out of a habit begun a year ago after Viola arrived, Rob, Robbie and Drew stood and welcomed her. Drew took a step forward to pull out her chair, but Robbie beat him to it.

"Morning, Miss Lila Rose." The boy, only ten years old, gazed up at her with something akin to puppy love. Cute.

"Good morning, Master Robbie." Her smile brought a blush to the boy's cheeks.

Drew liked it when she smiled at him, too. He shook off the thought. Any man would appreciate a pretty girl's attention.

Soon everyone had full plates—in Rob's case, a second full plate—and dug into their ham, eggs, potatoes and pancakes.

"Drew," Rob said, "I want you to start painting the barn this morning before the wind picks up and blows dust into it. Have Cable and Garcia help you. I'll work on the levee with Ahern and Mendez—" he winked at his son "—and Robbie." He went on eating as if he hadn't just ruined Drew's day.

"Um, I'd thought I'd start training those horses this morning."

"No. Lila Rose will be in the training corral with her two horses this morning." Rob said it casually, as if to convey that there would be no discussion, then finished his last bite. "Viola, I spoke with Mother before I came down. She'd like to see you when you get a minute." He stood and kissed his wife on the forehead. "Robbie, you ready to go?"

"Yessir." The boy grinned as he gave Viola a hug around the shoulders. "Have a good day, Mom."

"Thank you, my darling. You too." Viola's eyes reddened just a smidge. She brushed a hand through his hair. "Wear your hat so your ears don't get sunburned."

"Yes, ma'am."

Despite his own hurt over his ruined day, Drew appreciated the love he saw between his nephew and sister-in-law. After Rob's first wife, Maybelle, had taken baby Lavinia and abandoned him and their son, the boy had often seemed like a lost pup. With only hardworking men in the household, he hadn't had much of a childhood. Then Maybelle died, and her distant cousin Viola brought Lavinia back to the ranch. It didn't take long for her to heal more than Rob's broken heart. She'd restored Robbie's boyhood as well.

If only somebody could restore Mother and Pop's marriage. Then maybe Drew would get some respect, maybe even love, from his father.

At least if he painted the barn to Rob's satisfaction, he'd earn his oldest brother's approval, if only as a brief "good work." That thought in mind, he headed out to the bunkhouse to fetch Cable and Garcia. He had no doubt they would appreciate a change of pace after the harder work of building the levee.

"I'll take breakfast up to Rebecca and Mr. Mattson." Lila Rose took a tray from a shelf above the sideboard and began to assemble the necessary items. When she'd helped her employer prepare for bed the night before, the lady had appeared uncharacteristically depressed but too tired to explain why. Lila Rose hoped to cheer her up this morning, or at least try to discern how she and Mr. Mattson were getting along and whether she could help in any way.

"Thank you, but Rob said Rebecca—*Mother* wants to see me." Viola spooned hot oatmeal into two bowls and covered each with a saucer, then emptied the coffeepot into a carafe.

Lila Rose stifled her disappointment. After all, Viola was the daughter-in-law, while she was only a companion. Was it time for her to earnestly seek new employment even though she had no idea where to begin? Or would that be deserting her employer at a bad time? She mustn't do anything hasty without speaking to Rebecca.

For now, she must settle for teaching the etiquette class, although she truly was not teaching anything the girls hadn't already learned from Viola. The Monday morning gatherings were still mostly social times.

Exhaling a quiet sigh and dismissing her own depression, Lila Rose reminded herself of the one task she could do well—training those two fine horses Rob had let her choose.

"While I go up," Viola said, breaking into her musings, "would you please make a new pot of coffee? I'd like another cup before I start my day." She lifted the tray and took a step toward the door.

"Um…are you sure you want me to make it?" Lila Rose shuddered comically. "If you recall, my last attempt was undrinkable. And, I hasten to add, yes—I did follow your instructions carefully."

Viola laughed. "All right, then. I'll make it when I come back down. Oh, look. Here's our sweet girl and her kitty." She put the tray on the table and hugged her stepdaughter. "Good morning, sweetheart. Good morning, Puff."

Always shy in the morning, Lavinia buried her face in Viola's apron. Obviously feeling a little too squeezed, Puff jumped down and headed for her water dish.

"There's something you do very well, Lila Rose." Viola lifted the tray again, a slight wince revealing that simple action had caused her some discomfort. "Please fix a plate for Lavinia and sit with her while she eats." She spoke over her shoulder as she left the room.

"Yes, of course." Lila Rose smiled at the pretty, dark-haired five-year-old. "What would you like, my dear? Pancakes? Oatmeal?" Plenty of both remained on the stove.

"Can I… *May* I please have a scrabbled egg?"

"Oh." *Scrabbled?* How adorable. But Lila Rose doubted she could successfully prepare a *scrambled* egg. She spied a cold fried one on the platter. "Will this do?"

Disappointment clouded the child's face. She heaved out a big sigh. "Yes, ma'am."

No, that wouldn't do at all, not with Lavinia being so sweet in her disappointment. Lila Rose must at least try.

"Tell you what—you help me. Please get an egg from the icebox."

While Lavinia obeyed, Lila Rose turned to the stove, where the large cast-iron skillet sat to the side of the burner Viola usually used. Using a tea towel to grasp the handle, she moved the heavy pan over to the hotter area, hoping enough heat still radiated from the low-burning firebox. Should she add wood to it? She decided against it. It appeared that plenty of ham grease still coated the bottom of the pan, so she wouldn't have to add any.

Cracking the egg should have been simple, but too many bits of shell landed in the bowl. With no little difficulty, Lila Rose fished them out with a knife point. Oh, my. Who knew that uncooked eggs could be so slippery?

"I want to scrabble it." Lavinia grasped a fork and whipped the egg, sloshing only a little onto the table. She held the bowl up to Lila Rose. "See? I did it."

"Very good." Even with her lack of kitchen experience, Lila Rose could see the yolk was barely broken.

She took the bowl in hand and gave the egg a few more whips, then poured it into the pan. The egg quickly bubbled around the edges while the center remained uncooked. Should she stir it? Taking the egg turner Viola always used, she nudged the edges. Grease poured into the middle of the egg and mixed with it. Lila Rose watched in horror as it all oozed into a greasy, unappetizing white-and-yellow mess. She couldn't feed that to Lavinia.

"Meow." Puff reached up with her front paws and dug her claws into Lila Rose's skirt.

"No, Puff." Lavinia carefully plucked the claws out and gazed up at Lila Rose, her brown eyes bright with trust. "Mommy always feeds her in the morning."

"Ah. Very good." Lila Rose scooped part of the mostly cooked egg back into the bowl and set it on the floor. The eager kitty gave it a sniff, then walked away. "Give it a minute, Puff. It will cool."

To her relief, before she wasted another egg attempting to scramble it for Lavinia, Viola returned to the kitchen. After surveying the scene, she smiled at Lila Rose.

"Well, look at you. Fixing Puff's breakfast. Thank you so much. Now, why don't you go ahead with your day. I know you're eager to start training those horses." She scraped the remnants of the egg and grease from the pan into the bucket reserved for pig food.

"Thank you." Grateful for Viola's kind misreading of the situation and glad to escape the kitchen, Lila Rose walked toward the door. "Is everything all right with Rebecca?"

"Yes." Viola didn't offer any further response, so there was no need to pursue the subject.

Perhaps this evening, Lila Rose could coax Rebecca to confide in her, as she'd done these past four years. She missed those times.

On the way out, she was gratified to see Puff devouring the ruined egg now that it had cooled. The sweet kitty's appetite reminded her to grab some apples from the bin beside the icebox.

But as she stepped out the door and walked through the kitchen garden, the space between house and barn suddenly stretched out before her like a danger-packed continent inhabited by deadly snakes and other un-known perils. Would those coyotes she'd heard howl-ing in the night come looking for their next meal?

On legs that felt like wood, she began her trek, her gaze darting back and forth across the ground. Only by thinking of the joy before her could she force one foot in front of the other…and pray no snakes would attack her. If one did, could she outrun it?

Drew set the paint can and brushes on the plank table he'd built last week. He glanced up at Cable and Garcia, who stood on ladders, making good time scraping the side of the barn with metal scrapers. Once the rough parts were smoothed out, the painting should be done in two or three days, so long as the afternoon wind didn't whip up real bad and blow sand into the wet paint.

Midge and Sport, Robbie and Lavinia's two dogs, chased each other around the barnyard. They spotted Lila Rose at the same moment Drew did and made a beeline for her. He hadn't seen her interact with the dogs and was glad when she crouched and welcomed them with open arms. They licked her face and spun around in circles, each trying to get the most of her at-tention. Even at this distance, he could hear her musi-cal laughter.

He also heard Cable's low whistle. "Beats me how you Mattson men can attract such pretty women out here in the middle of nowhere. If you ain't gonna spark her, how about letting me?"

Garcia laughed. "If *mi querida*, Estrella, didn't al-ready own my heart, I would ask the same."

Drew shot an annoyed look at the two of them. "Just get on with your work."

His gruff order only brought out snickers.

He did his best not to look as though he was watching Lila Rose, but his eyes decided to turn in her direction. Still petting the dogs, she appeared to be adjusting to the outdoors.

Oops. Forget that. Now that she'd stood back up and started walking his way, she searched the ground in front of her as if expecting it to open up and swallow her. Should he go over and walk her to the corral? Nope, no way would he give Cable and Garcia more reasons to josh him.

Besides, she was coming out here to train two of *his* horses. He would ignore her and let her figure things out for herself. Nothing out here was gonna hurt her, but she'd have to learn that herself without any help from him.

His conscience pricked him. It was his fault she was even here, far from the city life she was used to. And despite not having any ladies on the ranch until last year, when Viola had brought Lavinia back from Charleston, he and his brothers had been raised to treat ladies with good manners. Protect them, even. Lila Rose sure did seem to need protection, though he doubted she would admit it.

She reached the open barn door and gave him a little wave, then ducked inside. Which brought on another annoying thought. They had ten stalls in the barn. Two for the milk cows, one for Rob's stallion, one for Lavinia's pony, one for Robbie's little bay gelding, Corky, three for hay storage. Somehow Viola had taken it upon herself to designate the two empty ones for the horses she and Lila Rose had chosen for sidesaddle training. Never mind that Drew's gelding, and Will's horse when he was home, had to be turned out with the herd in the large corral or the front pasture. To make more stalls available, they could move the hay to the loft, but it was already filled to the rafters from this year's first cutting.

Women. All Viola had to do was bat those pretty blue eyes at Rob or put a hand to her back like she was in pain, especially these recent months, and he would rearrange the entire house or barn to her liking.

Drew would do his best to treat these ladies with good manners, but he would never, ever let a woman persuade him to jump through hoops to please her.

Lila Rose waited while two barn cats chased a mouse from the tack room. While mice could startle her or a horse, she had no fear of them—but no fondness, either. As she entered the room, the smell of leather swept over her, bringing on a wave of nostalgia. Other than Mama, Lila Rose's only happy childhood memories were of her beloved horses. She never thought she'd be able to train one again, and now she had two.

The large room was well organized and clean, the dirt floor neatly swept. No cobwebs hung in the corners. And only a few dust motes danced in the light streaming in through the small rectangular window near the ceiling. Various halters, bridles, lassos and even spurs hung on wall pegs. The saddles sat on wooden stands, and the saddle blankets were laid over racks. Hoof picks, medicine for injuries and tins of leather-cleaning oil all sat on shelves. She even found a lunge whip tucked in a corner. The Mattsons must have a ranch hand who kept all this in order, just as Father had hired a groom for his barn. That groom, George, had taught her everything she knew about horses…until that horrible day.

Dismissing her gloomy thoughts, she donned her leather riding gloves, grateful she hadn't disposed of them when she left Father's lost farm. At last she had a use for them. Although a little stiff, they soaked up the leather oil she applied and should soon be supple again.

She selected two halters and grabbed the lunge whip, then headed for the stalls to lead the two geldings out to the circular corral beyond the large one. Viola had chosen the black horse with a white blaze and named him Prince. Even though the red bay wouldn't belong to Lila Rose, she had been granted the privilege of naming him. With his training mate boasting such a noble name, she could do no less for him. He would be Duke.

"Good morning, my handsome boys." She retrieved two apples from her pocket to catch their interest.

The horses put their heads over the sides of their adjoining stalls and nickered a welcome, then gobbled down the apples. She rubbed their foreheads and murmured nonsense to them.

"Now, let's go have some fun." She put halters and lead ropes on them and led them out into the sunshine. And paused.

The circular corral lay beyond the larger one in which the main herd was kept, a long way to walk through weeds and stumps where dangers might be hiding.

"Need any help, Miss?" Mr. Cable, one of the ranch hands who'd been scraping the side of the barn, jumped down from his ladder and approached her.

Beyond him, she could see Drew watching, his dark eyebrows bent into a frown. But he didn't counter the offer.

"W-why, thank you, Mr. Cable."

"Please, call me Ranse." He gave her a charming smile. Dare she call it flirtatious? "Let me take those." He reached for the lead ropes.

"Um, well. Thank you, Ranse." She fumbled for a gracious way to decline his offer without embarrassing him in front of the other man, Mr. Garcia, who was watching their interaction with all too much interest. "But I want them to bond with me and, as I'm sure you know, bonding begins on the first day of training."

"Yes, ma'am. I understand." He stepped back, still grinning.

Over his shoulder, she could see Drew trying to hide a smile. Was he pleased that she had declined Ranse's offer of help? *Humph.* She should have accepted it.

No. That would have been childish and might cause a misunderstanding on the ranch hand's part.

"Now, if you'll excuse me..." But the moment she started walking toward the far corral, she wished she'd accepted that offer. Not to be with him, of course, but to have some protection against the snakes. Too late now. Perhaps the vibrations of the horses' hooves would frighten any snakes away. After all, that black racer hadn't stuck around the day Suzette dislodged it from its sleeping shelter beside the log. Would a rattlesnake do the same, or would it chase her?

Oh, she truly must get over this fear. The horses would pick up on it. With a deep breath in and a long breath out, she glanced upward. "Lord, thank You for this wonderful opportunity to work with these lovely horses. Thank You for these clear blue skies. Thank You for Your care for me." *And please protect me—and, of course, these dear boys—from snakes.*

By the time they reached the training corral, her pulse had slowed, and she was able to coax her two charges into the ring without any trouble. After tying Duke to the railing, she led Prince around the perimeter, cooing to him in a soft voice. After a while, she repeated the exercise with Duke. Gradually, she moved toward the center of the ring and let out the lead little by little, using the lunge whip to guide each horse in turn.

If they hadn't already been saddle broken, the two-year-olds might not have taken to her training as quickly. And they were still young enough to respond to her next steps. If they did well, she could begin teaching the young ladies to ride sidesaddle sooner than expected.

Despite himself, Drew watched as Lila Rose began her training. She was doing a good job, using many of the same techniques with the two geldings that he would have. Due to a mild breeze blowing up from the river, her pleasant alto voice carried across the distance. He could listen to her all day. *What? No.* But at least it would be better than hearing the mindless chatter of these two ranch hands he was stuck working with.

He'd been worried when Cable offered to help her. The cowboy had a way with the ladies, so Drew was relieved when she turned him down so graciously. A local gal might have said "get lost" to the cowboy, but her city-bred manners smoothed the situation over. Drew had to appreciate that.

The morning wore on, and heat began to beat down on them as they worked farther down the side of the barn, where the breeze couldn't reach them. Working in that breeze, Rob and the rest of the hands continued to add dirt to the levee. For once, Drew wished he were working on the levee instead of the barn.

"Let's take a break." He took off his hat and wiped sweat on his sleeve, then took a drink from the nearby bucket. He emptied the dipper over his head and shook off the extra water.

After doing the same, Cable and Garcia took refuge in the barn to get out of the sun. Drew wandered toward the slope leading to the river to see how the levee work was proceeding. Rob and his men had also taken a break and were lounging on the piles of dirt. Robbie sat under the lone cottonwood tree that grew nearby.

"Lord, make that levee work," Drew prayed. "Make it hold back the flood like it did last year." They'd only lost a little of their lower pasture and none of their livestock, thanks to an early warning from Martinez.

Before he got too lost in thought, Drew headed back up the hill. Across the way, he saw Lila Rose still busy with the horses. Had she taken a break, too? Maybe not. He'd suggest that for tomorrow, then keep an eye on her to be sure she did. Mother would be devastated if heatstroke overcame her companion.

When she brought the horses back to the barn, he noticed the bright pink of her cheeks and the scattering of freckles across her pretty little nose. Gals didn't seem to like freckles, but he'd always thought they were kinda cute. Still, she should have worn a hat. Did she even have one besides that dainty bit of nonsense she wore to church—a mere decoration that wouldn't protect her from anything? Should he offer to take her to town so she could buy a brimmed bonnet to shield her fair skin? Why was he even thinking these things?

Maybe he would go to the barn dance at the Gentrys' place coming up in a couple of Saturdays and spend some time with the local gals, ones he'd grown up with, ones who might flirt with him something terrible but who knew how to take care of themselves. That would take his mind off the pesky single female he couldn't avoid here at home.

No, that wouldn't work. Other than Cable and a couple of the other single hands, the only other person from the ranch who might want to attend the dance was Lila Rose. Viola would insist that he invite her, but he sure couldn't ask her to go with him and the boys. Where was Suzette when he needed her? His new sister-in-law knew how to manage these situations.

Then another plan came to mind. Yep. That might just work…*and* keep him out of trouble.

Chapter Nine

Lila Rose led Prince into his stall, gratified to see Drew or one of the men had already mucked it out. The same was true of Duke's stall. *Thank You, Lord*. She wouldn't have to ask Drew to see that the chore was done. What an efficient operation these Mattsons ran.

She brushed each horse in turn, and each leaned into her, clearly enjoying the attention. This was one of her favorite parts of training because it showed the animals their time together was not all work.

After removing their halters, she took them to the tack room and laid them over an empty saddle stand, where Drew could find them easily and clean them for her.

Satisfied with her morning work, she ambled outside. *Oh, my.* After being in the barn for close to a half hour, she now felt the sun's heat even worse than before.

"How'd your training go?" Drew spoke over his shoulder as he brushed paint onto the wood siding.

"Very well, thank you." She noticed that beyond him, the two ranch hands had paused in their work to listen to the conversation. Both wore friendly smiles, not at all flirtatious.

Drew's smile was more of a grin. "You get pretty hot out there?" His blue eyes sparkled in the sunshine.

Her heart skipped. But how silly. She had seen this man every day for weeks now. Why should she react this way?

"Yes, very hot."

"You got a hat?"

"A hat? Do you mean a bonnet with a brim? No, I haven't." She turned to leave.

"We could get you one." His persistent concern charmed her even more than his eyes.

But then, the other men appeared to be hiding their amusement at this exchange, so the charm dimmed. In fact, the friendliness of all three caused Lila Rose's cheeks to heat even more than the weather warranted. Why all this fuss about a hat?

"Thank you, but I'm sure Viola has something I can wear." She dabbed her handkerchief against the perspiration on her forehead. "By the way, I noticed one of your cow ponies in the front pasture by himself."

"Yeah, that's old Fred. He's past his prime and can't move as quick as the steers, so Rob retired him after buying the new stock."

"So he's not a troublemaker?"

"No, not at all. Fred's real docile."

"Does he get along with the rest of the herd?" How sad to put him out alone. Horses needed their herds.

"As I said, never gave us any trouble."

"Hmm." She considered this for a moment. "Would you please bring him down to the barn? His calm disposition may settle the friskiness of the younger horses. If so, I'd like to see if he can be trained to the sidesaddle."

Drew gave her a long look. "Yes, ma'am. I'll be glad to do it."

When she reached her room to freshen up, a glance in the mirror revealed the reason for Drew's teasing. Not only were her forehead and cheeks bright pink, almost red, but also dreaded freckles had popped out on her nose. Freckles so obvious that no face powder would hide them.

Those men weren't being friendly. They were laughing at her! How utterly mortifying.

Well, she couldn't take time for self-pity, no matter how embarrassed she was. All she could do was gently apply her face cream to her burning skin, then put on a fresh shirtwaist and hurry down to the kitchen to help Viola prepare lunch for the men. And none too soon. Weariness shone on Viola's face and in her posture.

"Lila Rose, would you please take the lunch hamper out to the men?"

Just what she did not want to do. Although she hadn't seen any snakes so far today, the slithery beasts surely would reside between here and the river. But how could she refuse to help Viola? Even if doing so gave the rest of the ranch hands a chance to laugh at her ruined complexion again. Her eyes unexpectedly began to sting.

"Yes, of course." Hiding her tears from Viola, she gripped the wicker handle and lifted, only to realize how her work with the horses had tired her arms, especially her left one. She forced a smile. "Smells wonderful."

Viola nodded and gave her a weary smile.

Back out in the sunshine, she realized her mistake. She should have asked for a hat. Too late now. Arms aching, she walked across the barnyard, grateful for the company of the two adorable black-and-white dogs who had joined her. Her father had kept hound dogs for hunting, but when she tried to play with them, he forbade it. Even so, she'd often snuck little treats to them. Against Father's wishes, Mama had permitted her to have a little golden spaniel as long as she kept it away from Father. One day, as they walked near the river, a cottonmouth had emerged from the water and aggressively slithered toward her. Goldie had barked and jumped in front of her, taking the snake's bite intended for her. She shook off the sad memory. It would be dreadful if these friendly dogs got bitten as well, but perhaps they would warn her if a snake appeared.

Halfway across the barnyard, her aching arms forced her to set the hamper down for a moment. Lifting it again, she felt pain shoot up her left arm to her shoulder. Huffing out a breath, then inhaling another, she continued her trek…until Drew came running toward her.

"Here. Let me." He gripped the wicker handle.

"No, no. I'm fine." She tried to keep walking.

He gave her that silly grin that annoyed her so much.

She stopped. Why was she being so foolish? "Very well. Thank you."

As they continued toward the river, each holding on to the hamper, it occurred to her that she could turn back and let him take it the rest of the way. But somehow, she was enjoying this bit of companionship with him…until she remembered his amusement over her freckles. She stopped.

"I think you can manage from here on out."

"Oh. Awright." He stared down at her with those intense blue eyes.

She looked away. "There are plenty of sandwiches, fried potato wedges, pickles, lemonade…" Why was she going on like this?

"Yep. You ladies always feed us well."

She didn't contradict his assumption, even though if it were up to her, no one would be fed around here.

"Say, I have to go into town later this afternoon for two more buckets of paint. You wanna go with me?"

She blinked. "Well…"

"Hey, Drew!" Rob called from beside the river. "We're hungry. Get on over here."

Lila Rose used that interruption to make her escape. As much as she would like to go to town, she doubted it would be proper for her to go alone with Drew.

On the other hand, if Rebecca needed something from the dry goods store, perhaps she would countenance such a trip. The thought made her heart skip in a most annoying way.

She found Viola eating lunch with Lavinia at the kitchen table when she returned.

"Oh, good. You're back." Viola gave her a weak smile. "Would you mind taking lunch up to Mother and Pop?"

"Yes, of course." Lila Rose hadn't been able to spend much time with her employer since they'd come here three weeks ago, so she welcomed the opportunity.

Loading a tray with cups of coffee, small bowls of soup, sandwiches and cutlery, she made the precarious trip up the staircase. Her arms still ached from her morning workout, but she managed to make it to the master bedroom without dropping the tray. To her relief, the door stood open.

"Take that poison away!"

Shocked at Mr. Mattson's angry outburst, Lila Rose started to turn away...until she saw he wasn't yelling at her. Instead, he was resisting Rebecca's attempt to spoon medicine into his mouth.

"Good afternoon." She used her cheeriest voice. "Here's your lunch." She set the tray on a side table, praying for some pleasant words to break the tension in the room.

"Thank you, Lila Rose." Rebecca sounded as weary as she looked, poor dear. She began to sort the items on the tray, setting some on a lap tray for her husband.

Hungry though she was, Lila Rose sat on the edge of a straight-backed chair. "You'll never guess what I did this morning." She gave them each a sweet smile, inviting a response.

"You must tell me—*us*." Rebecca took a sip of her coffee.

"Ain't it obvious, woman?" Mr. Mattson scowled at his wife but turned a paternal smile toward Lila Rose. "You been training them new horses, ain't you?"

To Lila Rose, it seemed he was deliberately using poor grammar, perhaps to goad poor Rebecca. While she would be pleased to scold him for treating his wife so badly, it would achieve nothing.

"Indeed I have. How did you guess?"

He snorted out a laugh. "Easy, missy. You soaked up quite a bit of sun. Hope it's not too painful."

"Oh, my dear." Rebecca stared at Lila Rose with alarm. "I should have noticed. Does it hurt? Do you have some salve or some face cream? Why, you could have suffered heatstroke!"

Their concern brought tears to her eyes. "Please don't concern yourselves. I'm quite well. In fact, I had a wonderful time. The two horses Rob has assigned to me are quite biddable and seem eager to please. I'll have them trained very soon. Rebecca, will you go riding with me?"

"She don't ride." Mr. Mattson stuffed a bite of sandwich into his mouth, then spoke around it. "Never could get her on a horse. Never could get her to do much of anything..."

He sounded like Lila Rose's father, who never appreciated all Mama did for him.

Rebecca set aside her bowl of soup. "Excuse me." Head held high, she walked from the room.

Although Lila Rose longed to scold this mean old reprobate, she stood to follow her employer instead.

"Sit down and tell me more about the horses." Mr. Mattson waved a hand toward the chair Rebecca had just vacated. "And how did you come to know about horses?"

She sensed his interest lay in whether she was qualified to do the job, so she sat.

"My father owned a horse farm. During the war, he provided horses for the army. By some turn of events I never understood, he managed to keep the farm after Appomattox and continued raising Tennessee Walkers."

He scowled again, perhaps because she mentioned the war, so she hurried on.

"Of course, as soon as I was old enough to avoid getting stepped on...and could escape my governess..." She paused and gave a comical wince, which brought on the hoped-for chuckle. "I spent all my days in the barn with Father's groom, George. With the patience of Job, he taught me all about training horses." She hesitated but decided to tell him the rest. "Father lost the farm through gambling…and drinking."

"Humph." He glanced briefly toward the window. "No brothers?"

"No, sir." That sad fact had angered Father even more than the South losing the war…as if both had been Mama's fault. "I am so thankful that after my parents' deaths, the Lord led me to Rebecca. She has been like a mother to me."

His eyes glazed over. "You can take this tray."

"Yes, of course." Obviously he wouldn't listen to any favorable comments regarding his wife.

She found Rebecca in the kitchen, helping Viola with early supper preparations. The poor dear needed to get out of this house, if only for a few hours. Drew's invitation provided the perfect solution.

"Rebecca, Drew told me he needed more paint, so he invited me to go to town with him. I should probably buy myself a bonnet, so I think I'll accept. Would you like to go?" She noticed the approval in Viola's eyes and extended the invitation to her as well.

"No, thank you." She tilted her head toward Lavinia, who sat at the table, practicing her letters on a slate. "But I know someone who would like to go."

The child looked up, a grin on her sweet face. "Me?"

The matter decided, Lila Rose fetched her parasol and braved the expanse of the barnyard to find Drew.

Drew hadn't meant to invite Lila Rose to go to town with him. The words had just popped out of his mouth.

But then, as he finished using the last drops of paint in his can, he considered that her presence might actually help with his plan. She hadn't agreed to the trip, but maybe Viola or even Mother might need something from the dry goods store that only another lady would feel comfortable buying. He needed to go soon, or the return trip would be after dark. Did he have time to go up to the house and invite Lila Rose again?

While Cable and Garcia continued to work on the wall, Drew cleaned his brush and hands with turpentine. "You men use up the rest of your paint, then go help Rob with the levee."

As usual, they grunted their reluctant acceptance of his order. Let 'em complain to Rob. Ranch work meant *work* all day, every day, no matter who gave the order.

"Good afternoon, Drew." The lady of his thoughts appeared before he could take the first step in her direction. "Your mother and I would like to accept your invitation to town. Oh, and Lavinia, too." She gave him a smile he felt down to his toes.

He was glad he was facing away from the men so they couldn't see his foolish grin. He forced it away. "Good. I'll hitch up the surrey and pick you up at the back door in about fifteen minutes."

She gave him that smile again, then traipsed back toward the house. It wasn't until the men began to chuckle that he shook off his stupor and headed into the barn.

To his surprise and approval, he noticed Prince's and Duke's stalls had been mucked out. That spoke well of Lila Rose. Despite being rather dainty, she didn't expect someone else to clean up after her, even taking care of the harder, dirtier jobs. But that good thought disappeared when he saw the halters laid out in the tack room. Maybe she'd just been worn out. He'd forgive her neglect this time and clean them himself when he returned.

As proper while driving toward town, Mother sat beside him on the surrey's front bench, with Lila Rose and Lavinia on the back bench. Still, Drew hoped someday the young lady would sit beside him. If his plan worked out, that might be in a couple of Saturdays. After watching her train the horses and especially noticing she'd cleaned the stalls, he no longer questioned his spontaneous feelings for her, no longer tried to deny he enjoyed her company.

"Thank you for this outing, Andrew." Mother's weary expression showed she needed it.

"We should have gotten you out sooner." He glanced over his shoulder. Lila Rose and Lavinia were discussing the scenery as they drove past. The lady was good with the children—another admirable attribute. "I know you enjoy attending church. You should go with us this Sunday. Pastor Daniel is a fine preacher. He might not be as educated as your big-city preacher, but he knows the Bible."

"I would love to hear him." She patted his arm. "But I fear it would be ill-advised to leave your father without someone to keep him in bed, according to Dr. Warren's orders."

"One of the hands could do it. They don't all attend church every Sunday, anyway."

"Humph." Mother sniffed. "Your father should require it of every man who works for him."

Drew didn't try to explain that someone also needed

to stay and guard the ranch against outlaws like those who'd kidnapped Suzette. That might alarm her. All the men understood the situation and didn't mind the rotating schedule that gave them each a chance to attend services, although he had a feeling a couple of them just wanted to talk with the eligible local gals rather than worship the Lord.

If his plan worked out, those hands would also see those gals next Saturday.

Lila Rose tried to keep her excitement hidden. Despite having frequented Charleston's finest department stores with Mama, she felt almost giddy as they entered this quaint dry goods store. Mercy, it had been far too long since she'd shopped.

"Drew!" Alice Arrington bustled out from behind the sales counter, a wide smile on face. "Lila Rose, how good to see you. Looks like you've been out in the sun. Miss Lavinia, aren't you growing so tall." She settled her gaze on Rebecca. "And you must be Mrs. Mattson." She reached out a hand. "I'm Alice Arrington. My pa bought this store from your Suzette's pa. And we're so glad you've returned to the Riverton community."

"Thank you." Touching Alice's hand, Rebecca gave her a reserved smile, perhaps a bit put off by Alice's chattering.

"Now, what can I do for you?" Alice gave them no chance to respond. "Lila Rose, I asked Pa about that sidesaddle, and he said it's fine for us to use it." She turned to Drew. "You want to take it back to the ranch?"

Drew appeared a little surprised. "Well, I'm not sure it's in the budget…"

"Nonsense," Rebecca said. "If the young ladies require a sidesaddle, they shall have it." She turned toward the center of the store. "Lila Rose, we will also choose some fabrics for summer dresses." With that, she took Lavinia's hand and walked across the room.

Lila Rose took a step to follow, but Alice grasped her hand. "I'm so glad to see you. All of us gals are so thrilled you'll be teaching us once Viola—" she glanced at Drew "—well, doesn't have time to hold class anymore. Say, have you heard about the barn dance at the Gentrys' two weeks from Saturday? You have to come—doesn't she, Drew?" She blinked at him in a slightly flirtatious way. "You *are* coming, aren't you?"

My, what a silly grin he gave Alice. Was he showing off that dimple on purpose? Lila Rose guessed he was responding to Alice's flirtation. Did he flirt with all the girls? So much for her foolish idea that he might think *she* was special.

But then he turned that silly grin toward her. "Lila Rose, I've been meaning to ask if you want to come along with me and the boys, but I haven't figured out how to make it proper."

"Oh…" She felt a pleasant flutter near her heart. So much for her unfounded suspicions that Drew was a flirt.

Rebecca returned. "Lila Rose, I meant for you to follow me so we can choose our fabrics."

"Yes, ma'am." She gave Alice quick smile. "Excuse me."

"Say, Mrs. Mattson…" Alice followed them across the store. "There's a barn dance over at the Gentrys' next Saturday. Can you help us figure out how Lila Rose can come with Drew and the boys, and it all be proper?"

Lila Rose's face warmed from the inside, making her sunburn feel even hotter. "Oh, it's not necessary." But she would love to attend the barn dance. She had always enjoyed the balls of her youth, the ones Father attended as he struggled to keep his place in the community. A barn dance wouldn't be as elegant, but the dancing and socializing might be just as much fun.

Rebecca studied Lila Rose, then turned her gaze on Drew. "Andrew, have you invited Lila Rose to this event?"

"No, ma'am. I haven't had a chance."

She looked him up and down. "Haven't had a chance? Living on the same ranch all this time? Humph." She touched a bolt of sprigged muslin. "Lila Rose, this is quite lovely. Just perfect for a Sunday dress." Her eyes took on a merry glint. "And a barn dance. That is, if someone invites you."

Lila Rose forced down a giggle. "Why, yes..."

Alice huffed out a breath. "Well, he doesn't really have to invite her 'cause I just did." She sounded more apologetic than impudent. "Besides, nobody needs an escort. We all just show up and have a good time. Mr. Gentry plays a mean fiddle and can go on all night."

"Hmm. Then I see no reason Lila Rose should not attend. I shall go along as a chaperone." Rebecca turned back to the row of fabrics. "Now, let's decide about our new dresses, shall we?"

Her pronouncement surprised and pleased Lila Rose more than she could say. It apparently pleased Drew as well, because once they finished their shopping and started back to the ranch, he had to return to the store and buy the paint he'd made the trip for in the first place.

They all laughed at his forgetfulness, even Drew. Father would have blamed Mama for his own mistake, but Drew didn't seem to have any such misplaced pride. With each day, she liked him more and more, but that could only lead to heartache when she returned to Charleston.

That is, *if* she returned.

Chapter Ten

Drew's plan to get one of the other gals to invite Lila Rose to the barn dance had taken care of itself. Not that it had been all that clever, but as the conversation unfolded at the store, he could see the Lord was answering his prayers. He didn't even feel foolish for neglecting to remember the paint. It gave them all a good laugh when he had to turn the surrey around and return to the store. Mother said he must really want to attend the dance if it made him forget what he was doing. She didn't often tease, so he didn't mind being her target when she did.

Best of all, she seemed to perk up as the afternoon wore on. He needed to get her out more, maybe take her to visit some of the other ranch wives. Pop was being so hard on her, so unforgiving. Why couldn't he just forgive Mother for leaving close to nine years ago? She was here now, wasn't she? And she'd come willingly. While the rest of the family and Lila Rose brought some joy to her days, Pop's anger always ruined it in the evening. Drew prayed that wouldn't be enough to make her go back to Charleston.

He'd noticed Lila Rose didn't seem to be pulling Mother back toward her old home anymore. Maybe that was why he no longer tried to quash his kind thoughts toward her. Who was he joshing? His feelings of fondness and respect grew without any effort on his part. Now he would have the pleasure of her company at the barn dance.

Despite his parents' long separation, with no women residing at the ranch for most of that time, he and his brothers had learned to treat ladies with respect and to guard their reputations. Never for a moment had he guessed Mother would offer to accompany them to the dance. Only the Lord could have worked that out.

In fact, he should have tried to get Mother out of the house sooner. For the three weeks she and Lila Rose had been at the ranch, neither had been beyond the front fence. Mother hadn't even been down to the river. Maybe he should take her for a long-overdue tour of the grounds.

On Sunday, she agreed to attend church and obviously enjoyed it. She sang with enthusiasm, complimented Pastor Daniel on an insightful sermon and chatted with several ladies she'd known years ago. Most important, she warmly greeted Annie Sharp, Cal and Jared's mother-in-law, who had come to the ranch three weeks ago. According to those two ladies, nothing would do but that Annie and Job, along with Drew's brothers and their wives, would once again come over for Sunday dinner. As she had last time, Mother cooed over the two one-year-old babies, showing them the same affection she gave Lavinia and Robbie.

Once again, Drew didn't have to figure out how to

improve Mother's situation. The Lord seemed to be smiling on his decision to fetch her back home. If not for Pop's stubborn refusal to forgive her, perhaps Drew could live without his father's approval. No, that was something he would work for until his dying day. Never mind that he couldn't figure out what he'd ever done to displease Pop so badly. Too bad Pop hadn't heard this morning's sermon on the prodigal son and his forgiving father. Was there anything in the Bible about prodigal fathers?

Lila Rose had grown used to the noise and busyness of this large family, but with so many people in the house, she couldn't figure out how she could help prepare the midday meal. The sisters, Julia and Emma, helped Viola in the kitchen, so Lila Rose wasn't needed there. The four brothers crowded into Mr. Mattson's room and talked ranch business. Rebecca rested in her room. The children ran outside to play.

After setting the long table for twelve, Lila Rose settled in an armchair in the parlor and worked on the hem of her new gown. Viola had helped her cut it from one of her own homemade patterns that was more in keeping with local styles rather than eastern-city fashions. Stitching the dress up on Viola's Singer had been a pleasure.

Near her feet, the two babies lay on blankets, sound asleep. Soon she found herself watching them rather than her stitches. How precious they looked with their quiet breathing, their dark lashes resting against rosy cheeks. Although she'd begun to think of herself as a spinster shortly after Mama died, watching these adorable infants stirred a longing deep inside her. Would she ever have her own children? Would she ever even marry?

"I see you're enjoying my grandchildren," Rebecca whispered as she entered the room and settled in her rocking chair.

"Oh, yes. Aren't they precious?"

"Indeed, they are." A wistful look came over her face. "To think that I could have missed all of this if I hadn't come here. That I did miss it with Lavinia, along with most of Robbie's childhood…" She sighed. "Oh, well. It does no good to revisit the past. What's done is done."

"Are you happy here, Rebecca?" Lila Rose set her sewing on the Singer cabinet and gave her employer her full attention.

She sighed again. "I must admit, there have been many improvements. Viola has done a wonderful job of making this a home for…for everyone. I'm pleased to see my sons healthy and doing so well. But, to answer your question, no, I am not happy here. I didn't come expecting to find happiness. Perhaps you recall Dr. Martin's sermon on Proverbs 31 this past February. After listening to him, I began to rethink my reasons for leaving Ralph and my boys, and to pray.

"When Andrew showed up the very next day, I could see the Lord's will clearly before me. I knew I must keep my wedding vows and become a long-overdue blessing to my husband." She dabbed her handkerchief at sudden tears. "I am so pleased that you were willing to come with me, and so pleased to see you adjusting to life in this rough land. But at any time, if it becomes too difficult for you, I will send you back to Charleston to manage my house for me."

Did Rebecca comprehend what her offer meant to Lila Rose? Now she had a place to go, should she no longer be needed. Relief flooded her heart, and she gazed fondly at Rebecca. "I will stay as long as you need me."

"Or at least until after the dance." Uncharacteristic humor glinted in Rebecca's eyes, and she glanced at the unfinished gown on the sewing machine.

Lila Rose laughed a little too loudly, and one of the babies stirred and whimpered, then the other one.

"Oh, dear…"

"Never mind." Rebecca bent down to pick up Emma's daughter, Elizabeth. Instead of cradling her, she handed her to Lila Rose. "My babies always wanted to cuddle after a nap." She picked up Julia's son. "Come to Grandmother, little Joseph." She set her rocker in motion.

"Hello, little darling." Lila Rose brushed feather-soft hair from Elizabeth's chubby cheek.

The child looked up and began to fuss.

"Oh, dear. She didn't expect to see a stranger holding her."

"Don't worry." Emma swept into the room and took the baby. "She just needs to be changed." She eyed Rebecca's bundle. "Joey probably does, too. Want to help?"

"Of course." Rebecca stood and followed Emma from the room.

Lila Rose's arms felt suddenly empty, a sensation she'd never before experienced. Now she knew without a doubt she wanted a child of her own. But how could that ever be when she had no marriage prospects?

* * *

Arriving at the Gentry barn while the early-June sun was still high over the horizon, Drew parked in a shady spot under some cottonwood trees so the horses wouldn't overheat. He helped Mother down from the surrey, then turned to offer a hand to Lila Rose. However, Ranse Cable beat him to it.

"Miss Lila Rose, may I have the first dance?" Still holding her hand, Cable cast a smirk in Drew's direction.

Even though Drew could see Cable didn't intend a serious challenge, he wanted to kick himself. He should have claimed that first dance with Lila Rose on the way here or even before they'd left home. With six Double Bar M ranch hands riding behind the surrey, he should have realized they would all want to dance with the prettiest gal in the Riverton community.

"Thank you, Mr. Cable." Lila Rose's smile seemed a bit guarded. "I believe—"

"Now, Miss, please call me Ranse."

"Very well. Ranse." Her chin lifted slightly, and her smile disappeared. "I believe Mrs. Mattson holds my dance card." She glanced at Rebecca.

Dance card? The local gals didn't use dance cards. This was an informal shindig, not some grand city ball.

Mother was obviously in on Lila Rose's game. "Indeed I do. And when we get inside, I shall take it out and add your name, Ranse."

"Thank you, ma'am." Cable touched the brim of his hat, winked at Lila Rose and then headed toward the barn.

Drew breathed out a silent sigh. Despite that improper

wink, Ranse Cable was a good man, a reformed gun-
fighter who'd fought in the Colfax County War some
years ago. But he was older than Rob by several years
and a little rough around the edges for a lady of Lila
Rose's upbringing. Still, Drew couldn't deny him a
dance when there were fewer single gals than single
men in the community.

"Shall we go in?" Mother gave him an expectant look.

"Yes, ma'am." He offered her one arm and Lila Rose
the other, and they began to walk. "So, Mother, whose
name is first on Lila Rose's card?"

"Humph." Good humor colored her tone. "Why, you,
of course. You are her host, so it is only proper."

Good ol' Mom. Chuckling, he smiled at Lila Rose.
"You all right with that?"

She gave a little shrug, still not smiling. "I trust Rebecca to guide my social life."

"Oh, you do, do you?" He laughed out loud. "Now
what's all this nonsense about dance cards?"

"You'll see."

To his surprise, every gal who came to Viola's etiquette classes—and some who didn't—sported small
cards and stubby pencils tied to their wrists with fancy
ribbons. It didn't take long for all the cowboys to catch
on and hurry around signing up with the ladies of their
choice. Just as Rob's wife had hoped, she was bringing culture and civilization to Riverton, even when she
decided not to attend this dance herself. Maybe dance
cards would put an end to the occasional fight that broke
out when two men wanted to dance a particular number with the same gal.

Breathing in the mouthwatering aroma of beef roasting in the pit behind the barn, Drew ignored the rumble in his belly. There'd be a lot of dancing before they ate. He led Mother and Lila Rose to chairs near the refreshment table and served them cups of punch. "Say, I'd better join in this card signing, or I'll only be dancing that first dance. Please excuse me."

Not that he wanted to dance with any of the other gals, but he owed it to Alice for breaking the ice and inviting Lila Rose. After signing her card, he found Iris, the banker's daughter, and signed two spots on her nearly empty card. A shame more of the other boys couldn't see beyond her smallpox scars to her sweet and generous personality. He signed the last spot on Dolores's card. Seemed everyone was grateful to her for inviting everyone to this barn dance. Well, some of the cowboys might be interested in hitching up with a gal who would inherit this ranch. And Drew could see from the refreshment table she'd put her cooking skills to use. Too bad Lila Rose hadn't brought any of her own baking, but he supposed sewing that pretty dress had taken all her time these past two weeks.

"Here we go, folks. Let's dance." Fiddle in hand, Wiley Gentry took his place on a small platform and, with a firm downstroke, began a lively tune.

Behind him, Elgin Gregson joined in on his squeezebox, with Bill Acheson on guitar. Hawk Bondi stepped up in front of them and began to call.

"All join hands and form a circle... Circle to the left... Now circle to the right. Now swing your partner. Now ladies to the center...and back again. Now gents to the middle for the right-hand star...then back again.

Promenade to the left… Promenade to the right. Form that bridge and all duck through."

After a few missteps, Lila Rose caught on and managed to follow Hawk's directions. His hands at her waist, Drew grinned his approval. She was probably more used to waltzes and other fancy dances, but nobody could have more fun than he was having with her now. Even Mother had accepted an invitation from Mr. Arrington after his wife, sporting a sprained ankle, had encouraged her to join the fun.

When the gals appeared to be winding down, supper was announced, and everybody lined up to fill their plates. Even Mother and Lila Rose managed to eat without benefit of a table, instead setting their loaded plates on their laps with a napkin underneath. Drew leaned against the railing of a stall near them, plate in hand. Mother had put his name in three slots on Lila Rose's card. Had she worried her companion might not have other men lined up to dance with her? Surely not. Anyway, he'd enjoyed their two dances so far and looked forward to holding her in his arms for the final number. That would be a waltz—not his best footwork, but at least it was a chance to hold her closer than during the square dances.

At last the time came for him to step up and claim that dance. Her face glistened with sweat—or, as Mother insisted, *perspiration*—but her smile was as bright as when they'd stepped down from the surrey three hours ago. Her sunburn from the week before had faded to a nice tan typical of the local gals. Only those cute little freckles remained, and he admired every one of them.

The music began, and he set his hand at her waist. A pleasant sensation traveled up his arm. Then, when she placed her hand on his shoulder, a knee-numbing buzz swept over the rest of him. Her smile and blue-eyed gaze bored into him. He barely felt his feet moving across the dirt floor. Somehow he managed not to stumble.

"You having a good time?" He didn't need to ask because she'd smiled, laughed and danced all evening. But he couldn't think of anything else to say, not when what he wanted to do was kiss her right here and now so everybody knew she was off-limits to everyone but him.

Now what on earth made him come up with that idea? Yes, she was pretty. But it didn't take too much thinking to realize he was falling for this city gal. No matter how hard he tried to stop it, he had the sinking sense he was headed for a broken heart.

A pale half-moon hung high in the sky, and stars twinkled around it. Lila Rose hugged her shawl around her shoulders, remembering with pleasure the feel of Drew's hand at her waist as they'd danced the final waltz. The surrey rolled over the rutted road, the rhythmic clatter of the wheels harking back to the lively reel they'd shared. What a lovely evening!

No orchestra she'd ever heard could have been more heart-stirring. In fact, the entire event was every bit as enjoyable as the finest ball she'd ever attended. She couldn't recall the name of every cowboy she'd danced with, but they'd all behaved like gentlemen. Of course, Rebecca and the other older ladies had kept a watchful eye on everyone to be sure nothing improper happened.

And Lila Rose couldn't wait to tell Viola that the dance cards were a success.

When Ranse's name came up on her card, Lila Rose had a moment of concern. But the cowboy had proved more brotherly than flirtatious. He teased her about Drew. Then he teased her about her rosy cheeks his words had caused. Then, when he returned her to her chair, he took both her hands, gazed into her eyes and whispered, "Miss Lila Rose, don't you go breaking his heart. He's a good man, and he's had enough grief."

Before she could respond, he walked away to claim a dance with Iris Blake.

Break his heart? Did that mean Ranse thought Drew loved her? And all this time, she'd been worried about her own feelings. She admitted, if only to herself, that she had grown fond of him, that she would never want to cause him grief. His father did enough of that. Even Rebecca, Viola and Rob noticed, although they never spoke of it. Yet their faces showed it.

She'd had a lovely time this evening, especially when she danced with Drew. *Especially* during that final waltz with him. She could see he enjoyed it, too. At one point, she'd thought he might kiss her. And she'd wanted him to! *Oh, my.* That would have caused a scandal. Maybe that was a sign she should cool her friendliness toward him. But how could she do that when Ranse, Viola and even Rebecca seemed to constantly be pushing her toward him?

Far too tired to make a serious decision, she was glad to turn all her attention to Rebecca when they reached the ranch. She treasured these moments each evening when she could catch up with her employer while helping her into her nightgown. They'd had little time to talk during the barn dance.

First, they needed to check on Mr. Mattson. Rob had put him to bed, and they found him sleeping as comfortably as the cast on his leg permitted.

"Perhaps I should sleep in the chair in here," Rebecca whispered.

"I don't think so, Mother." Rob took her elbow to usher her from the room. "You need your rest, too." He gave Lila Rose a significant look.

She returned a nod. Until this evening, Rebecca had been wearing down little by little under her husband's daily tirades. Was it time to urge a return to Charleston?

"How was he?" Rebecca stood outside the door as though unwilling to go to her own room.

Rob chuckled softly. "He complained about everything except Viola's cooking. Wanted to know when you'd be home. You know—same old Pop."

"Wanted to know when I'd be home?" Rebecca's tone was an odd mixture of sadness and hope.

"Yep." Rob urged her down the hallway. "See? He can't do without you. Good night, Mother. Lila Rose."

He kissed Rebecca's cheek, then left her and Lila Rose in her room.

"Wanted to know when I'd be home." Rebecca's repetition of the words held more wonder now, as though she was embracing the idea.

Lila Rose's heart ached for her. This situation resembled her own parents' marriage all too much. Father always apologized to Mama after hitting her, but then he'd hit her again the next time he lost at gambling. Or was drunk. Or whenever he was displeased by anything. Mr.

Mattson was in no condition to do that to Rebecca—but after he was back on his feet, how would he behave?

And just how much like his father was Drew? Maybe that's why Mr. Mattson treated him so badly.

She finished preparing Rebecca for bed, then walked toward the room she shared with Lavinia. At the same moment, Drew came up the stairs. After leaving her and Rebecca at the back door, he'd driven the surrey to the barn so he could tend the horses.

"You have a good time tonight?" Even in the shadows, she could see his smile.

"Yes, thank you. And you?"

He gazed down at her, his posture much like it had been during their waltz. For several moments, they stared into each other's eyes.

"Ahem." Rob peered out of his room. "Good night, Drew. Good night, Lila Rose." Good humor colored his tone, along with a note of authority.

Drew huffed out a breath. "'Night, Rob." He took the three steps to his own room and disappeared behind the door.

As she walked to the end of the hall, heat flooded her cheeks. What must Rob be thinking? She would have to be careful not to give even the appearance of an etiquette breach, especially because she had no intention of falling in love with Drew.

That is, if she could somehow manage to hold on to her increasingly unruly heart.

Chapter Eleven

Unable to sleep, Lila Rose sat on the trundle beside Lavinia's four-poster bed and tried to read her Bible by the light of her kerosene lamp. But memories of the evening danced in her head, making it hard to concentrate. She picked up her journal and recorded those happy thoughts, then returned to her Bible, praying as always for the Lord to direct her life...and her heart.

From outside came the bawling of cattle that wafted up from the lower pasture on the night wind. A coyote howled, and another answered, causing her to shiver. She would never get used to the dangers of this wild country.

Then she became aware of a new sound to add to her unease—tiny squeaks emanating from underneath Lavinia's bed. Mice? Horror struck her. She must protect the child from rodent bites—but how? As she looked around the room for a weapon, a louder noise, a *meow,* came from the same direction. A furry calico head popped out from beneath the bed skirt, quickly followed by the rest of the adorable cat. Puff walked toward the closed bedroom door and looked at her expectantly.

"Meow."

"Well, hello, Puff," Lila Rose whispered. "So that's where you've been."

Early that afternoon, Lavinia had called for her cat downstairs and outdoors but hadn't found her. Now the mystery was solved.

Lila Rose opened the door and let Puff out, then closed it behind her. The mews continued, so she knelt and peered under the bed. In the dim light of the lamp, she could see tiny forms wiggling about on a ragged quilt piece.

Puff had had kittens! What fun! From the jerky way they moved, they appeared no more than a day old. She'd often missed her sweet cats from the farm, where they gave her comfort after her father's tirades. He'd allowed them to live there only to keep down the rat and mouse populations.

After unlatching the bedroom door so Puff could return to her babies, Lila Rose lowered the lamp wick until its light was extinguished, then settled back on the bed.

Early the next morning, Lavinia could hardly contain her excitement over the kittens. She reached under the bed and tugged the quilt closer.

"Let's not pick them up right away, dear," Lila Rose said. "Why not find a box that will keep them safe once their eyes open and they start to wander?"

"Yes, ma'am." Eyes shining, Lavinia threw on her Sunday dress, which Viola had laid out the night before, and dashed from the room. "Wake up, everybody! Puff had her babies!"

Lila Rose barely had time to don her own Sunday dress before Rebecca, Robbie and Viola gathered outside the door to view the three adorable kittens: one black, one gray and one yellow tabby. Viola sent Robbie to fetch a small wooden box from the pantry. Rebecca grabbed her sewing scissors to trim away the soiled parts of the quilt. As she tugged it close, a small calico lump rolled to the floor.

"Oh, dear." Viola sighed as she lifted the tiny form. "This poor little one didn't make it."

"Nooo!" Lavinia squealed and began to cry. "Why did it die, Mommy?" She buried her face in Viola's apron.

"I'm so sorry, my darling." Viola hugged her close with her free arm.

Drew poked his head in the door. "What's all the fuss?"

Lila Rose stepped over to him and explained about the stillborn kitten.

He knelt and took Lavinia into his arms. "Don't cry, little sprout." He brushed her uncombed hair back from her face. "Cheer up. You have three healthy little kittens to play with and..."

"No!" Rebecca's voice was edged with tears. "Can't you see she's heartbroken? You must let her grieve." She gasped in a breath, almost a sob. "You must..." She lifted Lavinia away from Drew and let the child weep into her shoulder. "You must let her grieve," she repeated as tears rolled down her own cheeks.

"I—I'm sorry. I—" Drew stood back, misery and puzzlement on his face.

Viola patted his shoulder and forgave him with a sympathetic look.

Lila Rose had never seen Rebecca cry. Why was she so easily overwhelmed by the child's tragedy? Perhaps her exhaustion from caring for an angry husband had caused her emotional response. Was it time to return to Charleston, where they would encounter none of the heartaches her employer experienced here at the ranch?

After Robbie returned with the box, Lila Rose helped Viola cut away the soiled parts of the quilt and arrange the remnant in the box. Puff hovered around, making sure her babies were well taken care of. At last, she settled down with them in the box and nudged them toward her belly.

"There you go, little mama," Viola said. "Time to give your babies their breakfast."

Rob appeared at the door. "Speaking of breakfast." He winked at his wife. "Milking's done, horses fed. If we're going to church, we need to get a move on."

"Yes, of course." Viola gave him a kiss, explained the situation and then wrapped the lost kitten in the cutaway bits of cloth. "Robbie, will you help me?"

"Yes, ma'am." The boy followed her down the stairs.

Rob turned his attention to his daughter, who now sniffed into Rebecca's lace handkerchief. "I'm sorry about that little kitty, darlin'. I know how you feel. I feel real bad whenever a newborn calf doesn't make it."

She gave him a weepy smile.

Poor Drew. His shoulders slumped even more. He'd only meant to comfort Lavinia. Now he hung his head and chewed his lip as though he'd done something wrong. Lila Rose offered an encouraging smile. He returned a rueful grimace.

"Lila Rose," Rob said, "you want me to move those kittens out to the barn so they won't keep you awake at night?"

"Nooo!" Lavinia cried. "Please, Daddy." Her tears flowed again.

"Yes, please leave them here. They won't bother me in the least." Lila Rose gave Lavinia a reassuring smile, earning herself an approving look from Drew.

How could she keep her distance from him when they so often seemed to communicate silently this way? How could she keep from falling for him when a simple look sent such pleasant feelings spiraling through her?

"I should help Viola with breakfast." She pushed past Rob and Drew, whose tall, broad-shouldered bodies had blocked the door. Although she would have preferred to stay and comfort Rebecca and perhaps find out why she'd been so moved by Lavinia's grief, there was work to do, as Rob had pointed out, if they planned to attend church. She might not be able to cook, but she could set the table. She'd even perfected peeling the ever-present potatoes and breaking eggs without too many bits of shell falling into the bowl. But biscuit-making remained a mystery to her. And forget about bread, a daily staple for feeding the family and cowhands. One could not make sandwiches with bread that fell apart.

She found Viola in the kitchen, her face lined with weariness, although it was early morning. How much longer could she keep house before the baby she carried forced her to rest most of the day? And who would manage things once that happened?

Lila Rose had already taken over the dusting and sweeping. But this large family would be very hungry if they depended on her to feed them. And of course it would be too much for Rebecca to take on the chore.

While it wasn't her responsibility to figure it all out, Lila Rose couldn't help but worry. Rebecca had already said she would remain at the ranch until her next grandchild arrived. Lila Rose couldn't blame her. Robbie, Lavinia and the babies from her two youngest sons brought her so much joy. How selfish it would be for Lila Rose to insist she go back to Charleston.

"Lila Rose, would you mind putting the ham in the pan?" Viola sank down into a kitchen chair and propped her head on one hand.

"Yes, of course." She donned her apron and, taking care not to dip her sleeve into the grease, laid the slices into the sizzling pan. After a minute, she turned them, then forked them onto a platter.

"Now the eggs." Viola put a hand on the table to stand.

"Sit still. I can do it." Lila Rose took a deep breath to gain confidence. "This time I'll pour off the grease."

"Thank you." Viola gave her a weary smile. "I think the biscuits are done."

Lila Rose opened the oven and used a folded tea towel to remove the pan, then laid the towel over the perfectly browned biscuits.

She broke and whipped the dozen and a half eggs Robbie had fetched from the chicken coop early this morning. After reducing the amount of grease in the pan, she poured in the beaten eggs. The creamy mass quickly bubbled up around the edges and center. Using a wooden spoon, she stirred and stirred, but they still cooked far too fast and stuck to the cast iron.

"I'm sorry." Viola came to her side. "I should have told you to set the skillet on the back of the stove while you prepared the eggs." She took a metal spatula and scraped the bottom of the pan, saving the eggs from burning. "Don't worry. They're only a little brown."

Lila Rose managed to successfully spoon marmalade from a jar into a bowl before calling Rob, Drew and the children to breakfast.

From the way the men dug into their food without complaint, she surmised the eggs had survived her near mistake. Drew even sent her a smile of appreciation.

"Viola, let me take the tray up to Rebecca and Mr. Mattson." This was something Lila Rose could do without failure, but she also wanted to be sure her employer felt well enough to attend church.

Viola gave her a grateful nod.

She approached the partially open door and saw Mr. Mattson displaying his usual cross mood, with his shoulder turned slightly away from Rebecca and his complaints about something or other filling the air. Rebecca sat in her nearby chair, bent over her knitting and ignoring his grumbling.

"Here's breakfast." Lila Rose used her cheeriest— perhaps too cheery—voice.

"Good morning, little lady." Mr. Mattson shifted on the bed. "Forgive me for not standing to greet you." He said that every time she entered the room. Did he say it to his wife? Doubtful.

"Good morning, sir." Lila Rose set a plate on his lap tray, then served Rebecca.

Her eyes still a little red after weeping over the kitten with Lavinia, Rebecca thanked her.

Mr. Mattson asked his daily question. "How're those horses doin'?"

"Very fine." She had been working with them for over a week. "I plan to try the sidesaddle tomorrow after Viola's etiquette class."

"Good, good." He took a bite of eggs, then looked up at her with a frown. "You make these?"

Rebecca stared at him. "What a question. What does it matter—"

"Yes and no." Lila Rose spoke quickly before an argument could erupt. "Viola and I worked together." Oh, dear. That gave her more credit than she was due.

"Well, they're mighty tasty, missy. Hardworking cowboys always need a good cook around to keep 'em fed."

Rebecca rolled her eyes. She'd barely touched her own breakfast. "You go on, dear. I'll bring the tray down when we're finished."

"Will you go to church this morning?" Lila Rose hoped she would take this chance to get away for a short while.

"No, I don't think so, dear. Last night wore me out."

"You ought to go." Mr. Mattson scowled at his wife. "The family needs to show up for church."

"If you recall…"

Lila Rose made her escape before the usual argument heated up any further. Oh, how she wanted to get Rebecca away from her grouchy, unforgiving husband. But as she descended the stairs, the thought occurred to her that she should pray for their reconciliation rather than another separation.

Such a prayer would not be in her own interests, but nonetheless, she would obey this prompting so clearly from the Lord, no matter what happened in her own life. Having Rebecca's promise that she could live in her house in Charleston gave her a measure of security. But would she miss her employer—*and* her employer's middle son—too much?

On Monday, with the barn painting finally completed, Drew and his helpers now pitched in to work on the levee. With this past winter's heavy snowfall, the Rio Grande would undoubtedly flood pretty bad, as it had last year. Folks upriver had been mighty helpful, sending telegrams when the waters began to rise and overflow the river's banks in Colorado. Drew didn't much care for shoveling dirt all day under a hot May sun, but Rob was determined to add another fifty feet to the levee before mid-June.

Trouble was, working down here at the river, he couldn't keep an eye on Lila Rose while she trained those horses. He felt a hint of pride over her success, though he still had to oil the harnesses after she used them. Funny gal—that she would shovel out the stalls, a much harder job, then leave the harnesses uncleaned. In fact, she didn't shy away from anything Viola asked her to do around the house, so he wouldn't mention the harnesses. It was a small chore to do for her after the way she was helping Mother cope with Pop. If only she could help *him* get on the old man's good side.

Today being Monday, he supposed the gals would arrive soon for their etiquette class. About that time, the unmarried cowhands usually made excuses to go up the hill to the barn, but anyone could see their real interest lay in the little cottage where Viola held her class. In fact, Patrick Ahern had stayed up at the house after fetching his mother and Rosa Garcia from town for laundry day, saying he needed to help his mam carry the clothes from upstairs out to the washtubs. While that might be true, he more likely wanted to wave to Dolores, whose dance card he'd signed more than once last Saturday evening.

The Irishman turned out to be quite the fancy dancer and could also belt out a romantic ballad to make any gal swoon. Drew was glad he didn't have a sister who might easily fall prey to the man's charms. So far Lila Rose hadn't responded to his attempts to flirt with her. He'd like to think it was because she preferred him to Ahern, if her ready smiles in his direction were any indication.

He could only hope that was the case. As for her being a city gal, he could see she was adjusting to ranch life more than she might even realize. Maybe he should let her know how he felt about her…if he could only figure out exactly how he *did* feel.

"Lila Rose, do you mind conducting the class today?" Viola had lingered at the breakfast table with Lavinia while Lila Rose washed the dishes. "I doubt I'm even up to walking over to the classroom."

"Of course." Lila Rose dried the last plate, then cast a worried glance at her friend. "Will you be all right?"

Viola laughed softly. "Oh, yes. I'm fine. Just tired from our trip to church yesterday. I'm sure I won't have any trouble making lunch for the men. Mother Rebecca is here to help me, as are Agnes and Rosa. If you can come back in time to carry the hamper down to the river, I'd much appreciate it."

"Yes, of course."

On the way to the cottage, Lila Rose decided to forgo the usual studies. Instead, once inside, she addressed them. "Ladies, I believe it's time to begin our riding lessons." She'd worn her denim riding skirt because she'd planned to ride after lunch, but why not include the girls? "Shall we go?"

Squeals of delight followed her announcement, and soon the eight of them were traipsing across the grassy pasture, then the dusty barnyard, to reach the barn.

"Yoo-hoo!" Dolores lingered outside the double doors, waving to the men who were shoveling dirt by the river. She skipped inside to join the others, a big smile on her face.

"Was that a certain Irishman you were waving to?" Alice smirked. "How many times did you dance with him on Saturday night?"

"Humph." Dolores pretended to be offended. "Only three—same number of times that Lila Rose danced with Drew."

"But who's counting?" Iris giggled. "Patrick and Drew made the rounds with all the young ladies…and some of the mothers, too."

"And didn't we all have a good time?" Lila Rose used the "teacher" tone she'd heard Viola use. "Now, let's have a good time with these lovely boys." She handed Dolores a halter and opened Prince's stall door. "As you already know how to tack up a horse, will you please show us your method? Dolores, you can take care of Duke." She handed her a halter. "I'll take care of Fred."

"Ew." Iris sniffed. "It sure does stink in here."

"Silly girl." Dolores laughed. "Of course it does. The horses stand in their stalls all night doing what comes naturally, so their stalls have to be mucked out in the morning. We can do that."

"Not me." Iris shuddered. "As I said—*ew.*"

"Never mind." Lila Rose had noticed the banker's daughter was a bit prissy. With a wealthy father, she would have a groom to take care of the unpleasant responsibilities of an equestrian. In fact, she herself had never cleaned a stall. George said it wasn't fitting for a lady to do it, so he'd always kept the stables clean.

"Drew always makes sure the stalls are mucked while I have the horses out." Just saying the words gave her a warm feeling of being...what? Protected? Cared for? The warmth flooded to her cheeks, no doubt making them red.

To keep the girls from noticing, she marched toward the tack room. "Let's get the sidesaddles. Dolores, will you help me?"

After the three horses were tacked up, they led them outside the barn to the mounting block. Lila Rose stepped up and mounted Duke, first sitting on the saddle, then lifting her right leg over the top pommel and securing her left leg under the lower pommel, with her foot in the stirrup. It felt good to be back on a horse. But she was here to teach, not ride for her own pleasure. She stepped back onto the mounting block and brought Fred over.

"Iris, Fred is a gentleman, so you don't need to be

afraid of him." She beckoned to Iris and helped her sit on the saddle and position her legs correctly.

Fred shifted his stance, and Iris gasped and grabbed the leather edge.

"You're doing fine, Iris." Lila Rose patted her knee. "Try to relax. Dolores, you're next."

"Sure thing." Dolores mounted Prince awkwardly. "This is so strange." She quirked her lips to one side. "I'druther throw my leg over his back and ride like I've always done."

Alice laughed, but Iris gasped once more.

"My mother says ladies should never say...well, *leg.*" She blushed as though she'd said a bad word. "Very immodest!"

Elena, only fifteen years old, blinked in confusion, as did Angelina. They conversed briefly in Spanish, giggling.

Juanita laughed, too. "These gringas have strange ways."

"I would not say my mother has strange ways!" Iris huffed out a breath. "She is always an elegant lady."

"Yes, of course." Lila Rose didn't know Mrs. Blake well, but seeing her at church, she'd noticed a bit of snobbery. Still, it wouldn't do for her to spoil Viola's class by letting an argument erupt among the girls. "Now, watch carefully. I'll show you how to signal to your horse what you want him to do."

While Lila Rose demonstrated her techniques to the girls, she noticed Ranse coming up the hill and entering the barn. Drew must have asked him to clean the stalls. How grand it was not to worry about such an unpleasant chore. She must remember to thank him.

Chapter Twelve

Drew pumped fresh water into the trough outside the barn, splashed water on his face and hands and then grabbed the clean milking buckets from the hooks beside the cows' stalls. After a long day of hauling dirt down from the hill and pounding it into place on the levee, he was glad to have a sit-down chore, if only for a few minutes.

He glanced inside the tack room and saw the harnesses laid over an empty saddle stand, as usual. Tired and grouchy from working in the hot sun all day, he grumbled to himself over Lila Rose's thoughtlessness. Surely, with all her experience with horses, she knew their tack needed as much care as the horses themselves. Maybe it was time to tell her that instead of suffering in silence and letting his resentment grow.

Milking done, he carried the two full buckets across the barnyard and into the house. To his surprise, the kitchen was empty. None of the usual mouthwatering smells hung in the air. No pots sat on the barely warm stove. Drew's belly complained with a fierce growl. He strained the milk through cheesecloth into two-gallon glass jars and left them on the table beside the icebox, then washed out the buckets in the sink before heading to the parlor. No one was there. Muted voices from upstairs reached his hearing, and he hurried up the front staircase. Rob met him at the top.

"Go get Doc Warren." His voice sounded strangled, as though he could barely speak. "Hurry."

Drew glanced into the bedroom Rob shared with Viola. Faces contorted with worry, Mother and Lila Rose bent over Viola, who lay on the four-poster bed, her face hidden behind the wall. Still, he could hear her soft moans. Robbie and Lavinia stood in the hallway, clutching one another, their eyes wide with fear.

Fear for his beloved sister-in-law gripped Drew so severely he couldn't move. "Is she—"

"Go!" Rob slapped his shoulder.

Gasping in a deep breath, Drew charged down the stairs and raced out to the barn. Buster, his gelding, was out in the pasture with the rest of the herd. No time to chase after him. Drew went instead to the stall where Raider, Rob's stallion, was kept. Now if the one-man horse would just cooperate in this emergency...

The horse resisted the bit at first but finally took it, soothed by Drew's calm encouragement, which was so disconnected from the racing of his heart. Raider twisted sideways to avoid the blanket and the saddle but at last relented. Drew led him outside and jumped on his back, digging in his heels to race toward town.

The pounding of Raider's hooves brought clarity to Drew's thoughts. He should pray—*did* pray—for God's mercy on Viola. On them all, but especially Rob, La-

vinia and Robbie. Losing Viola would be the worst tragedy of their lives.

From the moment she'd arrived at the ranch one year
ago, Drew and three of his brothers had known she was
the right woman for Rob, someone who could heal his
broken heart after his late wife had abandoned him and
put him off women for so many years. Rob had been
pretty stubborn, trying all sorts of ways not to fall for
her, but he'd finally given in to good sense and admitted he loved her. She'd, of course, felt the same. Then,
when her brother and sister had come to the ranch to
take her back to Virginia to marry her off to their slimy
business partner, Rob, Will and Drew had sent them
running, tails between their legs.

For their wedding, the church had been packed to
overflowing with well-wishers. While some of the local
single men had been disappointed due to their admiration for the bride, not one person in the entire community objected to the marriage.

Tonight the road to town had never seemed so long,
even when he'd had to fetch Doc when Pop had his
heart attack. But at last he arrived at the man's house.
He jumped down from Raider's back before the horse
came to a halt and raced to the door.

Good ol' Doc, always ready for an emergency, came
to the door with black bag in hand. "Who is it? Ralph
or Viola?"

"Viola. You take Raider. I'll bring your buggy."

"Good. And bring Cassandra." Doc's sister had served
as his nurse since learning her medical skills from Clara
Barton during the war.

Just over an hour later, Drew and Cassandra arrived

at the ranch. Heart in his throat, he parked Doc's phaeton at the back door next to where Raider was tied. Anxious as he was, he still needed to tend Rob's horse.

While Cassandra made her way inside, Drew led the stallion to his stall in the barn, took off the saddle and put it on a stand in the tack room. The halters Lila Rose had left for him to clean still lay over the other stand. Somehow her neglect seemed insignificant in light of Viola's precarious health.

Like Mother, Maybelle and now Viola, many women had a hard time out here in the West. One more reason for Drew not to lose his heart to a city gal like Lila Rose.

But when he returned upstairs and saw her helping Doc and Cassandra with his sister-in-law, he knew he'd already lost it.

When Drew appeared at the top of the stairs, Lila Rose's heart skipped, as though his presence would somehow save Viola and her baby. Which was ridiculous, of course. Doc and Cassandra possessed actual skills to save Viola and keep her little one from arriving too soon.

How grateful they all were for the nurse. Rebecca, already exhausted from caring for her husband, now had the added worry of Viola's crisis. Usually calm and capable in times of stress, she had broken down in tears more than once. At last Cassandra sent her to her room to rest.

Rob paced outside the bedroom, and the children sat huddled in the hallway. Robbie tried reading Mother Goose tales to Lavinia, but she soon lost interest.

And of course they were all hungry. Lila Rose had

no idea how to cook the roast Viola had planned for supper, but she could make sandwiches.

"If you need me," she said to Cassandra, "I'll be in the kitchen."

Focused on her job, the nurse gave her a curt nod.

Out in the hallway, she took her first deep breath in what seemed like hours. "Children, let's see what we can find for supper."

"Thanks," Rob murmured as she passed him.

Looking at Drew, she raised an eyebrow, inviting him along. He understood and followed her toward the stairs. Maybe he knew how to cook. After all, someone had fed the men on this ranch before Viola arrived.

The workings of the kitchen had been a mystery to her when she arrived nearly two months ago. Even though she'd often visited Ingrid in the kitchen back in Charleston, she'd never really paid attention to her meal preparations. Viola, on the other hand, seemed to dance around the room doing this and that and whipping it all up into delicious meals with ease. Lila Rose could never hope to emulate her.

"There may be something in the icebox." She opened the door and found, along with the uncooked roast, a covered bowl of chopped chicken. "This is probably for tomorrow's lunch, but I can make sandwiches for tonight." But then how would she feed everyone tomorrow? And how would she make Viola's delicious mayonnaise to mix with this chicken?

"Mommy has some cheese," Lavinia said. "Can we have cheese sandwiches instead?"

Relief flooded Lila Rose. "Oh, what a fine idea. Drew, would you slice the bread? Well, wash your hands first." She gave him a teasing smile. Surely his slices would be better than her uneven attempts.

He returned a weary grin, "Glad to."

"We don't have time to make mayonnaise." Did her comment border on a lie? She couldn't make mayonnaise if they had all the time in the world. "Besides, butter goes better with cheese."

"Butter goes better." Robbie emphasized the B sounds and made a comical face, causing Lavinia to laugh. "Hey, I just remembered. Mom made some sugar cookies last night." He opened the cookie crock and withdrew several handfuls.

Lila Rose's eyes stung with sudden tears. The children had been so brave all afternoon and evening. *Lord, please let Viola and her baby be all right. These children need their mother. They need that new baby.*

Among the four of them, they pieced together a humble meal to deliver to the family upstairs. Rob waved away the plate of sandwiches Lila Rose offered, so she set it on a table and prepared a smaller plate.

"Will you take this to your father?" she asked Drew, nodding toward the room at the end of the hallway.

"Um, I'm not sure he'll be pleased to see me."

She stared up at him, seeing the hurt in his eyes. "Then go with me in case he needs some help I can't provide for him."

"Um, sure." He followed her like a faithful puppy.

They found Mr. Mattson propped up in his bed, arms crossed, brow furrowed in anger and broken leg stretched out under the quilt.

"Well, what's going on down there?" He jutted his chin toward the door. "Nobody tells me anything."

After a glance at Drew to see whether he would answer, she said, "The doctor is doing all he can for Viola. I know you're praying with the rest of us that she and her little one will come through this."

His frown softened. "Well, you can't never tell about these things. Annie Sharp buried three stillborn boys before she had Emma and Julia. And…" He shook his head and stared toward the window, then waved a hand dismissively. "Life goes on."

For a moment, Lila Rose stared at him, struggling to squelch her anger at his uncaring attitude. "Here's your supper. I'm sorry it's rather plain fare." She put the plate on his tray and set it on his lap.

"That's all right, missy." He picked up a cookie. "If Viola ain't back on her feet tomorrow, you can take over the kitchen and fix something a little fancier."

She gave a rueful laugh. "Guess I'll have to try, won't I?" She certainly wouldn't worry them all at this difficult time by admitting she had no idea how to cook.

"Go on, now. Get outta here and let me eat in peace."

"Anything I can do for you, Pop?" The hope in Drew's voice made Lila Rose's heart ache for him.

"Yeah. Like I said, get outta here."

Drew's shoulders slumped. "Yessir." He sighed wearily as he left the room.

Lila Rose permitted herself to glare at the old man for three solid seconds before turning in a huff and leaving him to his miserable existence.

In the hallway, she found Drew and Rob listening to Doc.

"Viola and baby are doing all right for the moment. But she must stay in bed and avoid stress. Cassandra will stay overnight and monitor her condition, but I'll need her back in town tomorrow morning to help with a surgery."

Rob slumped against the wall and huffed out a long breath.

Drew clapped him on the shoulder. "Let's grab a sandwich. We need to keep our strength up. You, too, Doc." He indicated the platter on the table just inside the room.

"Thanks." Doc glanced toward Mr. Mattson's half-open door. "I may eat after I check on Ralph."

Rob followed him down the hallway. Drew hung back.

"You need to eat, too." Lila Rose pointed to the platter.

He gave her a rueful look but picked up a cookie. Just like his father, sweets first. She wouldn't tease him about it now. Maybe someday.

She peeked into the room. Cassandra stood by the bed, straightening the covers and speaking soothing words to the patient. To avoid disturbing them, Lila Rose went downstairs to the kitchen, where the children still sat at the table.

"Did you get enough to eat?" She had no idea what she would feed them if they said no.

Gazing up at her with solemn eyes, both nodded.

"Then I suppose it's time for bed."

They traded a look and appeared about to resist.

"After story time, of course." She had observed Viola reading to them each evening. Would they let her do it tonight?

"Yea!" Robbie stood and took his plate to the sink.

"Yea!" Lavinia copied his actions.

"All right. Fetch the book, and I'll meet you in the parlor."

The children raced upstairs and returned, leading Drew, who carried the book. Even though she'd seen him less than ten minutes before, Lila Rose's heart hiccoughed. His lopsided grin did nothing to still her racing pulse.

They settled on the couch with the children between them. After taking turns reading several rhymes, they let Lavinia choose "Little Red Riding Hood" for their final story. Lila Rose read the narrative and Red Riding Hood's words, and Drew performed a very fine Big Bad Wolf, adding a gravelly sound to his baritone voice to sound properly menacing. Robbie laughed and copied his uncle. Lavinia pretend-squealed and laughed and bounced where she sat.

Drew's love for the children was obvious. What a fine father he would make someday. She tried to dismiss the thought, but it didn't work. Like his brothers, he was a good man and deserved every bit as much happiness as they enjoyed. The woman Drew married would be blessed to have him. Did Lila Rose want to be that woman? Could she give up her city life altogether and live here on the ranch, with snakes and coyotes and other wildlife? Would her work with the horses be enough to make up for the deprivations and dangers of this land? The limited shopping opportunities?

Silly questions, of course. Drew hadn't said or done anything to indicate he thought of her that way. Well, there was that one *almost* kiss, but she couldn't—

wouldn't—let that persuade her into thinking he was falling for her.

After praying with him for their beloved stepmother and the brother or sister they both were eager to add to the family, Robbie and Lavinia gave no resistance to going to bed. They all met Rob and Doc at the bottom of the stairs and stood back to let them pass. Doc carried his black medical bag in one hand and a sandwich in the other.

"Be sure to have your father do those exercises several times a day," Doc said as they headed through the house and toward the back door. "Take it slow, and make him keep that splint on."

Rob's reply was unintelligible as they disappeared out the door.

After putting Lavinia to bed, Lila Rose rejoined Drew outside Viola's room. "The doctor's orders sound like good news about your father."

"Huh." He shook his head. "Rob doesn't need any more responsibilities around here, and you know Pop isn't going to let me help him exercise, the stubborn old mule." He stared at her, his face turning red. "I'm sorry. I shouldn't speak of my father with such disrespect. And I shouldn't involve you in this family's problems."

She patted his arm. "If you'll recall, I've been involved since greeting you at Rebecca's door in Charleston." She grimaced at the memory. "By the way, have I ever apologized for my rudeness that day?"

He chuckled. "No, I don't believe you have." He crossed his arms and gave her a chiding look. "Well?"

She snorted out a laugh—not the most ladylike thing to do. "Drew Mattson, I am so sorry for mistaking you for a vagrant due to your shabby, unkempt appearance and, as a result, trying to keep you from invading my employer's home. Can you ever forgive me?"

Now it was his turn to snort out a laugh.

"Shh!" Cassandra came across the room. "Viola needs rest and quiet. Please take your flirtation elsewhere." She quietly shut the door.

Flirtation? Heat flooded Lila Rose's cheeks. In the dimly lit hallway, Drew's face also appeared a little red.

"I have dishes to wash." She hurried toward the stairs, eager to make her escape from this embarrassing situation.

"I'll help." His footsteps sounded on the treads behind her.

She couldn't keep the foolish grin from her lips. Now that Viola's crisis appeared to have passed, would it be wrong to engage in a little flirtation? What would Rebecca say? Lila Rose had a slight suspicion her employer would like to see them fall in love. Until Viola was back on her feet, however, Lila Rose mustn't trouble Rebecca over something so trivial.

Drew dried the last dish and put it on the shelf, then hung the tea towel over the wooden rod on the wall. Lila Rose had been quiet while cleaning up the kitchen. Was she embarrassed by Cassandra's comment about their "flirtation"? He'd enjoyed those few moments of teasing, but he would hardly call it flirting. Maybe he should cool the situation.

"It looks like the cream has risen from tonight's milking." He nodded toward the two glass jars. "Guess we should skim it off so you can make butter in the morning. I mean, if you wouldn't mind. The butter churn is in the pantry."

For a moment, panic crossed her face. Then she blinked those pretty blue eyes, giving his heart a flutter. He was falling for her. No doubt about it.

"Make the butter? I did try that, but…" She straightened her shoulders as though preparing for a huge task. "Yes, I can do it."

He chuckled. She sounded as though she was trying to convince herself. "Of course you can." He found the ladle Viola used and scooped the cream into a smaller jar, covered it and put it in the pantry beside the churn.

Before he could devise a new topic to chat about, Rob returned from seeing Doc off.

"You heard Doc's instructions? Pop needs to get back on his feet and exercise a little at a time."

"Yep." Drew covered one milk jar and set it in the icebox, then set the other jar in the mudroom for Robbie to take out to the pigs in the morning. "You know he won't let me help him."

Rob grunted. "Brother, I'm sure sorry about that." He looked toward Lila Rose, who appeared to be taking inventory of the kitchen, no doubt planning what to fix for breakfast. "I don't know what gets into the old man sometimes."

At least his brothers noticed Pop's unfairness and didn't let it affect their relationships with Drew. "If you take care of his exercising, I can handle some of your chores."

"Good. I just saw Ahern. The men were concerned…" Rob's voice broke, and he cleared his throat. "They were worried about Viola. They'll keep working on the levee.

I'd like for you to start training those new horses for herding."

"Glad to." Drew wouldn't tell him he'd already started.

A sniff from across the room caught their attention.

"Lila Rose," Rob said, "thanks for pitching in, especially with the children."

She gave him a shaky smile. "I'm happy to do whatever is necessary."

"Thanks." Rob headed toward the door. "Can you have breakfast ready by six?" He left the room before she could answer.

If her momentary panic a while ago had surprised him, the look of utter terror on her pretty face now caused him real concern. Maybe cooking for the whole family was too big a challenge. Or was getting up at five o'clock to cook the problem?

"You all right?"

She swallowed and gave him another wobbly smile. "Oh, yes. Just fine."

But as he lay in bed trying to sleep, one nagging thought kept winding through his mind like a snake. Lila Rose was a city gal used to having servants. Although she'd never acted uppity, maybe behind all those smiles and polite words of hers, she thought she was too good to feed a family of cowboys. If that was the case, he'd better find out right now before he lost his heart.

Who was he kidding? He'd already lost his heart to her. And he had no way to keep her from breaking it.

Chapter Thirteen

Lila Rose had never realized it was Viola who filled the bedroom pitchers with hot water early each morning. And now she discovered the stove had no fire, and of course there was no hot water in the tank beside the firebox. How did Viola even start the fire under these circumstances?

She scooped the cold ashes from the firebox into a tin bucket she found by the back door. Laid in wood and kindling. Took matches from the box in the pantry. Tried to get a flame going. Each time she struck a match, it went out before the kindling would ignite. She didn't realize she was crying until a fat tear fell onto the firebox door.

"Need some help?" Drew appeared behind her, fully dressed but unshaven.

"Um...yes, please." She managed a shaky laugh. "I've never had success starting fires."

As he took the matchbox from her, he chuckled. "A trick I've learned is to use a little twist of paper." He found some butcher paper in the pantry, tore and twisted it, and soon had the fire going. "It's my fault it went out. I should have built the fire up last night and banked it."

His kindness in taking the blame caused more tears.

"As I'm sure you know, it'll take a while for the stove to heat up the water. We won't die from a cold shave." He pumped water into the second bucket from the mudroom. "Hmm. Maybe next time, don't use the milk bucket for the ashes."

"Oh, no..."

"Don't worry. I'll just dump them in the ash barrel outside the back door. We use them to make soap, so you didn't ruin the bucket."

He spoke in such an offhand way, as though she hadn't made a serious blunder. Make soap from ashes? She had no idea. In fact, she would have tossed them out into the pasture.

"Robbie'll be down shortly to gather eggs. While he's out at the chicken coop, I'll have him bring in a ham from the ice shed. We'll make it a simple breakfast. You go ahead and start the biscuits." He lifted the full bucket from the sink and headed for the stairs.

Start the biscuits? Lila Rose stared at the flour barrel, unable to see clearly for the tears blurring her vision. *Lord, what do I do now? These people need to eat, and I have no idea how to feed them.*

"Good morning." Cassandra sailed into the kitchen fully dressed, her dark brown hair in a severe bun. "I need to leave soon. Let me help with breakfast."

"Oh. Thanks." *Thank You, Lord.* "Maybe make the biscuits?" She couldn't keep the wobble from her voice.

Staring down at her from her almost-six-foot height, Cassandra narrowed her gaze. "Listen to me, young lady. You need to buck up. The last thing these folks need is a weepy female." She set about gathering ingredients and mixing the biscuit dough.

Lila Rose hadn't been scolded since Father died, so Cassandra's brusque dismissal of her feelings chafed. But the nurse was right. No one should have to put up with her tears, especially when she was not even part of the family. She must keep quiet and make herself as useful as possible.

Robbie dashed through the kitchen with barely a "good morning" on his way to gather eggs. Drew came back downstairs, clean-shaven but with a few cuts. Was that due to using cold water?

After the stove heated up, Cassandra made coffee. Lila Rose watched carefully so she could make it tomorrow. Maybe she should create a list of the various mundane chores that kept a house running smoothly and then try to make sure they were completed.

Eager to get back to town, Cassandra took over the remaining breakfast preparations. By the time Rob returned from whatever had taken him outside earlier that morning, breakfast was on the table.

"I won't mince words, Robert." Cassandra spoke with the same no-nonsense tone she'd used on Lila Rose. "You must keep Viola in bed, both for her own health and for the life of her baby."

His eyes reddened, and Rob took a gulp of coffee. "Yes, ma'am. I understand." He dug into his eggs. "We appreciate all you've done. Drew, take Miss Cassandra to town after breakfast. Robbie, after you do your morning chores, I'll need you on the levee. Lila Rose, can you manage things here at the house? Get breakfast to everyone upstairs? See to Lavinia?"

"Yes, of course." A little thrill and perhaps a hint of pride filled her heart. Rob always gave each family member an assignment at breakfast. This was the first time he'd included her in his orders. An unfamiliar sense of determination came over her. Yes, somehow she would manage this house. And if she was quick about it this morning, she could still get out to the training corral and work with Prince and Duke and Fred this afternoon.

Midmorning, when Rob came up to the house to exercise his father, however, she began to doubt herself again. Not that he said anything, but he did bring down the chamber pots, take them outside to dump in the outhouse and rinse them at the outside pump. How had Lila Rose failed to notice the need to empty chamber pots in every bedroom? Another task Viola had performed without a word. From now on she must undertake this unpleasant chore so Rob could get on with his day sooner.

A myriad of other tasks, large and small, confronted Lila Rose at every turn. When lunchtime drew near, she realized the men would require sandwiches. The cooked chicken still needed mayonnaise. Butter would make a poor substitute this time.

While perusing the supplies in the pantry, she found a cookbook, handwritten and well-used. To her relief, it contained several simple recipes, including one for mayonnaise. The two extra eggs they hadn't consumed for breakfast would be a start. In addition, the recipe listed vinegar, prepared mustard, salt, sugar and oil.

Oil? She couldn't find any. Would butter work? Or bacon grease? Or the cream Drew had skimmed from last night's milking? At least there was a small tin of mustard seeds, along with plenty of sugar and salt.

She whipped the eggs until her right arm ached, but they never thickened. A quick look at her pin watch revealed that she needed to move on. She stirred in the other ingredients, including the thick cream. That helped a little. It would have to do. Adding the chicken also improved the texture.

She sliced up the last two loaves of bread, spread the mixture and wrapped each sandwich in butcher paper. Instead of working the horses this afternoon, she would have to make bread.

Which reminded her to stir the fire and add wood from the rack beside the stove. Should she put the roast in the oven now? How long would it take to cook? The endless list of questions made her head ache.

When she'd taken breakfast upstairs, she'd planned to ask Rebecca for help. But Rebecca had moved her nursing duties from Mr. Mattson's room to Viola's. Lavinia played with her cat near the window, and the ladies were deep in discussion, so Lila Rose decided not to bother them with her questions. They had enough to think about. But after her difficult morning, she could only pray they might advise her regarding preparations for supper when she took them their lunch.

The men must be fed first, so she filled the wicker hamper with the sandwiches, added a dozen baby carrots from the kitchen garden—which was badly in need of watering and weeding, not to mention the rosebushes—and hoped it would be enough for the men working so hard on the levee.

She was halfway across the barnyard before she remembered to look for snakes, but she quickly brushed off that worry. If she encountered one of the slimy creatures, she would simply give it a wide berth, keep walking and pray it wouldn't chase her.

Instead, she encountered Drew, who came striding toward her, a big smile on his face.

"Hey." He reached for the hamper.

She happily surrendered it. Whipping the mayonnaise had worn out her right arm more than training the horses had. As always, her left arm protested its overuse from carrying the hamper.

"How's your morning going?"

She shrugged. "I don't know how Viola manages."

His blue eyes twinkled in the sunlight. "Yet here you are with our lunch."

"Yes. Well." She had to look away from his intense gaze. "Enjoy your sandwiches."

She turned back toward the house, but he stopped her with a hand on her shoulder.

"Lila Rose, I don't know what we'd do without your help. Thank you for stepping in this way."

She gave him a weak smile. Once he tasted his sandwich, he might not be so grateful.

Drew could spare only a moment to watch Lila Rose walk away. Instead of her usual cute little sashay, she moved wearily, with shoulders slumped and head hanging. Needing to take the food to the men, he couldn't take time to encourage her now. Maybe later.

Lord, please help Lila Rose. She's being so brave and good to pitch in and help this way—a far cry from her pampered life in the city.

The men washed off in the river before gathering under the cottonwood tree to eat. Drew took a sandwich from the hamper. Moisture dampened the butcher paper and made it stick to the bread. As the men took their shares, their faces displayed the same disappointment Drew felt. Yet no one refused to eat.

Drew chewed a bite of the mushy concoction and grimaced at the vinegary taste. Even Old Fuzzy's cooking would be better than this. And that was saying something. The old cowboy cook had managed the kitchen for Drew's family for years until Viola came last spring. The lovable old coot gladly turned the kitchen over to her, and the family had eaten well since then. Drew knew he'd put on a few pounds, mostly muscle. Maybe with Lila Rose cooking, he'd lose some of that.

Holding his soggy, crumbling sandwich, Rob heaved out a sigh. "Interesting flavor."

"Uh-huh." Drew refused to criticize Lila Rose in front of the others.

Yet the other men took their exchange as permission to complain.

"I am thinking Miss Viola did not make this," Juan Garcia said.

"Miss Lila Rose may be *muy* beautiful," said Julio Mendez, "but, *caramba*, she cannot cook."

"Wonder where she learned to make such fine fare." Ranse Cable snickered.

"Me *mam* wouldna feed this to the pigs." Patrick

Ahern emphasized his words with his on-again, off-again Irish lilt.

Rob glared at him for a moment. "Well, why don't you just ride into town and fetch your *mam* so she can fix something better."

Ahern returned the glare. "I'll just do that." He stood and brushed his hands on his trousers. "An' I'll be takin' the phaeton, if you please, so she can ride here in a style as befits her prodigious talents."

"Be my guest." Rob chomped into his food, grimaced and stared at Drew as though he expected a challenge.

Drew shrugged and tried another bite. Still too soggy, too pickly, but he needed to eat to maintain his energy. Oddly, the promise of better food encouraged him. Agnes Ahern would probably feed them her tasty Irish stew, as she had last year while Viola was away nursing smallpox victims. Although it got tiresome after two or three days, it was always edible. And she did make delicious cakes and other desserts. Maybe she could teach Lila Rose a few tricks in the kitchen.

After eating, he picked up his shovel and resumed his work. With Agnes coming, the Lord had answered his halfhearted prayer for help for Lila Rose. Maybe he should pray more often. And with more faith.

"I'm so sorry," Lila Rose whispered to Rebecca. "I—I…" Her throat clogged as she looked down at the soggy sandwich she'd offered her employer.

Rebecca chuckled in her kindly way. "Never mind, my dear. Perhaps I can help you." She stood and checked Viola's covers. "She's sleeping. Let's see what we can find in the kitchen. Come along, Lavinia."

After going to the bedside to kiss Viola's cheek, the child followed her grandmother.

Tucked in the dark back corner of the pantry, they found tins of food, pork and beans, corn, peaches, and other fruit.

"Let's add some ham to the pork and beans." Rebecca found the tin opener and showed Lila Rose how to use it. "We'll heat it in the medium pot—" she pointed to the pans on the rack beside the stove "—and take it up to Ralph and Viola."

Encouraged, Lila Rose ventured a question. "By any chance, do you know how to make bread?"

Rebecca sighed. "I'm afraid it's been too long since I've done so. Perhaps Drew can buy some from the general store."

They prepared the ham and beans and took it upstairs to feed the invalids. Both required further attention, so Rebecca stayed with them. Lavinia clung close to Rebecca, worry filling her eyes. *Poor child.*

Back in the kitchen, Lila Rose decided it was time to begin the roast. She found a cast-iron pan large enough to hold the meat, potatoes, onions and carrots. With all assembled, she shoved it into the oven and closed the door. Huffing out a breath, she went to the parlor for relief from the hot kitchen and settled on the couch for a short nap.

Sunlight streamed in through the west window, awakening her with a start. How long had she slept? She rushed to the kitchen to check the progress of the roast. The stove was warm, not hot. She quickly stirred the smoldering bits of wood in the firebox, then added another small log.

"Oh, please catch on fire." She must not bother Rebecca again. Instead, she loaded the firebox with more wood and kindling and opened the flue. To her relief, in a few minutes, the fire was practically roaring. She kept it that way for the rest of the afternoon, taking time only to water the roses and pull a few weeds from the garden. To her dismay, she also managed to uproot several beets and carrots that should have stayed in the ground a few more weeks. At least they weren't a total loss. Perhaps she should boil them now.

Staring across the barnyard, she saw Prince, Duke and Fred with their beautiful heads draped over the top rail of the corral, their eyes seeming focused on her.

"Yes, my dear boys. I'd much rather be playing with you, too."

Why not do so? She shook the extra dirt from the vegetables and strode across the yard. All three geldings nickered a welcome. They'd missed her, too. Or else they saw the tasty treats in her hands and couldn't wait to eat them. Probably the latter. Fred shoved to the front. Prince and Duke shoved him back, all trying to reach her.

"Hey, now, stop that. There's plenty for all of you." She divided the vegetables among them, and they devoured them, leafy stems and all. She stroked their noses and murmured loving words. "At least I know how to feed you boys, don't I?"

Just being with the horses chased away her anxiety over her failures.

The rattle of buggy wheels caught her attention, and

she turned to see Agnes Ahern arriving in the phaeton. Patrick drove to the back door of the house and helped his mother down.

Lila Rose hurried across the barnyard. "Good afternoon, Agnes. Patrick."

"And a good afternoon to you, Miss Duval." Agnes carried her apron, a promising sign, but her frown indicated some hesitation.

"Miss Lila Rose." Patrick sketched a perfect bow, gave her his usual wink and then hopped back in the phaeton and turned it toward the barn.

"Agnes, I'm so glad to see you." Lila Rose's eyes stung, and her heart lifted with relief. "Did you come to help?"

Agnes's oval face brightened with a smile. "Aye, indeed I did, Miss Duval—"

"Please call me Lila Rose."

"Aye, then, Lila Rose. What can I do?"

Lila Rose laughed and sobbed at the same time. "Well, I think I have supper in hand, but we're desperately in need of bread."

"Come along, then, missy." She strode toward the back door.

Lila Rose hurried along behind her. To her horror, smoke and the smell of burnt meat hung in the kitchen air. "What—"

Agnes grabbed a tea towel and opened the oven door. More smoke billowed out, and she waved it away. "I'm thinkin' we might have to start over on supper."

"Oh, no." Lila Rose dropped into a chair and put her head in her hands.

"Never mind, me girl. Maybe we can save part of it."

And indeed she did. The blackened potatoes and carrots were beyond saving, but the center of the large roast, while dry, appeared edible. Agnes bustled about the kitchen just as Viola usually did, doing this and that so quickly, Lila Rose couldn't keep up with her. Soon bread was rising, fresh potatoes were simmering on the stove and a cake was in the oven.

By the time Rob and Robbie came through the kitchen, cleaned up from their day of hard work, the burnt smell had dissipated, replaced by the aroma of baking bread. Soon after, Drew brought in two full jars of strained milk and set them beside the icebox, reminding Lila Rose that she hadn't made butter from the earlier milking's cream. Too late now.

After supper, with everyone fed and the children settled in bed, Lila Rose sought a moment of quiet on the front porch. Sitting in the swing, she rocked gently and gazed out on the sliver of moon hanging in the darkening sky.

How different her life was now from her idyllic existence in Charleston. Yet despite her failure to manage the household chores, she now felt peace and even joy. She had thought to rescue this family, but she hadn't any idea of how to do it. God had stepped in, bringing the wonderfully talented Agnes to rescue them all.

"There you are." Drew stepped outside and settled beside her on the swing. He nudged her arm, sending a pleasant feeling up to her neck. "How you doin'?"

She should move away but couldn't. Didn't want to. Wanted to feel his strong arm touching her, maybe even around her. Was that thought terribly improper?

"I'm so grateful to Agnes. She's amazing."

He nudged her arm again, and she nudged back.

"Why didn't you tell us...*me*...you don't know how to cook?" Even in the dim light, she could see his teasing grin.

She laughed softly. "Why didn't you notice? I've been here for two months. When did I ever serve the family something I'd made?"

"Huh. Now that I think on it, that's true."

They rocked gently for several minutes, enjoying the quiet.

"So, just exactly what does a lady's companion do?"

Despite the unspoken suggestion that her occupation had little value, she could hear the teasing in his voice and wanted to answer in kind. "Fetch a handkerchief. Call the servants. Answer the door when unkempt cowboys come to call."

He laughed. "What else?"

She sighed. What did she do? What had she done for Rebecca back in Charleston? Perhaps he needed to know more about their lives. Something deeper.

"When I first met your mother, she suffered from depression. After she hired me, she gradually began to take an interest in life, probably because I urged her to get out more. She'd had her orphan boys she taught in Sunday school, but she saw them only on Sundays." Stopping the swing, she looked up at him. "Why do you suppose she chose to help the boys instead of orphan girls?"

He looked away with a furrowed brow. "Maybe she missed her own boys." The catch in his voice stirred her own emotions.

When she could speak, she said, "I've always thought that, too, although she didn't like to talk about it."

He took her hand. "I'm sure you were a great comfort to her, as you have been to all of us here."

"Do you think so?" She didn't pull her hand back. "Even though I can't cook?"

Grinning, he shrugged. "Weelll…"

She punched his arm. "Never mind."

"Hey, you two." Rob poked his head out the door. "I'm headed upstairs. You coming in anytime soon?"

Lila Rose's cheeks heated up. Rob must think she lacked proper manners. Or was it his brother he didn't trust to be alone with her on the darkened porch?

"Leave 'em alone, Rob." Agnes's voice came from behind him. "I'll be sittin' right here in the parlor as their chaperone. The window's open, so I can hear everything they say. Or if it gets too quiet."

Both brothers snorted out a laugh.

"And there you have it." Drew smirked.

"Yeah. Good night, then." Rob disappeared back into the house.

"Well, this has been lovely." Lila Rose hated to break the mood, but reality loomed. "I plan to get up early and help Agnes all I can." She stood and started toward the door. "Maybe I'll even learn to make something edible."

Drew joined her and turned her to face him. "Lila Rose, I—" Without another word, he took her face in his hands and bent to kiss her, gently at first, then rather fiercely.

Her knees weakened, and she clutched his arms, fearing she might collapse. She should push him away. Instead, she tugged him closer.

After a moment, he pulled back with a gasp. "I'm sorry. I'm sorry. I don't—"

Sighing, she put a finger to his lips. "Did you hear me complain?"

Chuckling, he bit his lower lip and stared away. When he refocused on her, he said, "Want to do it again?"

"I wouldn't mind."

But as he bent to kiss her once more, rapping sounded on the doorframe.

"Beggin' yer pardon, Drew, but have ye a mind where I might be sleeping this night? Patrick said I'd be needed here for a week or more."

Although Agnes spoke to Drew, her eyes bored into Lila Rose with a warning look.

Drew stepped back. "Um, I can bring up a cot from the bunkhouse and set it up in the parlor. That's what we did last year, wasn't it?"

"Aye, and I was quite comfortable, too. Be off wi' ye, then." She waved toward the end of the porch and gave him a little shove.

"Yes, ma'am." Drew sent Lila Rose an apologetic grimace before hustling off to obey.

Agnes gave Lila Rose a maternal smile. "An' I'm thinkin' you ought to be off to bed, me girl. I heard you say you plan to help me, so let's make sure you get plenty of rest."

"Yes, ma'am." Lila Rose took her cue from Drew in obeying this woman's orders.

"And, missy—" Agnes touched her arm. "—I know yer a decent girl, but sometimes things can get out of hand. Be warned by someone who knows that all too well."

A half hour later, as Lila Rose lay in bed, the memory of Drew's kiss still warm on her lips, she pondered Agnes's warning. How easily she could have succumbed to his charms if they hadn't been interrupted.

She hadn't meant to lose her heart to him, but perhaps now it was too late.

Chapter Fourteen

Drew met Lila Rose in the barnyard the next day as she carried the lunch hamper toward the river. He took it from her and peeked inside. "Please tell me you didn't make the sandwiches. Or the potato wedges."

"I'll have you know I peeled the potatoes." She gave him a saucy grin that almost rocked him back on his heels.

He sucked in a breath to regain his balance. "Oh, well, then. Guess I can just toss the hamper into the river—"

"Suit yourself. I'm sure the other men will make you pay dearly. Maybe even toss you in the river after it."

They both laughed, then grew quiet. For several moments, they stood staring at each other.

"You all right?" He'd barely spoken to her at breakfast. With Agnes and Rob hovering around, it would take some doing to have another private conversation.

"Yes. You?"

"Weelll—" He stared off for effect before gazing down at her again. He tried to think of some silly thing to say, but as he stared into those beautiful blue eyes, nothing came to mind except… "Lila Rose, I—care for you… I care a whole heap."

Her eyes widened. "I… I…"

"Hey, Drew!" Rob called out from the levee. "When you get a minute, we're hungry down here."

"Yeah, save your sparkin' till later." That from Ranse Cable.

The other men chuckled and made remarks Drew couldn't hear.

Lila Rose's cheeks turned bright red. She spun around and ran toward the house.

That afternoon she was back in the corral, working with the horses, but every time he took a step up the hill, Rob sent a scathing glare in his direction or gave him a task to do that was nowhere near the corral. He seemed to forget his own sparking with Viola that had begun less than a year ago. Seemed a brother should be more understanding.

That evening, when he brought the milk to the kitchen, he found her seated in front of the crockery butter churn, working the wooden paddle with fierce determination. Keeping an eye on Lila Rose's work, Agnes stood at the stove, stirring her Irish stew. The room was filled with its mouthwatering aroma, and Drew's belly rumbled in response.

Supper didn't offer a better opportunity to talk with Lila Rose. At Rob's invitation, Agnes sat with them to eat. She seemed to take that as permission to regale them with stories of her childhood in Ireland and her years of working in an earl's "grand estate" in England from the age of fourteen. Like her son, Patrick, she was quite the storyteller.

Drew noticed that Lila Rose stuck close to Agnes. Was she just trying to learn basic kitchen skills, an admirable goal? Or had she been put off by his spontaneous kiss last night? His declaration of his feelings today? His heart ached every time he considered how he'd blurted out that he cared deeply for her. Why had he been so unguarded both times? He hadn't meant to frighten her. Even with all his doubts, he remembered how she responded to his kiss and the way she seemed to love teasing him. Didn't that mean she felt something for him, too? With his lack of experience with females, he had no idea, and he wasn't about to ask Rob.

As the next few days passed, everybody kept busy with their responsibilities. Doc gave Viola permission to get out of bed but insisted she must only do simple chores that caused no strain. Mother stuck close to her to be sure she did as the doctor ordered. Between the two of them, they taught Lavinia reading, writing and arithmetic. Robbie caught up on his lessons after supper.

Rob had been exercising Pop, and now Doc said he could come downstairs as long as he kept the splint on and someone was with him. Pop still refused to let Drew help him—didn't even want to be in the same room—so all the work landed on Rob.

Pop couldn't avoid sitting with Drew at supper, but his eyes never turned in Drew's direction. He even seemed to ignore Mother, who sat directly opposite him at the other end of the long table.

Despite Pop's animosity toward the two of them, the

evening meals once again became a time of relaxation from work, a time to catch up on everyone's day.

"Say, missy..." Pop focused on Lila Rose. "You still working those horses?" He'd asked her that every day for the past month. Maybe he was getting senile.

"Yes, sir. They're doing very well. On Monday, the young ladies and I will begin their sidesaddle lessons in earnest. Several are bringing their own horses and the new saddles Mr. Arrington ordered. We'll ride around the ranch to see how they're doing, then maybe into town the following week."

"Ah, very good." He sent a cross look in Mother's direction before turning back to Lila Rose. "I might come out and watch you. Now don't you worry none about the cooking. You got other important work to do, teaching those gals to be ladies like Viola used to do." He winked at Viola. "Scripture commands older women to teach the younger ones—" he glared briefly at Mother "—if they stick around to do it."

Mother ignored him and kept eating.

"But if a *young* lady has something to teach, she can go ahead and do that, too." Pop, seeming satisfied with his rant, dug into his supper.

"Thank you, Mr. Mattson." Lila Rose shot him a brief smile...actually, more of a grimace. Drew could see she didn't care for his rudeness to Mother any more than the rest of them. "You'll be interested to know that, under Agnes's wise tutelage, I prepared the bread and butter you're eating this evening."

While exclamations of praise came from the others, Drew could only stare. True, the bread didn't have a perfect consistency like Viola's, but it held together and was tasty. The butter couldn't have been smoother and had just the right amount of salt.

"Well, it's too bad you won't be around here much longer," Pop said. "Viola could use your help. But I know you'll want to be heading back to Charleston with…" He nodded in Mother's direction but didn't speak her name.

Drew noticed that Mother winced slightly, yet still sat in her rightful place at the end of the table and sent a serene gaze toward Pop.

"I will stay until the baby arrives, then for as long as Viola needs me."

"Humph." Pop snatched another slice of bread from the platter in front of him and slapped on a large glob of butter.

"I'm real glad you're here." Rob, seated adjacent to Mother, set a hand on hers. "You've been good for all of us. Please stay as long as you like."

"As long as *she* likes?" Pop stood and threw his napkin on the table. "What about what I like? I'm the one who built this ranch. Me and you, Rob. Workin' and sweatin' with the cattle and buildin' this house like she wanted. Then she ran off at the first—"

"Are ye ready for dessert?" Agnes jumped to her feet. "Lila Rose and I have a surprise for ye."

Pop truly must be getting senile because the ruse worked. He sat down and snatched up his napkin again. "Well, don't just stand there. Bring it on."

Up to this point, poor little Lavinia and even Robbie, who had seen adults bicker before, had watched wide-eyed during this whole conversation. But at the promise of dessert, their eyes lit up with anticipation. The change of subject worked its charm on the children. From the looks on other faces, Drew could see they welcomed it as well. Good ol' Agnes.

Pop had always accused Mother of leaving the ranch because life got too hard. From the way she'd been working alongside the rest of the family, Drew doubted that was true. He'd even doubted it before he went to Charleston to fetch her home. Of course Pop wouldn't listen to anything he had to say, but maybe with Lila Rose's help, they could get to the bottom of why Mother had left and figure out a way to heal their broken marriage. At least Mother appeared to want that. Otherwise, why had she sat by Pop's bedside the past two months, taking care of his most intimate needs and suffering his verbal abuse?

Lila Rose treasured the moments when she delivered the lunch hamper to the men each day. She took slow, deliberate steps away from the house so Drew would notice her. He in turn hurried up the hill to meet her. They sauntered down to the other men, leaving the food with them before walking together to the river's edge.

They ignored the teasing from Rob and the other men. Lila Rose had come to realize it was all in fun. Besides, Rob approved of their growing closeness. While he demanded proper behavior, he gave them opportunities to talk, even allowing Drew to observe her work with the horses…as long as Robbie accompanied them.

The boy's presence gave them a chance to tease each other, but it was during their private chats by the river that they tried to devise a plan to uncover the truth about his parents' fractured marriage.

"What do you remember about that time?" She had decided only someone who had been present nine years ago could offer any clues.

He scratched his head. "That was a long time ago. I was fifteen and still trying to prove I could work as hard as Rob and Will." He paused and huffed out a breath. "Now that you ask that, I do remember Pop trusting me with plenty of responsibilities, especially keeping Jared and Cal in line. And he'd tell me when I did something right. Didn't even yell at me when I messed up."

She gave him a sympathetic smile. "You must miss that."

He shrugged, but she could see the hurt in his eyes.

"Your mother and I haven't had much opportunity for deep conversations these days because she's sticking close to Viola to be sure she doesn't do too much. But maybe I can find a way to get her alone and ask her what happened."

"Thank you." He gave her a tender smile and gripped her hand. "Now I have to ask you something."

Her heart skipped. "All right. What is it?"

"That night when I kissed you… No, that's not how I want to start." He glanced away and huffed out a breath.

She laughed. "Go on."

"That day when I told you how I feel about you…"

Her heart dipped. Now he would say he hadn't meant it.

"I do care about you, Lila Rose." He glanced toward the men, some twenty yards away. "I love the way you love my mother and take care of her. I love how you fit in with my crazy family." He chuckled. "And I love your determination to learn how to cook, although I'm worried all Agnes will teach you is how to make Irish stew." He brushed a strand of hair from her cheek, a gesture so gentle she wanted to weep. How different it was from her father's cruel beatings. "Most of all, I love that you are always true to yourself."

With each sentence he spoke, Lila Rose's heart lifted higher and higher. Did this mean he loved *her*? She couldn't trust herself to respond, so she stared down at her hands as she struggled to compose herself.

"Um, I'm sorry." Drew stood quickly. "I'm sorry. I shouldn't have—"

She jumped up and touched his lips. "I care deeply for you, too."

He gave her a crooked smile and blinked his blue eyes. "Really?"

She giggled at his boyish expression. "Yes, really. But I think we have some issues to work out before we can take things any further between us." She stared up into his wonderful eyes, and tears came to her own. "Forgive me for saying this—we don't want to end up like your parents."

"What?" He stood back a little. "We won't do that. Why would you worry about that?"

"Think about it, Drew. I'm from the city. I'm not sure I can spend my life here in the wilderness, and—"

"Wilderness? This isn't *wilderness*. You should have seen it before we broke ground." He stepped away from her and waved a hand toward the house, the barn, the river. "We're a short drive from Riverton, not far from Española and Santa Fe. Lots of good shopping there. I'll take you whenever you want to go."

"It isn't shopping I care about. You still have coyotes, wolves, grizzly bears." She shuddered. "And snakes."

He put his fists at his waist, clearly annoyed. "How many snakes have you seen here?"

"Well, just one, but—"

"Right. And it wasn't even a dangerous one. Didn't Suzette say it skedaddled once she poked the log?"

He wasn't listening to her heart, her fears. How could she make him understand how deeply the deadly wildlife terrified her? Every day she worked with the horses, she feared a snake would enter the pasture, maybe chasing a field mouse, and frighten or bite one of the horses.

"Hey, Drew!" Rob called from the worksite. "We saved you a sandwich. Better hurry, or Ahern will eat it."

"Oh, dear." Lila Rose started walking toward the men. "I've kept you from lunch."

He caught up and touched her arm. "We can talk more later?"

The doubt and sadness in his voice stung. "Yes, of course."

But how could she ever convince him that she couldn't live here in constant fear, no matter how much she loved him? She would stay until Rebecca returned to Charleston. If Rebecca reconciled with Mr. Mattson and settled back into family life here, Lila Rose would accept her offer and go back to live in her Charleston house. And there she would live safely…but brokenhearted and alone.

Drew endured the joshing from the other men without comment. They'd tire of it soon and go back to grumbling about how slowly the levee was taking shape, how they'd rather be training the new cow ponies to herd cattle, how this summer was hotter than last, and on and on. A cowboy's life wouldn't be bearable if he couldn't complain.

Drew wished their complaints were his biggest worry. Now that he knew Lila Rose cared for him in return, how could he make her see life here wasn't all that dangerous? Wasn't their growing fondness worth fighting for? Besides, most of the wolves and grizzlies had been driven up to the mountains, and the coyotes only came out at night. She would just have to overcome her fears, as Viola had. In fact, Viola had dismissed her encounter with a rattler last year as a trivial event. That's probably why Rob had fallen for her. Couldn't Lila Rose do the same?

Drew chewed his lip. What if Mother and Pop never reconciled or even found a way to live together in peace? Mother might give up and leave, taking Lila Rose with her.

Could he follow them? Could he give up the only life he'd ever known and live in the city? What would he even do there to support a wife? He had no idea.

He also had no idea what he would do if Lila Rose left for good. If Rob weren't so caught up in running the ranch and worrying about his wife and unborn baby, Drew might ask his advice. He was closest to Will, but Will wouldn't be back until September. Could Jared or Cal help him out? Maybe he should ride over to their sheep ranch on Sunday afternoon and unload his worries on his two younger brothers. Their wives had grown up out here, but they still might have some encouragement or maybe just a listening ear.

When Sunday arrived, Pop insisted on attending church, splint and all. It took the surrey and phaeton and three horses to transport everyone, including Agnes, to town. They crowded into the building just as Lacy Neal began playing "What a Friend We Have in Jesus" on the pump organ.

Mother, Viola and Lila Rose joined the singing before they even reached their seats. Pop made sure he was at the far end of the pew from both Mother and Drew. Did anyone else in the congregation notice the odd arrangement? If so, they had the grace not to stare or mention the matter during the fellowship time after the service.

"Rob, I'm gonna ride over and have dinner with the Sharps." Drew glanced at Lila Rose, who stood in the aisle, talking with some of the town gals. He wanted to get away before she noticed and maybe asked to go along.

"Sure. Just be back for milking." Rob continued his conversation with Mr. Arrington about supplies they needed for the ranch.

Drew took this chance to leave the building and catch up with Annie and Job Sharp. "Say, can I beg an invitation to dinner? I'd like to spend some time with my sweet little niece and nephew." It was true. He did love the babies. Now that they'd begun to interact with other people, they were all the more fun.

"Sure thing." Annie looked over his shoulder. "Why

don't we have the whole family over? I'm sure the girls and I can rustle up plenty for everyone to eat."

"Uh, well…"

Job nudged his wife's arm and whispered, "Don't you get it, sweetheart? The boy wants to talk to his brothers."

"Ah, I see." She winked at Drew. "Need some courtin' advice, do you?"

Drew tugged at his collar. Mother and Lila Rose were emerging from the church, and he didn't want them to catch on. Once word spread, everybody would want to join in.

"I'll meet you at your place." He hustled over to his horse and mounted up. Halfway out of town, he realized he should have helped load the ladies into the surrey and phaeton for their trip home, but it was too late to go back now.

Despite being lamb instead of beef, dinner proved to be just as tasty as anything Viola cooked. Drew supposed the ladies shared their cooking secrets with one another.

Because Job had figured out his purpose in inviting himself over, Drew played it up, even made it a joke around the dinner table.

"Y'all can't imagine how hard it is to be the last unmarried Mattson." He clicked his tongue and shook his head. "I just don't know what I'm gonna do."

While their wives and in-laws laughed, Jared and Cal nodded solemnly.

"Man, I remember those days," Jared said. "Couldn't even go to town without some silly female wantin' to invite me to supper or just to flirt."

"I did notice all those goings-on, but I never had the same problem." Seated beside his wife, Cal lifted her hand and kissed it.

"That's because you two were in love since you could barely walk, and everybody knew it." Emma eyed Jared and gave him a loving smile. "We didn't have quite the same smooth road, but we finally arrived."

Drew vaguely recalled their early sparking, their big breakup and, finally, their renewed romance. Now they appeared to live happy-ever-after, like folks in children's bedtime stories.

"So, since we're the ones with bumpy experience, how can we help you?" Jared asked.

Drew sighed. In a family this size, secrets were hard to keep. But he was blessed to have loved ones who also wouldn't betray those secrets to outsiders.

"I'm pretty close to falling for Lila Rose."

He expected a big reaction—teasing from his brothers, happy sighs from their wives. But they all just stared at him.

"Did you think we didn't notice?" Emma laughed. "She feels the same. What's the problem?"

Drew chewed his lip. "She's a city gal with no inclination to live on the ranch. And I can't see myself livin' in the city."

For what seemed like a few minutes, they sat in silence. At last, Job spoke.

"Son, were you listening to the sermon this morning? I know you were. Remember when Pastor Daniel read the words of our Lord Jesus? 'Greater love hath no man than that he lay down his life for his friends.' I believe there's no closer friend to a man than his wife."

He gazed down the length of the table at Annie. "I'll do whatever it takes to make her happy, no matter what I have to give up."

"That's mighty fine, sir." Drew tried not to sound impertinent. "But you and Annie seem to want the same things. You both love this ranch, this community. I can't see either of you leaving."

"That's true, brother. But what about Jared?" Cal, usually the quiet one, spoke up. "Do you know what he was willing to do for Emma?"

"Aw, Cal, don't get into that." Jared waved a hand dismissively.

"Yes, I will. I think Drew needs to know what you were willing to do when Emma needed to go to Cleveland and help her aunt rear her young'uns." He turned back to Drew. "He gave up his ranching plans so he could go with her. Even planned to work in the steel mills to support her."

Work in the steel mills? Drew couldn't imagine it.

"Well, the Lord worked it out." Emma stood and began to clear the table. "Aunt Maggie's widowed sister-in-law came to live with her. I didn't need to go, and we all got to stay here, right where we wanted to be."

The Lord worked it out. All the way home, Emma's words drummed into Drew's mind. Jared's willingness to leave the land he loved—the very fact that he became a sheep rancher instead of a cattle rancher—showed a deep, sacrificial love for his lady. Did Drew care for Lila Rose that much? Could he move away from all he'd ever known and establish a new life in the city?

Yes, he cared more than his simple cowboy words could say. But no, he couldn't leave, at least not until he'd reclaimed Pop's respect and approval. So he needed to do whatever it took to achieve that goal first. Otherwise, he'd just be running away rather than facing his hardest problem.

Trouble was, he had no idea how to solve it.

Chapter Fifteen

"Don't be afraid, Iris." Lila Rose held Fred's halter so her friend could mount him. "Remember, just like when you sat in his saddle the last time, he's a gentle boy and won't throw you."

Despite her trembling, Iris stepped up on the mounting block and sat on the saddle, then lifted her right leg over the upper pommel and put her left foot into the stirrup. After situating herself, she smiled.

"All right. I'm ready to go." She reached out a hand.

Lila Rose gave her the reins and held the lead rope so she could guide Fred around the corral. The placid gelding followed her. "That's a good boy, Fred."

They circled around along the fence for several minutes, with Lila Rose watching for any hesitancy in her student. Iris appeared to be enjoying herself.

"Are you ready to go it alone?"

Iris's eyes briefly widened. Then she smiled again. "I am."

Lila Rose unhooked the lead rope but continued to

walk beside Fred. Slowly, she let him move ahead of her and continue around the edge of the corral.

"If you want him to turn, remember your signals."

As Iris pressed her leg against Duke's side, she moved the reins. He obediently turned…perhaps a little too fast, because she tilted to the right and cried out. Lila Rose hurried to her side, but Iris had already regained her balance.

"I can do this."

Lila Rose laughed. "Yes, you can."

And so could all the other girls. After several weeks of practice in the corral, they all expressed sufficient confidence to ride around the ranch. With great excitement on the appointed day, they all tacked up their horses and mounted.

"All right, ladies, where shall we go?" Lila Rose adjusted her straw hat to better shield her face from the sun.

"Let's try the front pasture." Dolores tucked her skirt under her leg. "We can practice trotting there."

Lila Rose had never walked out to that pasture, but from a distance she'd seen plenty of field mice. Pictures of hungry snakes chasing after them slithered through her mind. What had she been thinking to suggest a ride around the ranch?

"Let's go down by the river," Alice said. "We can give the horses a drink."

"Oh, yes, I'm sure that's the reason you want to go there." Dolores smirked. "Never mind that handsome Ranse Cable is down there, working hard and showing off his muscles."

Alice sniffed, pretending to be offended. "I'm sure you wouldn't mind saying hello to Patrick Ahern."

Juanita patted the neck of her horse. "I would like to say *buenos días* to my brother Julio. We never see him at home now that he lives here in the bunkhouse."

When the other girls agreed to the plan, relief swept through Lila Rose. She'd never seen a snake during her visits with Drew by the river. "Very well."

She hadn't been to the riverside since her last disastrous talk with him last week. She'd merely carried the lunch hamper halfway each day and waited for him to fetch it. He, in turn, had sent someone else to pick it up. When they did encounter each other in the house, they said very little beyond polite greetings. Did his heart sit heavy in his chest, as hers did?

"Lila Rose." Iris spoke louder than her usual soft tone. "Are you paying attention?"

"Maybe she is thinking she will soon see Señor Drew Mattson," Isabella said.

The other girls laughed, but Lila Rose could only offer a weak smile. Hadn't they noticed how things had cooled between the two of them?

"I said we'll follow you." Iris nodded toward the river.

They took the path that led downward and were rewarded with the immediate attention from the men.

"Hello, ladies." Ranse swept off his wide-brimmed hat and sketched a courtly bow, his eyes settling on Alice.

"Buenos días, mi hermanita," Julio Mendez called out. He approached Juanita, and the two chatted in Spanish.

Likewise, Patrick and the other men set down their shovels and greeted the ladies. All except Drew. And of course Rob, who looked none too happy to have the work stop.

"Let's move on, ladies." Lila Rose refused to surrender to her roiling emotions. She should have anticipated this. "Hurry now. Let the men get back to work."

That earned her a nod of appreciation from Rob. She forced her eyes away from Drew's reaction and focused them instead on the sandy path along the river.

In the lush, green lower pasture, cattle grazed contentedly, not bothering to acknowledge the riders. The massive bull, whom they had named Charlemagne, must have been used to interlopers in his domain as well, because he also continued to eat. Rob had mentioned they would move the herd up the hill when the river rose a little higher.

Lila Rose tried to relax and enjoy the beautiful day with these ladies. Growing up, she'd had few friends because Father kept a tight rein on her and Mama's social lives. They could only attend functions that might lead to financial gain or some sort of influence. It never did him any good. His so-called friends got him drunk and took his money through gambling. He rarely came out ahead in selling his horses.

She dismissed those dreary thoughts. Attending church with Rebecca in Charleston and then living here at the ranch, she'd revised her opinion that most men were drunks and scoundrels. The Mattsons and their ranch hands had proved to be men of integrity who lived responsibly, even Drew. It could be his sense of responsibility that made him so determined to remain here on the ranch. She'd never had cause to consider him lazy. And now she was learning to enjoy friend-ships with other ladies. Life had become much fuller since she took over Viola's teaching position. In fact, she admitted—if only to herself—her life had become fuller since coming to the ranch. If it weren't for the dangers, she might even consider it enjoyable.

"Looks like the river is rising pretty fast," said Alice.

"I see that." Lila Rose had also noticed it. "The other day, Rob said they could keep working on the levee until it floods in full force."

"They always get a warning from upriver," Dolores added. "That's when they move the cattle to the upper pasture."

Right now it flowed peacefully, washing its banks free of leaves and small branches blown there by last winter's winds. If the flood held off, perhaps she and the girls could bring a picnic out here next week.

Her pleasant reverie was broken by the rattle of… leaves in the wind? No. Coiled at the edge of a cluster of dead branches, a snake the color of the sand rattled its tail, its hideous wedge-shaped head pointed directly at Duke's legs.

As he whinnied and skittered to the side to avoid it, a scream stuck in her throat. Terror shot through her. She couldn't think, couldn't react.

An explosion like a loud firecracker sounded from behind her, and the snake flew apart in bloody pieces. At the same moment, Duke reared on his hind legs, then spun around and crashed past the other horses. He refused her call to stop or her tug on the reins. She could only hold on tight and pray he didn't stumble on the uneven ground and break a leg.

He raced up the hill, avoiding the men's attempts to grab his reins and nearly knocking one of them down. He ran until he reached the front pasture, and she feared he would jump the fence. Instead, he slowed his pace and finally stopped—huffing, wheezing, shuddering, as though the memory of the snake still terrorized him.

She also trembled like a leaf in the wind, and her pulse raced as fast as his hooves had moved. Somehow she managed to direct him back to the barn. But when she tried to remove his saddle, the horror of the experience, the vision of that snake threatening to strike, overwhelmed her. She collapsed to her knees on the dirt floor and surrendered to hysterical weeping.

"Hey, Lila Rose, it's all right." One of the girls— Dolores?—gripped her shoulders and lifted her to her feet. "No harm done. We're all here, safe and sound."

How could she be so calm? Of course. She'd been reared on a ranch. Had no doubt seen many snakes.

"I'm guessing you haven't trained ol' Duke here not to react to gunfire yet." Dolores pulled a pistol from beneath her vest and laughed, as did the other girls.

Lila Rose stared at her. "*You* shot the snake?" Her voice squeaked. Did all the girls carry guns on their persons?

"Sure did." She shrugged. "Not my first one, either. You gotta be prepared out here."

The other girls nodded and voiced their agreement.

"When a rattlesnake came into my garden while I was weeding," Elena said, "I used my hoe to dispatch him."

The others offered tales of their snake encounters, and Lila Rose could see they were trying to console her. While she appreciated their kindness, she could not relate to their experiences. How did they endure the constant danger this land offered? In each of the situations they described, they hadn't been bitten only because they'd seen the snake first. What if they had stepped on one they failed to notice?

"Hey, Lila Rose." Drew sauntered into the barn, a teasing smirk on his lips. "Who won the race? You or Duke?"

Behind him, Rob and several of the hands chuckled.

Rob surveyed the group. "You girls all right?"

The others all said yes, even Iris.

At their laughter, Lila Rose's cause for trembling turned from fear to anger. She pushed past Dolores and strode across the barnyard, increasing her pace to a run as she neared the house. She could not stay here when even the other women dismissed her fears of all the very real dangers. What was the matter with these people?

She took refuge in the small bedroom she shared with Lavinia. While she shed more tears into her pillow, the three kittens joined her, crawling on her and beneath the quilt and meowing in their tiny voices. They were just over two weeks old now, not quite the age at which their antics could either cause much laughter or much trouble. So far, they couldn't wander out of the bedroom, but they did climb the curtains, leaving shredded hems. Small and helpless as they were, what would happen when they discovered the world beyond the bedroom door? Did Viola want Puff and her three babies underfoot once her own baby was born? Or would they be put out in the barn with the larger cats? Small as these little ones were, snakes might kill them.

I'm just like these kittens. Small, helpless to change my life, probably underfoot, with little to contribute.

Oh, dear. She was sinking into self-pity. That meant it was time to leave. But she would have to explain to Rebecca what had brought her to this decision. And poor Rebecca had troubles enough of her own. No matter how much she took care of Mr. Mattson, he still refused to speak a kind word to her. Like Lila Rose's father, he reserved his good manners for others. She would never tolerate such treatment, even if it meant she had to take the meanest of employment somewhere—anywhere—else.

With everyone seated around the supper table, Drew hoped to tease Lila Rose out of her scaredy-cat mood. She'd probably told Mother and Viola about the snake, but he couldn't resist the opportunity to make light of it for their benefits. Last year when Viola had encountered a rattler, she'd dismissed the incident as trivial. To hear Rob tell it, she'd said, "Shoo, silly snake." The whole family had split their sides laughing. Could Drew relate today's event with as much humor?

"You should have seen our city gal." He winked in her direction, but she was concentrating on her supper. At least everyone else—even Pop—was listening to his story. "One little snake, and him dead already, and she's off like a shot. Ol' Duke tore up that hill like he'd been shot out of a cannon."

The glint in Pop's eyes encouraged him. Was the

old man actually paying attention to him? Better make the most of it.

"Now, me and the boys did try to grab his reins, but, man, that horse was havin' none of it."

Pop chuckled, and Drew felt a kick of excitement and inspiration.

"The other ladies galloped past us like they were in the annual Independence Day race. The boys and I were hollerin' for our favorites to win." He felt the story growing. "Next month, we oughta use a rattlesnake instead of a gunshot to start the race. That'll make all the horses run for their lives."

Pop laughed out loud. In fact, more like *guffawed*. It sounded to Drew like everyone else was laughing, too. He glanced again at Lila Rose, who was staring at him through tear-filled eyes. Oh, man, now he'd really messed up. How could he fix it? "Well, I guess—"

"Son, that's the best tale you ever told." Pop chortled. "A bit more practice, and you'll be as good as Rob at spinnin' a yarn."

Was that actual approval in his eyes? Drew could hardly breathe. All these years of hoping—*praying*—and he was about to earn Pop's acceptance. He heard the shuffle of a chair but didn't turn to look. He could only see the gleam in Pop's eyes, the grin on his lips.

"Speaking of races," Pop said, "you gonna run that gelding of yours in the race this year to represent the family?"

"You can count on it." He hadn't thought that far ahead but wouldn't admit it. Not now. "You got any tips for me?"

"Let me think on it. I'm a little out of practice."

"Yessir. I'll appreciate all the help you can give me."

"Well, it's about time I got outside this house more than goin' to church." Pop cut a cross look in Mother's direction. "If I can escape my jailer, we'll see what we can do."

As Drew followed his gaze, he noticed Lila Rose's place was empty. Man, she must really be mad at him. But then, she was a city gal. As he'd noticed with Viola, city gals didn't take to teasing like local gals. At least Viola had come around when she'd realized they were just showing how much they liked her and wanted her to stay. Would Lila Rose come to understand that?

"We'll start tomorrow." Pop set his knife and fork across his plate, a sign he'd finished. "Agnes, did I smell apple pie this afternoon? How 'bout you serve that up with some fresh cream."

"Comin' right up, milord." Agnes had taken to calling Pop and Mother the lord and lady of the castle in her thickest Irish accent, which sometimes eased the tension coming from the two of them.

While she and Viola cleared the table and brought out the dessert, the conversation turned to other ranch business, with Pop fully engaged in everything Rob and even Drew reported. He hadn't been involved with the day-to-day work since his heart attack, so this renewed interest was a sure sign of an improvement to his health.

"Y'know, Rob," Pop said, "I think we oughta go back to having our family meetings in the evening. What do you think?"

Rob's eyebrows shot up. "Uh, sure. I've missed those times."

Drew's heart kicked up another notch. He had no

idea what had happened. Maybe the lighter splint Doc had put on Pop's leg improved his attitude. One thing was sure. His obvious approval, his laughter at Drew's story, his promise to help him prepare for the race all added up to a new day for Drew.

The empty chair across the table slowed his excitement. *Lord, I've prayed for this for years. But do I have to give up my hopes for working things out with Lila Rose in order to keep Pop's respect?* His change seemed to take place when Drew told his snake story, the very thing that drove her away.

Maybe it was for the best. If she couldn't take a little teasing, maybe she wouldn't fit into this family or even the community after all.

But if that were true, why did his belly ache and his heart feel like it had been replaced by a stone?

Chapter Sixteen

I should be in the kitchen, helping with supper cleanup, but I can't let Rebecca and Viola see me like this.

Seated on the trundle bed, Lila Rose tugged her dampened handkerchief away from the tabby kitten, who seemed determined to own it. The other two kittens wrestled on the floor while their mama bathed herself nearby. From her modest experience with indoor cats, she guessed the little ones would soon want to leave this confined space. Since the kittens' births over two weeks ago, Lavinia resisted every attempt to move them from her room to the barn. Perhaps she wouldn't object if they were taken to the mudroom, where they would be easy to feed solid food when they were ready for it and their box would be easier to clean. Should Lila Rose bring up the subject to Viola? To Rebecca?

She huffed out a sigh. It wasn't her responsibility to make such suggestions. Nothing here was her responsibility, not even teaching the girls their riding lessons. She would never be able to face them again after running away in tears. Not one of them had expressed understanding of her terror. Not one. Even if she told them her beloved Goldie had taken a cottonmouth's bite intended for her, had died in agony in her arms the next day, they would undoubtedly say what her father had said. She was a fool for caring so much for a dog.

"Miss Lila Rose?" Sweet Lavinia peeked in the door. "Gram'mother wanted me to fetch you for the family meeting."

"Oh. Oh, dear." Lila Rose grabbed a fresh handkerchief from the bureau drawer. Rebecca hadn't summoned her since they'd arrived here many weeks ago. Perhaps she was needed after all. "Tell her I'll be right down."

As the child scampered off, Lila Rose studied her face in the bureau mirror. Unlike this afternoon, when she'd sobbed into her pillow, this time she'd merely let the tears flow as they would. While they had left her face a little puffy, perhaps no one would notice.

Rebecca met her at the bottom of the stairs, strain obvious around her eyes but a smile on her lips. "I don't know what's happened, but this is significant. Ralph hasn't changed his attitude toward me…yet." She flinched, then shook her head. "But these family meetings often resulted in good things." She squeezed Lila Rose's hand, and Lila Rose squeezed back.

"You don't really need me, do you?"

"Oh, yes, of course I do." Rebecca kissed her cheek. "Come along." She led her to the parlor and to a seat beside her rocking chair.

Everyone gathered in the room, even Agnes, with Drew and Rob bringing chairs from the dining room to provide seating.

I won't look at Drew, no matter how often he looks my way.

She need not have worried. Drew's attention was focused on his father, his expression like an eager puppy. A pang of sympathy struck her. Somehow he'd regained Mr. Mattson's love, or at least his attention. What had happened to bring this about?

"It's good to see everybody." Mr. Mattson spoke as if they hadn't just shared a meal around the table. "We should do this every night, just like we used to."

"Yessir," Rob said. "Good idea."

Drew echoed the sentiment.

"If I recall, we used to start out with a Bible reading." Mr. Mattson waved a hand toward the huge family Bible on a shelf beside the divan. "Viola, you always give us such fine readings. Would you honor us with one now?"

"Of course." Viola started to rise but dropped back into her chair and gripped her rounded belly. "Rob, darling, please bring it to me."

He did as she asked. "I'll hold it." A twinkle lit up his eyes as he sat in a chair opposite her, the Bible resting on his legs. "You don't exactly have a lap to put it on."

Everyone but Lila Rose chuckled. Even Rebecca. Goodness, this family liked to tease. She did, too, but after they had all dismissed her encounter with the snake, she no longer felt a sense of camaraderie with them.

"What shall I read?"

"Let's see." Mr. Mattson scratched his chin. "How about the passage Pastor Daniel preached on a while back, the one Rob told me about? You remember it?"

Nodding, Viola turned the pages. "Luke 15, beginning at verse 11. 'A certain man had two sons. And the younger of them said to his father, "Father, give me the portion of goods that falls to me."' Oh, dear." Her face grew pale, and she gripped her belly again. "I don't think I can go on."

Rob handed the Bible off to Drew. "What's wrong?"

Tears rimmed Viola's eyes, and she grimaced with pain. "I don't know."

"Let's get her up to bed." Agnes bustled over and helped Viola stand, then felt her belly. "Send for the doctor."

"I'll go." Drew dashed from the room.

While Rob and Agnes tended to Viola, Rebecca gripped Lila Rose's hand. Once they were out of the room, she broke down in tears.

"I can't go through this again."

Robbie and Lavinia stared wide-eyed at her.

Lila Rose beckoned to them. "Children, let's pray for your mama." She turned to Mr. Mattson. "Sir, would you please help the children with their prayer?"

The genial expression he'd been sporting since supper had disappeared. "Huh. What's the use? It's clear this baby isn't going to make it. Rob and Viola need to face that—"

"Stop it!" Rebecca stood and hovered over her husband. For a moment, Lila Rose feared she would strike him. "How can you be so cruel?"

Lila Rose beckoned to the children. "Robbie, take your sister upstairs. I'm sure you know how to pray for your mama. Do that, then read a story. Can you do that?"

"Yes, ma'am." Robbie took Lavinia's hand. "Don't cry, sis. It'll be all right."

They scurried from the room.

"You see that?" Mr. Mattson waved a dismissive hand. "Rob and Viola have two fine, healthy children. What more do they need?"

"Oh!" Rebecca's shriek sent a shiver down Lila Rose's back. "You monster! That's what you said when our daughter died. You dismissed her death, her very life, as not worth caring about."

"Woman, you have five healthy sons. And you abandoned them when life got a little hard out here, even though you agreed to come out here with me. I had calves being born right and left—our livelihood! And I needed to tend them. But you deserted us. Ran off like a scared chicken right when we needed you most."

Rebecca now sobbed, as she had for Lavinia's still-born kitten. "I left because you have no heart. I love my sons, but you know how I wanted a daughter. Our precious little Maisie—"

"And now you can be thankful you have four daughters-in-law and two granddaughters." Mr. Mattson stood, grabbed his cane and limped past his wife. "I'm going to bed. And I don't need your help to get there."

Rebecca slumped down on the divan and sobbed as though her heart would break.

"Mother." Drew returned to the room and knelt in front of her. "I'm so sorry. I never knew I had a sister."

"You were supposed to fetch the doctor." Lila Rose couldn't keep the crossness from her tone.

He spared her a brief glance. "I sent Ahern. Mother, I'm so sorry."

Lila Rose sat back and let him console Rebecca…or at least try. She had never spoken of this lost baby, yet it must have eaten into her soul all these years. For her husband to dismiss her grief was worse than Drew's dismissal of Lila Rose's deadly fear about the snake. What was wrong with these men?

She wouldn't wait around to figure it out. As soon as possible, once Viola passed her crisis—no matter how it turned out—she would take Rebecca back to Charleston.

A heavy thump pulled Drew's attention away from Mother. He left her in Lila Rose's care and hurried from the parlor to the staircase to find Pop seated on a lower step, his splinted leg stuck out in front of him.

"Why'd she have to bring all that up?" Sorrow rather than anger filled his expression.

Drew could think of no response. Instead, he had a flash of memory about those dark days when he'd been maybe fourteen or fifteen years old and Mother had been very sick. Rob had kept Drew and his other brothers busy working the ranch so they wouldn't worry about her. One day, after Mother was back on her feet, he'd sent Drew to the house for something. There, he'd found his parents in the middle of an argument. Mother was packing a carpetbag. Pop grabbed her arms, shook her and yelled that she wasn't going to leave him.

Drew wasn't sure what else happened. All he could remember was stepping up to his father and slamming a fist into his jaw.

He'd hit his father! The horror of it swept over him. He thought he might vomit. Was that the reason Pop had treated him like an outcast all these years since? But Drew had forgotten that awful experience in the chaos after Mother left. Rob's wife, Maybelle, had fallen into a depression and refused to do the simplest household chore other than tend to little Robbie. Pop had brought in Old Fuzzy to help out, and the old trail cook did his best to keep them all fed. They'd all scrambled to keep up their responsibilities, so the ranch work consumed them all. Now he needed to make sense of what had happened to cause Mother to leave…and his own part in that awful day.

"Pop." He set a hand on his father's shoulder. "I have to ask you a question."

"Huh?" Looking older than ever, Pop turned his reddened eyes to Drew.

He took that as an affirmation. "All these years, every time you looked at me, you thought, 'This is the son who hit me.' Am I right?"

Pop leaned away from him. "You might be."

"Well, this is long overdue, but I need to ask you to forgive me."

Pop stared at him for a long time. "I did."

Now Drew returned the stare. "When? I mean…"

"It's been slow coming to me ever since Rob told me about Pastor Daniel's sermon a few weeks ago—the one about the prodigal son. It got me thinking."

That rankled him. "But I've never been a prodigal or wastrel. I've worked hard on this ranch."

"I know you have. But in that story, I saw a father loving his son no matter what he'd done, and it struck me right here." He thumped his chest. "I was going to tell you this evening in front of the whole family, but then Viola…" He cast a glance up the stairs. "Besides, I knew I deserved it. I was raised a gentleman, and my pa would have whipped me good if I ever raised a hand to a lady."

Drew digested this revelation for a moment. "Have you asked Mother to forgive you?"

Pop bristled. "If she asks me to forgive her for leaving, I'll ask her to forgive me for roughing her up." His posture slumped. "If that's what she came for, I'll do it to make her leave…if she's a mind to."

Drew snorted out a laugh and regretted it immediately. Did Pop want Mother to leave or not? "Sorry." He should stop now rather than risk losing Pop's renewed approval. "I'd better go out and check with the hands. Rob told them to bring the herd up from the lower pasture in the mornings."

"You boys been keeping an eye on the river?"

"Yessir." It felt good to have Pop consult him, respect him, as he did Rob. He didn't ever want to lose that again. "We watch it while we're working on the levee, and somebody's down there all night, every night."

"Good. Good." Pop gripped the banister and pulled himself to his feet.

"You want me to go up with you?" That sounded better than asking if he wanted help.

"No. I'll be fine. You go ahead and check on things outside." Pop glanced toward the parlor door and shook his head. "See you in the morning."

"Yessir." Drew watched him climb the stairs one at a time, pulling the splinted leg after the good one. Reaching the top, he turned down the hallway toward his room.

On his way out of the house, Drew walked past the parlor. Mother and Lila Rose still sat on the divan, their hands clasped and heads bowed. Lila Rose glanced up at him, sorrow in her eyes. He gave her a little smile, but she didn't return it. In fact, she looked away.

He released a long sigh. Just as he'd feared, gaining Pop's forgiveness and respect had dashed his chances with the woman he was falling in love with.

Had Drew realized she and Rebecca could hear everything he and his father had said? Did he care? She couldn't begrudge him his reconciliation with his father, something she had often prayed would happen. And if his smile meant anything, Drew seemed ready to reconcile with her. But she couldn't get past his dismissal of her fears. After growing up with a father who didn't understand or protect her, she wanted a man who would, or she'd have no man at all.

Where had that thought come from? She had long ago resolved never to be at the mercy of a husband who had the power to dictate what happened in her life. That was why she appreciated Rebecca's decision to stand up for herself. To learn that Mr. Mattson had physically abused her, even if only once, was terribly shocking. As was Drew's defense of his mother. Shocking and admirable.

"Shall we go up and see if we can help Viola?"

Rebecca nodded. "I must face it, even if she loses the baby. Perhaps I'll be able to offer some understanding and comfort."

Who had comforted her when her baby died? From

what Lila Rose could perceive, she'd grieved the loss alone.

They found Viola in Agnes's good care. The Irish woman certainly had more skills than washing laundry and preparing good meals.

"It seems the little one is tired of waitin' to see the sunshine, but wait he must—for a bit longer, anyway." Agnes lifted Viola up to a sitting position and gave her a drink of water. "O'course, the good doctor will be tellin' us what to do, but I'm thinkin' he'll be sayin' it's back to bed wi' ya."

"I'm so tired of being in bed." With a weary sigh, Viola slumped back against her pillow.

Moving closer, Rebecca felt Viola's forehead. "You don't seem to have a fever, but you're still pale." She caressed her cheek. "My dear, please rest." Her voice caught, and she brushed away a tear.

Her own emotions close to the surface, Lila Rose swallowed hard before asking, "What can I do to help?"

Viola gave her a sweet smile. "You've been such a help already. Please keep up our Monday classes, especially the riding lessons." She thought for a moment. "I know you were frightened by the snake today. We're so grateful neither you nor Duke was bitten. And just to clarify, despite family lore, I was terrified last year when I encountered that snake while riding Robbie's horse. I did not say, 'Shoo, silly snake.'" She rolled her eyes and shook her head. "These men and their exaggerated storytelling."

The others laughed, and Lila Rose managed a slight snicker. She wouldn't contradict Viola, but the issue wasn't the storytelling. It was their dismissal of very real traumas she and Rebecca had suffered. She would recover from her fright, but Rebecca still had not recovered from the loss of her newborn daughter all these years later. Yet Mr. Mattson, and even Drew, couldn't see the truth about what had driven her away from them.

Mr. Mattson had claimed his own offense had been grabbing Rebecca's arm and shaking her. Yes, that was very wrong and very unlike him. Rebecca had assured her that he was not abusive. The enduring offense was his ignoring her grief over her tragic loss. Could he not have spared her one kind word, one loving embrace to show he respected her feelings even if he didn't understand them? He seemed to be saying he had his sons to work beside him on the ranch, so what did he need a daughter for? No wonder it seemed he only cared about losing his cook and housekeeper when Rebecca left.

Dr. Warren arrived with Cassandra and prescribed just what Agnes had said... Viola must remain bedridden, with only short walks up and down the upstairs hallway. After listening to the baby's heart with his stethoscope, he raised his eyebrows briefly but offered no further alarms.

"While Cassandra tells Agnes here about Viola's care, I'll take a look at Ralph." Doc headed to Mr. Mattson's room. He returned after a half hour, carrying the splint. "Rob, we can get rid of this now, but you keep an eye on him so he doesn't do too much."

With the invalids tended to, they left, taking along with them several of the muffins Agnes had baked that afternoon.

To do her part, Lila Rose promised Viola that she would continue the etiquette classes with the young

ladies. And if she could muster up the courage for another riding lesson, she would give it, so long as Dolores
carried that pistol and rode at the front of their group.
And there would definitely be no picnics by the river.

As for her feelings for Drew, she must stifle them
and renew her promise to herself never to care for a
man who did not return the same measure of affection
and respect.

Now if only she could keep that promise…

Chapter Seventeen

True to his word, Pop came out to the barn to advise Drew on the upcoming Independence Day race. He even allowed Drew to help him down the stairs and across the barnyard.

"Now, you gotta watch that Martinez stallion." Pop rested a hand on the top rail of the corral and huffed out a deep breath. "No reason a gelding can't beat a stallion, but it's all about strategy. Our cow ponies can outrun a Thoroughbred that first quarter mile, but then they get tired. You gotta hold Buster back for the first few blocks around town so he'll have what it takes heading toward the finish. And watch for Martinez trying to block you."

"Yessir." Drew knew exactly how to beat Martinez, but he wouldn't tell Pop. They'd raced last year, and Drew knew all his neighbor's tricks.

"I guess Viola won't be up to entering one of her pies in the baking contest." His father chuckled. "And we sure don't want Lila Rose to enter."

Drew laughed. Pop's renewed interest in the ranch

and community—and especially his relationship with him—overrode any loyalty he might feel for Mother's companion. He had to forget his fondness for her and move on with his life. No matter how much it hurt. Now if only he could remember that when he saw her.

The river continued to rise, but there was no flooding yet. Still, Rob ordered the men to drive the herd to the upper pasture. It felt good to be in the saddle again, doing real ranch work instead of shoveling dirt day after day. The new calves needed branding—not Drew's favorite job but a necessary one to keep cattle rustlers from claiming the stock when they went up to the mountain pasture next summer.

Preparations for the Independence Day celebration commanded everyone's attention. Agnes, who had extended her stay for as long as the family needed her, planned to enter some of her fine baking. Mother surprised them all by saying she would enter some of her knitted items for judging. Did this mean she wanted to become more a part of the community? If so, his bringing her here from Charleston had been worth every bit of effort and time and money…and pain.

Best of all was the time Pop spent each day coaching him in tricks he'd known since childhood. Not that he'd ever say that. Instead, he soaked up the long-overdue affection like dry land soaked up the river's floodwaters.

The heavy flood began on June 29, with water flowing over the river's banks and onto the land, chasing all sorts of critters up the hill, including those snakes Lila Rose feared so much. As far as Drew could tell, she'd spent that day in the house. Otherwise, he was glad to see her keeping up the classes with the other gals, especially the riding.

He saw her at mealtimes and during those evening meetings Pop still insisted on having, but she never returned his smile and barely acknowledged his presence. Instead of getting used to it, he felt the cut deeper each day. Maybe it was time to confront her. No, *confront* was too harsh. *Cajole? Woo?* Once he'd decided to approach her, the word didn't matter because his heart took over, and he looked for the first opportunity to do so. He even enlisted Rob's help.

"All right, everybody off to bed." Pop shut the Bible and handed it to Rob. "We'll have a good day of work tomorrow."

Mother had stayed upstairs with Viola, and Lila Rose usually tucked the children into bed. At Drew's wink, Rob called them to his side.

"My turn, Lila Rose. I want to hear their prayers this evening."

"Yes, of course. Good night, my darlings." She gave Lavinia and Robbie kisses on their cheeks. After they left, she seemed at a loss for a moment, then headed for the front door.

Pop leveled a look on Drew and waved a hand toward the door. "What're you waitin' for?"

With that stamp of approval—and seeing Agnes settle in a chair by the open window with some mending—he followed Lila Rose. As he stepped out the door, she looked up from her place on the swing, and her eyes briefly widened. Should he tease her about coyotes? No, best not to tease at all. What should he say? How beautiful she was? How he missed their pleasant conversations? Missed *her*? He'd never before wanted to romance a lady. Had never even paid attention when other fellas did it. Maybe it was time to give it a try.

The three-quarter moon rising over the horizon lent little light to the landscape, and the warm summer breeze carried the smell of cattle now that they were in the upper pasture. Not the most romantic setting. But he forged ahead.

"May I join you?"

She didn't answer but scooted over in the swing to make room for him. For several minutes, he gently rocked them, still wondering how to start.

"How're your classes going?" Stupid question. She'd already told them about it last Monday evening.

"Fine. Thank you." She stared off into the darkness.

"Are you ready for the race on Wednesday?" She didn't look his way as she asked the question.

"Um, yes." He scratched his chin. "Buster really loves it when I give him his head."

She nodded. "So you think your cow pony can beat Señor Martinez's Thoroughbred? I noticed him last Sunday and would say he's close to sixteen hands."

"Fifteen and three-quarters." Drew chuckled. "But if Martinez wears his usual regalia, especially that sombrero, he'll have wind resistance and be carrying more weight."

That made her smile. "Well, I wish you the best." She stood abruptly and moved toward the door. "Good night."

"Lila Rose, I meant what I said when I told you about my feelings for you."

She stopped, her hand on the doorknob, and stared down. "Hmm."

Then she was gone. Drew sat back in the swing, his heart in his belly. Right when he thought they were moving closer, she up and left. What had he done wrong?

With the household focused on the Independence Day celebration, Lila Rose longed to participate. Under Agnes's tutelage, she had conquered biscuit-making, but that was hardly worthy of offering to the cooking contests. When she voiced her wish to the young ladies in her class, Dolores spoke up.

"We should take part in the parade to show off our sidesaddle skills."

"And dress alike," Alice said. "Something patriotic. Red, white and blue."

The other girls chimed in their support. Offering ideas from their wardrobes, they discovered everyone had a blue skirt, or at least a dark one. Everyone also had a white shirtwaist.

When the day came, Alice provided bright red material from her father's dry goods store to make sashes to go around their waists. She also provided straw hats to shield them from the sun. Lila Rose added a veil to further shield her face.

As they all mounted up for the event, Lila Rose had a moment of doubt. Father and even Mama had denounced public displays as unseemly for a lady. But that had been under the strict social rules of what it meant to be a *Southern* lady. Here in the West, rules gave way to expediency and, more often, fun. Who would it harm if she took part in a parade? No one was keeping score on her behavior, not even Rebecca. Well, maybe Agnes, who served as a chaperone whenever she thought Lila Rose and Drew required one, bless her heart. But as much as it pained Lila Rose, they wouldn't require one unless Drew saw the error of his ways. His father certainly hadn't tried to make up with Rebecca.

"Ladies!" Dolores waved her riding crop in the air. "Let's show them how it's done."

She urged her horse up the drive and under the arch at the ranch entrance, with the other girls following. Lila Rose was glad she'd wanted to lead. Everyone would recognize her as the daughter of a prominent rancher, which would take the attention off Lila Rose, who followed behind the others in case one of them had a problem with her horse.

They loped toward town and soon joined the others lined up for Riverton's second-annual Independence Day parade. While New Mexico Territory wasn't yet a state, Riverton residents still felt very much a part of the United States of America and wanted to celebrate the nation's founding.

The ladies' literary club rode in a surrey and held up the books they'd discussed. Tacked on the back of the carriage was a sign encouraging everyone to take up reading. Some of the older men who had been drummers or buglers or pipers during the war, for either the North or South, put aside their differences and created a small marching band. Children who attended the school in town wore patriotic costumes fashioned out of *papier-mâché.*

To the shouts and cheers of numerous onlookers, the parade wended its way through the few streets of town, past the dry goods store, bank, ice-cream parlor, law offices, barber shop and other businesses. When the other girls waved their gloved hands to the crowds, Lila Rose followed suit, especially to the ladies she'd met at church.

The final destination was the field beside the community church and across the road from the mission. Volunteers had set up booths for all the contests, and soon the field was swarming with participants of all ages. With her riding complete, Lila Rose tied Duke to a post and joined the other girls as they wandered from booth to booth. Rob had brought Rebecca's newly knitted baby blanket and placed it among those being judged. Agnes accompanied her son, Patrick, bringing her own pies and pickles. When Dolores and Iris entered the egg race, Lila Rose and the others stood on the sidelines and cheered them on as participants struggled to keep their raw eggs on their wooden spoons.

"Miss Lila Rose." Mr. Mattson limped toward her, leaning heavily on his cane. "Come along with me and watch Drew win this horse race."

"Oh, yes, Lila Rose, you must watch Drew race," Alice teased.

"Si, I think we all like to watch him, even if he is not racing." Elena giggled.

While the other girls made their silly remarks, Lila Rose refused to take the bait. "I'm always eager to watch a horse race. Too bad I didn't sign up to ride, too."

"Ha. Good answer." Mr. Mattson offered his elbow. "Come along now. It's about to start."

Lila Rose looped her arm through his, and they crossed the grounds to the edge of the road, where the start had been laid out in front of the judges' platform, with the Independence Day banner overhead. The riders would race around the streets of town, returning to the same spot. Eleven contestants had already lined up, and the second the starter pistol blasted, the horses bolted, and the crowd broke into cheers.

"Go, boy, go!" Mr. Mattson took off his hat and waved it in the air. "Look at him go, Lila Rose. Ain't you proud of him?"

As thrilling as the race was, her heart sank. How could she respond? To her relief, Mr. Mattson was too involved in watching his son to expect an answer.

Two blocks from the start, the horses disappeared around a corner at the edge of town. As the crowd quieted, their thundering hooves could be heard in the distance.

Within minutes, the thundering came from several streets over and grew closer, then the riotous cheering began again. The first horse around the corner was Drew's Buster, with Señor Martinez's Thoroughbred only a length behind. By the time the two swept under the Independence Day banner, they were too close to call a winner.

"He did it!" Mr. Mattson hopped around on his good leg, waving his cane in the air. "He won!"

"Hooray!" Lila Rose couldn't keep the joy from her voice...or her heart. Pride in Drew filled her. He would be so happy, and she was happy for him. Try though she might, she couldn't keep from loving him and wanting the best for him, even if they had no future.

The rest of the horses swept past, slowed and turned back to the judges for their results. The three male judges on the stand conferred, argued, conferred again.

Finally, Mrs. Gentry, whom they'd ignored, muscled her way into the conversation.

"Quit your jibber jabbering." She glared at the other judges. "It was a tie, and you all know it."

"She's right!" shouted someone in the crowd. Others voiced their agreement.

"Nonsense." Mr. Mattson huffed. "It all depends on the angle. I saw Drew's Buster an obvious nose ahead of that stallion."

"No, no, señor." The man beside them posted his fists at his waist, his belligerence clear. "It is Martinez who wins."

"Now, just a big minute here, fella—"

"Oh, look." Lila Rose grabbed Mr. Mattson's arm. "Drew and Señor Martinez are shaking hands."

"What…oh." He pushed out another breath. "Huh. Don't that beat all."

The sportsmanship on display was a sight to behold. Drew and Martinez were laughing and slapping each other on the back. They both agreed the prize of a five-dollar gold piece should go to the town's orphan fund.

As the day's celebration came to an end and families packed up to leave, Lila Rose savored the wonderful experience as something she would carry with her when she returned to Charleston. More than that, she would *miss* this experience and this community. Living a quiet life with Rebecca in the city could no longer compare favorably with the camaraderie and downright fun these folks had. Since she and Rebecca had arrived, not one person had ever made either of them feel unwelcome.

But when they couldn't even take a walk or ride around the ranch safely, what would protect them from the danger?

* * *

At the supper table, Pop praised Drew's race and insisted he'd won fair and square. Drew knew better. Being a cow pony used to chasing down steers, Buster had the necessary skills to take the corners more sharply. It gave him the lead near the end. But despite Drew's strategies, the long legs of the Thoroughbred had been the deciding factor, if only by an inch. Still, Drew basked in the praise of his family for several minutes before turning the attention to the ladies.

"Mother, your knitting won that nice red ribbon. With all the competition, I think you can be proud of that." He dared a look at Pop. "Right?"

"Humph." Pop grabbed a biscuit with one hand and dug into his stew with the other.

"Thank you, dear." Mother gave Drew a weary smile.

He should have taken her to town today, but she'd insisted on staying with Viola.

"But these pickles Agnes made," Mother said in a brighter tone. "My oh my, aren't they delicious? They certainly deserve that blue ribbon."

Agnes blushed, and her eyes twinkled. "Yer most kind, yer ladyship."

Everyone laughed.

"And we can't forget the beautiful ladies riding sidesaddle." Drew had been trying to think of ways to regain Lila Rose's interest in him, and maybe even her affection. Their mutual love of horses had to be the key. "Lila Rose, you all added a special element to the parade. Have you ladies thought about naming your group? How about Lady Riders of the Rio Grande?" He dared a wink.

Of course she blushed, but she also smiled. "What a nice idea. I'll speak to the other ladies."

Did her response mean she planned to stay? Or was she simply being polite?

Pop was too tired for a family meeting and went to bed early. His lighthearted mood and the support he'd given Drew seemed to indicate an overall improvement of his health and his view of life. Should Drew take a chance and talk to him about Mother? Or would that ruin the progress he'd made so far in their relationship? His failure with Lila Rose reminded him he wasn't the best diplomat. Best not to take a chance but let his parents work things out for themselves. If only they would.

But then, wasn't reconciliation the reason he'd fetched Mother home in the first place?

Chapter Eighteen

The weeks following the celebration were filled with ordinary ranch work. Lila Rose had found contentment in helping Agnes in the kitchen and with other household chores as they awaited Viola's delivery. As long as she stayed in bed, with only short walks in the hallway several times a day, the expectant mother should have no further crises. Busy with managing the ranch though he was, Rob still attended to his wife every day. Lila Rose no longer wondered whether any man could be a good husband. Rob Mattson was proof that a man could be kind and devoted, as were his younger brothers, Jared and Cal, and probably Will.

Was Drew different from them? No, he was just as gentlemanly and kind, something that had impressed her moments after they met. He wasn't angry and cruel, as Father had been. His only fault seemed to be his failure to understand and *respect* her fears. But that failure was sufficient to keep her from losing her heart to him. Or at least to try. She did care for him, but she would never admit it to him again, even when she observed his more endearing side.

One afternoon she almost lost her resolve when she saw Drew and Robbie whittling on the back stoop. One of three kittens, who all now lived under the stoop, crawled up Drew's trouser leg and shirt all the way to his shoulders. Not missing a word of instruction to his nephew, he gently unhooked the tiny claws from his clothing and cuddled the feisty cat, even as it bit into his calloused hand.

Lila Rose almost wept at his kindness, his gentleness. Father had never treated animals that way, especially cats. But she could not trust Drew to be as kind to her heart. It was easier to bide her time in silence, wait until the proper moment to persuade Rebecca to return to Charleston and avoid being alone with Drew as much as possible.

In early August, a cry from upstairs interrupted supper preparations. Agnes set down the chicken she was preparing, then washed and dried her hands.

"If I'm not mistaken, this is it. Take over here and fry this chicken, me girl." She nodded to Lila Rose, then winked at Lavinia, who sat at the table, practicing her writing on a slate. "You stay here, little one, Idont'cha worry none 'bout yer mam."

Lila Rose's pulse raced. "Should I find someone to fetch the doctor?"

"I'll send his lordship out to the barn. He'll find somebody." She bustled from the room.

Lila Rose stared at the chicken, which was only partially cut up for frying. She'd mastered several kitchen skills, but cutting up a chicken was not among them. Could she serve a decent supper without Agnes?

A whimper from the table pulled her attention away from her own concerns. Lavinia stared at her with wide eyes. "Will Mommy be all right?"

Lila Rose longed to promise that Viola would be fine, but what if she wasn't? Pretending things were fine never achieved anything. Mama had lied about Father's abuse, leaving Lila Rose with a sense of betrayal when his abuse turned toward her.

"Why don't we pray for her right now?"

Lavinia gave her a solemn nod, so Lila Rose sat with her and asked the Lord for the baby's safe delivery. Because the child had comprehended the birth of her kittens, Lila Rose hoped her words were not inappropriate. "Now, you pray."

"Yes, ma'am." Lavinia bowed her head again and pressed her small hands together. "Dear Jesus, please help Mama and our new baby. We love her and need her, and I really want a new baby sister." She thought for a moment. "I guess a brother would be all right, but I already have a brother." She opened one eye to glance up at Lila Rose. "And please help Miss Lila Rose not ruin supper 'cause Daddy doesn't like her cooking. Amen." She looked up, eyes wider still. "I'm sorry—"

Lila Rose snorted out a laugh and pulled Lavinia into an embrace. "Oh, my darling, I don't like my cooking very much, either." She brushed back the child's dark curls and kissed her forehead. "But if you help me, I think we can put something tasty on the table." Even if that meant pulling last night's leftover Irish stew from the icebox.

Mr. Mattson hobbled down the stairs and through the kitchen faster than was safe. Lila Rose added a prayer for him not to sustain another injury in his haste. Doc had removed his splint only a few weeks ago and had warned him to be careful.

Soon Rob dashed into the house and up the stairs. Within less than a minute, he was back in the kitchen, scooping a pitcher of hot water from the tank on the stove.

"Refill it." His cryptic order showed the depth of his anxiety, and he was gone before she could respond.

She pumped water into another pitcher and filled the water tank, then added wood to the firebox. As Agnes had taught her, she opened the flue just enough to draw the fire to the fresh logs.

Now for that chicken. Using a sharp knife, she located the joints and cut downward on the cutting board. That worked fine for the legs and wings, but the body of the bird remained a mystery. She huffed out a breath. How did Agnes—or Viola, for that matter—manage to make such even cuts and nice-sized pieces? Humph. This was *her* chicken now. She would cook it as she saw fit. And if no one liked it, too bad.

Drew sat with Pop, Robbie and Lavinia, waiting for Lila Rose to serve up the supper she'd prepared. The mouthwatering aroma of seasoned chicken hung in the air, but that didn't promise the food would taste good. No matter what, he would eat it and praise it, even if he had to pay the price later with a bellyache.

Footsteps sounded on the staircase, and Rob lumbered into the dining room.

"Any news?" Pop asked.

Drew and the children stared up at their dad. If the young'uns felt as anxious about Viola as Drew did, he sure would understand. This business of birthing human babies was just as hard as birthing calves. Good thing the doctor had come right away and was now tending Viola.

"Viola got mad at me and threw me out." Rob sat and ran a hand across his stubbled cheek.

Pop chuckled. "Yeah, they do that sometimes." He looked toward the kitchen door and shouted, "Lila Rose, what's keeping supper?"

Was that all he cared about? Drew had been mighty careful of late not to anger Pop or, for that matter, to get mad at him. But sometimes the old fella showed complete indifference to the sufferings of others, especially the womenfolk.

"Here you go." Lila Rose, looking pretty as a painted picture in her blue day dress and white apron, set the large soup tureen in front of Pop. "I hope you enjoy it." She sat in her usual spot across from Drew.

After praying over the food, Pop removed the lid, releasing a curl of steam from the contents. "Sure smells good, just like Viola's cooking. Don't tell me she made this before—" He glanced at the children. "Maybe Agnes made it." He served himself a portion of the chicken stew, which had little biscuit dumplings sitting on top.

Rob looked too tired to care who cooked it, but he ladled out portions—first for the children and then himself. Lila Rose insisted that Drew serve himself, so he put a healthy portion in his bowl.

"Tumbleweed!" Pop uttered the exclamation he hadn't used in years. "This ain't Viola's or Agnes's. Lila Rose, did you cook this?"

"This?" She blinked her eyes in the cutest way. "Why, yes, now that you ask—I did."

Pop chortled. Then choked and coughed so hard Drew had to pound him on the back and give him a drink of water. When he recovered, he stared down the table at Lila Rose. "Young lady, this is mighty fine fare. Seems you've been taking lessons. Ha! We'll make a rancher's wife out of you yet."

Rob spewed a mouthful of coffee across the table, and Lila Rose began to cough like she was choking. She stood and stormed from the room. Drew thought his head would explode. How could Pop ruin everything like that?

He stood to follow her, but Pop grabbed his arm. "Sit down, boy. She's just shy. Give her time." As usual, he was oblivious to his mistake. "Eat up, young'uns. We'll have a special story time this evening." He glanced toward the kitchen. "Guess it's too much to expect some dessert."

Lila Rose forced her shaking hands to begin kitchen cleanup. She must get control of herself. It would not do for her to break any of Viola's lovely dishes just because she'd been insulted.

Did Drew actually expect her to marry him? No doubt he and his father had talked about that very thing, as though she were a piece of merchandise. Did his father's continued approval depend upon it? He'd disregarded her fears, and now he assumed that, being a spinster, she would be so grateful to have a husband that she'd be quick to accept his proposal. A proposal offered only because they thought she'd learned to cook.

The children cleared the table, then returned to their grandfather for the promised story. Rob and Drew went about the evening chores. Her anger diminished as she worked, but Lila Rose couldn't bear to go to her room. Instead, she sought out her usual spot on the front porch swing. With Agnes busy upstairs and unavailable to act as chaperone, surely Drew wouldn't join her in the dark. That would be the last straw.

But he did come out. "Pop's reading right there in the parlor."

"Is he now?" She stood and walked toward the door. "Good for him."

Drew gently touched her arm and whispered, "Lila Rose, that supper was mighty good, but I don't think like Pop does. He makes it sound like being a rancher's wife is a job, but it isn't. It's a marriage like any other, with two folks respecting and loving each other and wanting to build a life together." He waved a hand toward the swing. "Will you sit with me for a minute?"

His whispered words, his gentle touch, sent a pleasant shiver down her side…and lured her like a kitten following a string. Maybe she'd been wrong about him agreeing with his father. She sat, hoping Mr. Mattson would not be able to make out their words.

The motion of the swing soothed away some of her weariness from the day. "Has Rob checked on Viola?"

He chuckled softly. "I guess so. She finally let him back in the room."

Lila Rose would have laughed, too, if the situation

weren't so dire. Why was this baby taking so long to make an appearance? She'd seen kittens being born, but she'd never observed a woman in childbirth, so she couldn't imagine the possible complications.

"Listen, I know it's not easy for ladies, especially city gals like you and Mother, to live on a ranch. It's hard work, and everybody needs to pitch in." He took her hand, and her traitorous heart warmed to him. "You've been a big help to the family, and we all appreciate it. *I* appreciate it." He exhaled a long breath. "I'm not saying what I mean to say."

Now she did laugh. Maybe she was foolish to let herself be so affected by his charming clumsiness, but she couldn't help herself. "Tell me, Drew. What do you mean to say?"

He grinned. "What I've wanted to say before." He paused and took a deep breath. "I love you. And I want to marry you—not because of that fine supper you fixed tonight, but because you're a good, kind woman." He shook his head. "That still doesn't say it right."

"Do you want to marry me and spend your life with me?"

He looked surprised. "Well, sure. That's it." He grinned again. "I want to marry you and spend my life with you."

"Why?"

"Hang it all, Lila Rose. Why are you making this so hard for me?"

"I'm trying to help you."

"Oh, is that what you call it? All right, so will you?"

"Will I what?"

"Will you—" He threw an arm around her, pulled her close and planted a kiss on her lips.

A pleasant tingle shot through her. She couldn't move. Couldn't speak.

Too soon, he broke away. "So, will you marry me?"

"I—I…"

A loud whoop from upstairs resounded throughout the house. Laughter followed…then a baby's cry. Then another baby's cry.

"Oh, Drew!" Lila Rose jumped up and hurried toward the door. "I think it's twins!"

Chapter Nineteen

Drew couldn't move, couldn't think. He'd finally summoned the courage to propose to Lila Rose, or at least to mend their strained relationship, and he'd been left in the dust because of a baby's cry. *Two* babies' cries.

He should kick himself. They'd all been praying for Viola and her baby to come safely through the birth. And maybe they even had a bonus baby. *Thank You, Lord!*

He charged up from the swing and into the house, following Pop, who was running up the stairs way too fast. He faltered, and Drew reached out to steady him.

"Thanks, son." Pop huffed. "Was that two baby cries, or is my hearing going out?"

"Sounded like two to me."

"No wonder she had problems. Jacob and Esau all over again."

"What?" Why was Pop bringing up that Biblical story at a time like this?

"Jacob and Esau, boy. Don't you remember the story?

They fought with each other even before they were born. No wonder Viola had such a hard time."

Drew just shook his head. Pop knew the Bible from front to back. Too bad he couldn't apply the love of God to Mother.

They reached the top of the stairs, walked the few yards down the hallway to Rob and Viola's room and bumped heads as they tried to peek inside.

Rob sat at the head of the bed, an arm around Viola's shoulders. She held one cloth-wrapped baby and gazed lovingly at him...her? Across the room, Doc and Cassandra washed up from their work while Mother cuddled the second baby. Her eyes moist, Lila Rose beamed a pretty smile at the little one.

"Well?" Pop stepped over to the bed and peered at the one Viola held. "Boys or girls?"

"One of each." Rob's chest puffed out proudly. "This one's the boy."

"Where'd you ever come up with twins? No twins in our families, is there?" Pop glanced at Mother, a rare acknowledgment of her presence.

Busy cooing at the baby, she didn't look up.

Her face pale, Viola leaned against Rob. "I have a brother and sister who are twins. I suppose that's the answer."

"And now we can use both names we picked out." Rob touched a finger to the infant's hand, and the little one's tiny fingers curled around it. "This is James Ralph. We'll call him Jemmy." He nodded toward the infant Mother was holding. "That's Jennifer Rebecca. We'll call her Jenny."

Everybody voiced praise over the chosen names, even Pop.

"I'll write their names in the family Bible," Pop said. "Or maybe you can do it, Viola, when you're up to it. You have a real fine hand."

Lila Rose whispered to Mother, and Mother handed little Jenny to her. The sweet look on Lila Rose's face as she gazed down at the infant smote Drew in the chest. She'd be a good mother herself, just as she was an excellent companion to Mother. Loving, caring, unselfish, hardworking. All the qualities a man hoped for in a wife.

Then there was that undefinable thing that drew a man to a woman—not just the physical but a matter of the heart. Love. A desire to be with her, to share joyful moments like these. To support her when life got difficult. Like Rob with Viola, with this difficult birth. Like Will, when he'd risked his life to save Suzette from the outlaws. Like Jared and Cal, when the Sharps' barn burned down and they had worked side by side with Emma and Julia to rebuild it. That was the life Drew wanted, hoped for, longed for with Lila Rose.

Only trouble was, she hadn't said yes to his proposal.

Lila Rose glanced over at Drew, who stood in the doorway, gazing at the baby in her arms. The adoring look on his face warmed her heart. She smiled at him, and he grinned broadly.

"You want to hold her?" She didn't want to let go of the precious newborn, but that was selfish. After all, Drew was Jenny's uncle, a member of the family.

"Sure thing." He stepped over and reached out, taking Jenny into his arms so gently it brought tears to Lila Rose's eyes.

The men in this family certainly did love children— a quality she admired. Drew's tenderness toward this newborn breached her last bit of resistance. Yes, she would marry him. Somehow she would overcome her fear of snakes and coyotes. And even if one of those deadly creatures attacked her, at least she would have known the love of the man she loved in return.

"All right, folks…" Doc Warren finished reassembling the contents of his black bag and picked up his hat. "Viola, we'll leave you in the good care of Rebecca and Agnes. The rest of you, clear out. That means you, too, Rob. Go milk a cow or something. You have two healthy babies, and their mama's healthy, too. Cassandra'll come back tomorrow and check on you. Now clear out. I mean it."

Everyone laughed at his officious manner, but they also obeyed his order. While the others followed Doc and Cassandra from the room, Drew appeared reluctant to hand Jenny over to Rebecca.

"My oh my." He held a hand to his chest as he descended the stairs beside Lila Rose. "What a grand day. You all right?"

She laughed. "Oh, yes. More than all right."

If she returned to the front porch, would he follow? Repeat his proposal? Only one way to find out. "I won't be able to sleep, so I'm going to sit on the porch a bit longer."

"Mind if I join you?"

"We won't have a chaperone. Your father went to his room."

He stopped. "Oh, yeah. Well, I guess we could sit in the parlor. Would that do?"

Rob's boots thumped on the staircase, and soon he poked his head in the parlor door. "I'm getting more hot water for upstairs. Drew, refill the tank and check the fire for me so we have plenty of hot water in the morning." He looked between the two of them. And grinned. "If you two want to visit a bit longer, that's all right, but I'll be checking back in ten minutes." He gave Drew a warning look. "And I expect to hear conversation all that time." He headed toward the kitchen.

Lila Rose's face burned as it had when she'd spent the day in the sun. "Maybe I'll just go to my room." She took a step toward the stairs.

Drew touched her shoulder. "Will you give me those ten minutes?" The hopefulness in his tone stopped her. "Let's sit on the divan."

This was it. He would propose again, and she would hasten to say yes. Once they were seated, she looked at him expectantly.

"Lila Rose, I know you grew up a bit spoiled, with servants to do all the work. But you've surprised us all—even Mother—with the way you've pitched in during our family trials. You fit right in with ranch life, never minding getting your hands dirty. Well, except for not mucking out the stalls for your horses and cleaning up your tack—"

"Spoiled?" She couldn't believe her ears. Her happy mood shattered. "You think I grew up *spoiled*? Just because I didn't learn how to cook or clean house?" She stood, glared down at him. "Why do you blame me for not cleaning the stalls when you order the men to do it?

The very idea that you think I'm spoiled! It only goes to show you know nothing about me and have never even tried to learn."

Against her better judgment, she unbuttoned her cuff, pulled her long left sleeve up to her shoulder and pointed to her arm. "You see this scar?" She hated for anyone to see the long, deep disfigurement and never wore gowns that would reveal it. "My father did that. He beat me with a whip when he found out our groom, George, was teaching me to train horses. He beat George, too, and my mother. And that wasn't the only time."

Trembling with anger, she yanked the sleeve back down again. "Yes, he *spoiled* me. Spoiled me for marriage." She blinked back tears and saw the shock on his face. Too bad. She wouldn't stop now. "I will never live under the thumb of another cruel or thoughtless man. No matter what it costs me, it's better to be a spinster than to let a man rule my life who laughs at my concerns and dismisses my fears…and wrongfully thinks I'm spoiled!"

Unable to say more, she hurried from the room and raced up the stairs before he could stop her. But no footfalls followed her, so he must have decided to let her go. All the better. She hadn't accepted his proposal, so now she wasn't bound to stay here any longer. As soon as Rebecca wanted to leave, they could go back to Charleston. Even if Rebecca wanted to stay, Lila Rose would accept her offer and go back to live in the house by herself.

Careful not to disturb Lavinia, she prepared for bed, ignoring the gentle tap on the bedroom door and Drew's soft call. Eventually, he stopped, and the noises from the hallway ceased, except for occasional tiny baby cries from Viola's room.

Lila Rose tried to say her bedtime prayers, but no words would come, only tears. Even though the kittens now lived outside under the kitchen porch, Puff still remained. She jumped up on the bed and patted Lila Rose's tearstained face. But that only made her cry all the more.

How could he have been so stupid? So thoughtless? He'd never asked Lila Rose anything about her childhood and just assumed she'd been pampered, probably because she hadn't learned to cook. While he'd meant to praise her willingness to learn, he'd opened his mouth and let his brains fall out.

That scar on her arm horrified him. He had a few scars himself from childhood scrapes and falls, but no one had ever taken a whip to him. She was such a little thing, so dainty. Her father must have been a monster. Drew's hand curled into a fist, but he couldn't pummel a dead man. And, as he'd learned after hitting Pop, violence didn't solve anything—just made more problems.

Lord, is there any way I can fix this? Any way I can win back her love?

What else had she said? She wouldn't live with a man who laughed at her concerns, dismissed her *fears*. The rattler. How could he have disregarded the signs? Every time she walked across the barnyard, she stared at the ground fearfully, as though expecting to encounter a snake. And then she actually had. And he'd laughed. Had related the story to the family at supper, expecting her to laugh, too, as Viola had done. Instead, he'd wounded her. Like Pop, he'd ignored the deepest concerns of the woman he loved.

He scrubbed a hand down his face. In these parts, everybody came across dangerous critters from time to time. Those who had reason enough to stay learned how to deal with them. What could he have done differently—something that would have helped Lila Rose, would have given her a reason to stay? Maybe what Rob had done with Viola. Like training a skittish horse, he should have calmed her. Should have offered to teach her how to live in this wild land, how to protect herself when he couldn't be with her. Now, with her refusing to talk to him, it looked like he wouldn't ever be with her again. But his worst failure? He should have been seeking her approval all along instead of Pop's.

Tonight Agnes would be staying with Viola to care for the babies so their mama could get some rest. Bless that dear woman. What would the family do without her? Rob planned to sleep in Drew's room, if the new dad could sleep at all. But if he could sleep, he'd be snoring. Drew grabbed a blanket and headed downstairs to the parlor. To his surprise, Pop and Rob sat in their usual chairs, deep in conversation.

"Mind if I join you?"

Pop waved a hand to the chair next to Rob. "Not at all. Rob was just schooling me on how to be a better husband to your mama."

Drew hid his surprise as he nodded to his oldest brother, the only one of the five of them who could ever confront Pop about anything. "Don't let me interrupt." He sank down into the chair and tried to keep his expression neutral. This was exactly what he'd hoped for when he brought Mother back from Charleston. Maybe Rob could heal their parents' broken marriage. And maybe Drew could learn a lesson or two about women as well.

"I still say a woman's supposed to be like that gal in Proverbs 31." Pop picked up the pipe he hadn't smoked in nine years and fiddled with it, as he often did. "Your mother should have stayed here—but no, she left right in the middle of calving season, right when the success of this ranch depended on everybody doing their job. You gonna tell me that was all right?"

Rob shook his head. "You're not looking at this the right way, Pop. Remember when Jared and Emma were having their troubles before they got married? I remember what you told him. That women need to be listened to, not told how wrong they are." He exhaled a long breath. "I don't remember everything about the time when Mother left, but I do know she'd just lost our baby sister. I remember her wailing like her grief would never go away." His voice broke as he spoke, maybe thinking about his own newborns.

"Yeah, I remember." Pop stared down at his pipe. "Bad things happen in this life. You just gotta go on. She should have been grateful for you five boys—"

"Don't you hear yourself?" Rob scooched up to the edge of his chair and lifted his hands in a pleading gesture. "Mother was never slack in her love and care for us boys. She willingly gave up her nice life in Charleston and came out here to help you build this ranch, doing all the work Proverbs 31 wives do. Then, wasn't she around forty years old when she finally gave birth to the daughter she'd been praying for? And that sweet little baby died. Don't tell me you would shrug it off if Lavinia died. Or baby Jenny. Do you value Julia's son more than Emma's daughter? I know you don't because you made a fine cradle for each of them, not a finer one for little Joseph."

As Rob spoke, Pop stared off across the room. Gradually, his defensive expression softened. "What do you want me to do?"

"It doesn't matter what I want. Or what my brother wants." He reached over and bumped Drew's shoulder with his fist. "What does the Lord want you to do? Instead of schooling your wife of thirty-two years in what she should be doing—which, I might add, she's been doing since she arrived, nursing you and all—how about taking a lesson from Ephesians 5? 'Husbands, love your wives as Christ loved the church and gave Himself up for her.'"

"The verse before that says she's supposed to submit to me—"

"Wait a minute, Pop. What did the Lord say to Peter when he complained about John? He said don't worry about John, just follow Him. You and I need to follow what the Lord tells each of us to do, and that's to love our wives. He'll tell them what to do."

When had Rob gotten so wise? He should be a preacher. And Pop was listening to him. Maybe he could tell Drew how to fix things with Lila Rose. Or maybe the Lord could. Drew revised his idea of seeking approval from Pop instead of the Lord. It was God, who already approved of him in Jesus, that he should seek to please.

"Let's get to bed." Rob stood and stretched. "Gotta get up early. G'night, Pop. Drew."

After he left, Pop sat still for a bit, gazing off toward the wall.

"You all right, Pop?"

"Huh? Yes, I'm all right." He shook his head. "No, I'm not. Your brother's given me a lot to think about."

He seemed eager to talk, so Drew kept quiet.

"I saw a lot of death in the war. Came near to dying myself. After a while, a man gets numb to it so he can keep going, keep doing his duty. I suppose I figured your mother would do the same. I should have seen how she grieved for that baby girl."

That must have been why she understood Lavinia's grief over the stillborn kitten.

"So, what are you gonna do?"

Pop shrugged, then sat up, determination written on his face. "Same as what I did for you. I'll forgive her."

"Um. Good start." But had Pop missed the most important part of Rob's preaching?

"Then I'll tell her how grateful I am for taking care of me all this time."

Drew's heart lifted. "She sure did a good job."

"She did." Pop's eyes cleared, and he gave Drew a half grin. "You think she might like a new hat? Some fancy jewelry?"

"Like a peace offering?" Maybe a gift would help Drew win back Lila Rose, too.

"I'm just joshin' with you, son." Pop chuckled. "Your mother never cared much for presents." He stared off.

"I'll have to think on that Bible verse and figure out ways to love her like Jesus loves the church."

"Yessir. That's a good idea."

Lila Rose might not be his wife, but it couldn't hurt for Drew to do the same thing for her.

Chapter Twenty

The morning after the twins' births, Lila Rose took one look at Rebecca and knew she would never leave those babies and return to Charleston. As she held one of the twins, her face aglow with maternal pride and love, she made plans with Viola for how she would share the many tasks a new mother must accomplish.

Happy for her employer and knowing it was all for the best, Lila Rose still dreaded the coming separation. For the briefest moment yesterday, she'd thought she had a new family, one in which she could freely love and be loved in return. She even admitted to herself that Drew probably loved her in his own way. But his assumption that she was spoiled added to his dismissal of her fears and revealed his deeper attitude toward her—that she didn't deserve to be heard, didn't deserve to be valued just for herself. Father had never listened to her or Mama. While Drew wasn't a brutal man, his dismissiveness equated to the same thing, diminishing her value as a person.

She would wait a few days before telling Rebecca of

her decision so as not to interfere with her enjoyment of the babies. In the meantime, she would resume her training of the horses…and avoid Drew as much as possible.

As the summer wore on, that became easier. August weather was hot and dry in New Mexico Territory. Work at the ranch picked up, so Drew and Rob spent their days, morning to night, harvesting hay for the winter and building an addition onto the house for Agnes, who had proved indispensable to the family. Patrick couldn't have been happier, as he often told Lila Rose while he mucked out the stalls for the horses under her care.

"I appreciate your help, Mr. Ahern. You've been doing this all along, haven't you?"

"Yes, ma'am. Me and Ranse takin' turns. A little slip of a gal like you shouldn't have to do such dirty work." He winked. "And please, call me Patrick."

"You're very kind." Although his wink appeared more brotherly than flirtatious, she must put some distance between them. "I saw you talking with Dolores after church. How is she?" She knew very well how Dolores was, having seen her only the day before.

His grin broadened. "Pretty and sweet as ever. Don't know if her pa likes me so much, but he don't seem to hate me, neither." As often happened, his Irish brogue was displaced by a cowboy drawl.

"Well, you have my best wishes." She led Prince from the barn and out into the sunshine.

Drew stood just outside the door, a scowl on his face. Her pulse began to race…until she remembered they had no future together.

"You keeping my men from doing their work?"

She brushed past him, refusing to answer. Then it struck her. He was jealous. For some odd reason, she liked that idea. Not that she wanted to see him suffer, but it showed he still cared for her. If only that care led to his seeking to know her better, to understand her. But if they had no future together, why would she hope for that? She truly must cease these foolish musings.

He fell into step beside her. "How's old Fred doing?"

Against her better judgment, she smiled at his silly question. Apparently, he wanted to keep talking with her. "See for yourself." She pointed her riding crop toward the field where Fred and Corky grazed. "They've formed their own little herd with Prince and Duke, and Fred's the alpha."

Drew chuckled. "Yep. He's a good ol' boy."

She stopped and stared up at him. Mercy, if only he weren't so tall and handsome, she wouldn't have so much trouble controlling her feelings for him. "Don't you have some work to do?"

"Hey, Drew!" Rob called from back near the barn. "We've got work to do."

She laughed. "That answers that."

He huffed out a breath. "Lila Rose—"

"Drew!" Rob sounded a little cross this time.

"I'm comin'!" Sounding as cross as his brother, he spun around and loped away.

Lila Rose's heart sank. Against all that was good for her, she'd been enjoying their conversation. If she didn't get away from the ranch soon, she might surrender to these fond feelings for him and end up married, consigning herself to a lifetime of misery.

* * *

"I wanted to say this in front of the whole family." Pop had called a meeting and was now sitting in his usual chair in the parlor, with Mother seated beside him rather than in her rocker. He took her hand, and Drew's heart kicked up like a mule. This was what he'd been praying for.

"Rebecca," Pop said, "I want to thank you for taking such good care of me when I had my heart attack and after I broke my leg. Don't know what we would have done without you. What *I* would have done." He lifted her hand and kissed it. "I'm sorry I was so hard to put up with."

Mother smiled and gazed at Pop like he'd hung the moon. "And I want to thank you for providing for me all these years. I should have written…"

Drew wanted to jump up and shout *hallelujah*, but that would ruin the mood. If his parents were finally reconciled, everything he'd worked and prayed for had come to pass. Even if he lost all chances with Lila Rose, he would be thankful that the Lord had prompted him to go to Charleston and bring Mother home.

"And I should have written," Pop said. "Sending the money was the least I could do. Now, I won't say it didn't wound me deeply when you left. It wasn't just all the hard work you did. It was *you*, the woman I love, being here and standing shoulder to shoulder with me to start this ranch. Being here in the house at the end of a long, hard day. Listening to my grumblin' when things got hard. When you left, a big hole opened up in my life and my heart." A frown crossed his forehead, and he looked down. "But losing that baby girl—" His voice caught, and he cleared his throat. "I'm so, so sorry I acted like it didn't matter to me. It did. It broke my heart. But like a fool, I failed to see how broken your heart was. I was caught up in the cares of this ranch and felt I had to press on so I wouldn't lose it, too." Tears shone in his eyes. "Will you forgive me for not seeing you're more important to me than any ranch?"

She lifted their joined hands and pressed them against her cheek. "I will. Those were hard times for all of us. Now, thanks to Drew—" she sent him a loving smile "—here we are, together again."

Everyone turned their attention to him, and heat rose up his neck. He shrugged and stared down at his hands. "Just glad it all worked out."

"Now, what's goin' on with you and Lila Rose?" Pop turned his attention to Mother's companion.

Drew gulped down a protest. He couldn't embarrass her in front of the whole family.

Her face turned pale, and she started to stand.

"Hush, Ralph." Mother glared at him. "Sit down, my dear. We can tell them now." She let her gaze scan the room. "Our dear Lila Rose is returning to Charleston. She will manage our house there."

"We certainly will miss you." Viola appeared unsurprised by the announcement.

"Sure will," Rob said. "You've done some mighty fine work with those horses. You sure I can't hire you to stay on and train a string of ladies' horses for us to sell?"

"I—I…"

"No, hang it all." Drew jumped to his feet, unable to stop himself. "I want you to stay here and marry me."

The room went silent. Even the children stared between him and Lila Rose with mouths hanging open.

"Well." Mother stood. "Time for bed, everyone. Drew, you and Lila Rose may stay here for as long as you need to." She herded the others out like she was driving cattle. When Lila Rose started to follow her, she said, "No. You are to stay here and work this out." She kissed Lila Rose's cheek. "I think you can be trusted without a chaperone, but if it makes you feel better, Agnes will be sitting at the top of the stairs." After shooting a warning look at Drew, she followed the others.

In the silence that followed, he had no idea how to begin. What if he said the wrong thing *again* and ruined this last chance with Lila Rose?

"I'm so happy for your parents." She didn't look at him. "This is what you hoped for, and you did a good thing to bring your mother home. You must be so pleased."

"Yes, I am." Drew chewed his lip. Then inspiration struck. "I'm glad you agreed to come along, too. You're good for Mother. For all of us. You fit right into this family." No, that was the wrong thing to say. "What I mean to say is—"

Now she glared at him. "What do you mean to say, Drew Mattson?"

He swallowed hard. He'd said this before, but would she hear him this time? Really hear him? "I love you, Lila Rose Duval. I want to marry you. But I'm always putting my boot in my mouth. You have to tell me what you want to hear."

She rolled her eyes and released a long sigh. "That's

not how it works. If I tell you what to say, it won't be from your heart."

"Well, I've already told you what's in my heart. What more do you want?"

"Oh!" She stood and walked toward the door.

He jumped up and gently took her hand. "You're not being fair. I think you love me, but I can't guess what will make you happy." He tugged her toward the divan. "Please sit down and tell me."

To his relief, she did as he asked.

"All right, I will." She still refused to look at him. "I'm afraid to live out here. I still have nightmares about that rattlesnake. They must be all over the place." Now she looked up at him, tears shining in her eyes.

"I'm afraid because I don't know how to solve this problem. No one has ever looked out for me. Even my dear mother was too weak to shield me from my father or even take care of herself. Rebecca gave me a home and security, and for the first time in my life, I felt safe. Then, from the moment we arrived in New Mexico Territory, I had this underlying fear. After that snake encounter, it's no longer beneath the surface. I was chased by a cottonmouth when I was a girl, and my dog, Goldie, died saving me. Every time I walk out to the barn or work with the horses, I'm terrified I'll encounter another one and it will chase me and bite me or one of those wonderful horses."

She stared down at her hands. "And there you have it. You people live here in this wild country, and the dangers of these horrid creatures never seem to cross your minds. But I will never be able to live here without fear."

Lord, what can I say now? What had Rob done for

Viola? He'd given her a derringer and taught her how to shoot it. But Lila Rose seemed almost as afraid of guns as she was of snakes.

Wait. What had she said? A snake had chased her. Her dog had died saving her? Now she was scared another would chase her. Thank the Lord he hadn't laughed at her.

"I'm real sorry about your dog. That must have broke your heart." He paused a moment to let his words sink in. When she nodded her appreciation, he continued. "It's a good thing rattlesnakes aren't like cottonmouths. No, sirree. Rattlers are as scared of you as you are of them." He worked hard not to grin as he said it. "They'd just as soon avoid people and other animals and go about their business of finding smaller critters to eat."

She skewered him with a look. "Don't tell me that snake wasn't out to bite Duke."

"Well, sure he was. You rode up on him unexpected. If he'd seen that big horse coming his way, he would have skedaddled to avoid getting trampled. But a snake doesn't have good eyesight. He depends on smell and ground vibrations to warn him of danger, and he'll look for the best way to escape. If he can't, that's when he shakes those rattles as a warning. If that's not enough to scare you off, then he bites."

She continued to scowl at him, but little by little, her expression softened. "So you just need to see him—*it* first. That's why Suzette said never to step over a log without jostling it to chase out any snake that might be there." She shuddered. "The snake she chased out scared me witless, but at least it wasn't poisonous."

He dared to put his arm around her and gently

squeeze. To his relief, she let him. Even rested her shoulder against him.

"It's a good thing you're cautious. We all are. Pretty soon, it becomes a normal part of life, like looking for buggies and horses before you cross the street in town." He chuckled. "That's why we make sure Robbie and Lavinia have their dogs with them when they're roaming around the property. The dogs will sense any snakes and scare them off."

"So no one ever gets bitten?" She sat up and gave him a sly look, like she knew the answer.

"It does happen sometimes. And I won't lie. It can be awful bad for anybody who gets bit. But so far nobody around here has died from it—just been sick a long while."

She nodded and stared off across the room.

"Lila Rose, none of us can know the future, but I can make this promise to you. If you'll marry me, I'll take care of you. I'll listen to you. Nothing will be more important to me than you." He inhaled a deep breath. "Please say yes."

She was quiet for so long he feared another rejection. Then she clasped her hands in her lap and leaned her head against his chest. "Yes, I will marry you."

His heart jumped up into his throat, but before he could speak, she moved away, grabbed his hands and stared into his eyes.

"I will make this promise to you. If life gets hard and you forget what you just said or you can't always keep your promises, I will stick by you. I'll never leave." She giggled. "And I'll pester you until you do remember what you've promised."

"Oh, I see. If I'm not the perfect husband, you'll become a nag." What was he saying? Now he'd ruined everything.

"No, silly." She smacked his shoulder. "I'll—"

He tugged her into his arms and kissed her long and deep. To his relief, she didn't pull away but responded in kind. Mercy, she was a sweetheart. *His* sweetheart.

"If you'll pardon me intrusion—" Agnes appeared in the doorway. "This here is my sleepin' quarters until me new quarters is done, and I'm a bit weary. If you want breakfast bright and early, best be off, the both of ye." She waved a hand toward the stairs. "G'night to ye."

Lila Rose's cheeks turned bright pink, and from the heat he felt in his own face, Drew figured he was blushing, too.

"Yes, ma'am." He stood and pulled Lila Rose up into his arms, giving her another kiss that lasted about two seconds before Agnes interrupted again.

"Ahem!" She brushed past them and pulled her cot and bedding from behind the divan, refusing his help. "Off with ya now."

They made it to the top of the stairs before Drew felt the need for another kiss. Lila Rose didn't resist. At last, she broke away.

"See you in the morning."

He grinned. "And every day after that."

"I knew it!" Suzette slapped her hat against her leg and waved away the pesky flies buzzing around the barnyard. "I took one look at you, Lila Rose, and knew you were the right one for our Drew. When's the wedding?"

The dust hadn't settled from the return of the cowboys before Suzette and Will demanded an accounting from Lila Rose and Drew.

"We were just waiting for you to arrive home so you could be my bridesmaid." Lila Rose had sought Rebecca's and Viola's advice on whom to choose, and they'd all decided on Suzette. The other Mattson wives would be busy with their babies, and the girls from the Monday class would understand her choice of a sister-to-be standing up with her.

"Will, you kept my secret, so will you be my best man?" Drew put his arm around Lila Rose's shoulder and tugged her close. "I—*we* couldn't have done it without you."

"I'd be honored, brother." Will was as dusty and sweaty as his wife, but neither of them seemed to notice. After four months in the mountains with the herd, they seemed more in love than ever.

"Where are the rest of the cattle?" Lila Rose looked toward the front gate, where two cowboys drove the last few well-fed steers under the Double Bar M archway.

"We don't bring them all back here," Will said. "We load 'em on the trains in Riverton and ship 'em to Denver. These are for our winter eatin'."

"Goodness, I have so much to learn."

"And we want to hear all about your courting." Suzette grasped Lila Rose's hand, then dropped it. "Oh, sorry. I should wash up first."

Retaking Suzette's hand, Lila Rose laughed. "Never mind. I work with horses, so I'm used to a little dust." She wouldn't mention the smell of hard work emanating from both Will and Suzette. Viola had warned her to expect it.

"And how about Mother and Pop?" Will's brow furrowed. "We've been praying all summer they would reconcile. Is Mother still here?"

Drew laughed. "You'll be happy to hear that your prayers were answered."

Will whooped, and Suzette clapped her hands.

"Suzette, I know you'll want to see those new babies. Want to come now?" Lila Rose never tired of showing off the infants, her officially soon-to-be niece and nephew—though in her heart, they already were.

"Mercy, no." Suzette shook her head, and dust floated into the air. "I'll head over to our cottage and clean up first."

That afternoon, Viola, Rebecca and Agnes laid out a lavish supper on the front lawn with all their cooking skills on display. Rob and Drew had dug a pit for roasting a side of beef and a small hog. Having churned the butter that morning, Lila Rose made the biscuits everyone liked and added them to the meal. While she never expected to cook as well as the other ladies, she loved to contribute what she could.

All the ranch hands, including those who had been on the summer drive, joined the family for a grand feast and for catching up with all the news. Lila Rose wasn't certain, but she thought Suzette and Will might be adding to the family in another four or five months. Of course, she wouldn't ask them, but it did give her hope that she and Drew would also add another baby to the family in the future.

One thing was sure. Watching Drew with all his

nieces and nephews, she knew she never had to worry that he wouldn't care for his own children with love and tenderness. She could truly put the past and her bad memories of her childhood behind her and move on to a wonderful future beside the man she loved.

Epilogue

"I've never seen a prettier bride." Rebecca adjusted Lila Rose's veil and stood back to survey her work. "There. I think you're ready." She kissed Lila Rose's cheek.

"I'm so grateful Viola loaned me her gown." Lila Rose ran a hand down the satin skirt. "I don't know what I'd have worn otherwise."

"I can see this gown will be worn in many future Mattson weddings," Rebecca said. "It fits you very nicely, except for the length. I'm glad we could raise the hem a little."

"Wouldn't want you to trip on your way to the altar." Suzette, always ready with a quip, primped a bit in the mirror at the end of the cloakroom. Her sprigged muslin gown had been let out in the waist, confirming Lila Rose's suspicions.

The organ music began, and her heart jumped. "Oh, I'm so happy, Rebecca."

"In another hour, you will have to call me Mother."

Tears sprang to her eyes. "You've been a mother to me already."

Rebecca's eyes shone. "And you have been the daughter I've always longed for." She looked at Suzette. "As are you, my dear."

"You gals ready to go?" Mr. Mattson—Pop—stuck his head in the door. "Come along now. Don't keep that young man waiting."

Rebecca preceded them down the aisle and sat in the front row. Suzette followed. Then Lila Rose looped her arm through Pop's and walked toward her future with her beloved Drew.

March 1889

The train chugged into the Riverton station, and Lila Rose peered out the window. Yes. There they were. She and Drew disembarked and hugged Will and Suzette.

"Did you get the house sold?" Will asked.

"Sure did, and we got more than expected for it," Drew said.

"Mother will be pleased to know the pastor of her church bought it and plans to keep Ingrid and Eric employed as housekeeper and groundskeeper." Lila Rose glanced at Suzette's small waist, and her heart sank. "Oh, my dear—"

"What?" Suzette followed her gaze and looked down. "Oh, no. Don't worry. Little Will is home, sucking his thumb and giving Mother a lapful of joy."

"That's a relief." Lila Rose had her own secret, but she would wait until she spoke to Drew first before sharing with the others. She gazed up at her dear husband. "Let's go home."

The house had been crowded, but Rob had promised

they would sort it out while the newlyweds were on their honeymoon to Charleston. As the surrey neared the ranch, she studied the landscape.

"Oh, Drew, look!" She pointed to the new building not far from the cottage, another cozy-looking little house. "Will, is that for us?"

"Yep." Will chuckled. "We had to work pretty hard over the winter to get it done, but Rob was anxious to get you out of the house, like he was with us."

Suzette giggled. "Now they have a nursery for the babies, and Robbie and Lavinia can still have their own rooms."

"Hey, brother, stop here." Drew jumped down and helped Lila Rose to the ground. He led her to their new house and opened the door, then swept her up in his arms. "Welcome home, Mrs. Andrew Mattson." He set her down and tugged her close.

"Welcome home, Mr. Andrew Mattson."

As he kissed her in his delightful way, she had a vague curiosity about what the rest of the cottage looked like.

But enjoying his kisses as she was, she decided the tour could wait.

* * * * *

Dear Reader,

Thank you for choosing to read Finding Her Frontier Home. This story is set on a fictional ranch beside the Rio Grande near the fictional town of Riverton, New Mexico Territory.

This book is a sequel to my 2022 Love Inspired Historical novel, Finding Her Frontier Family. Both stories began with my 2015 LIH novella, Yuletide Reunion, which was published in the anthology A Western Christmas. In the novella, I created a family of brothers who own and work on the fictional Double Bar M ranch. Like any author who falls in love with her characters, I wanted to give each brother his own love story. This one is Andrew's turn.

Why do I write stories about the Old West? I grew up watching Westerns on black-and-white television: Wagon Train, Rawhide, Maverick, and my favorite, Gunsmoke. Then there were those thrilling John Wayne Westerns my dad took me to see. Is it any wonder I fell in love with cowboys and the Western way of life? Although my life didn't lead me to live on a ranch, my imagination takes me there with every book I write. I'm so glad my readers enjoy my stories.

I love to hear from my readers, so if you enjoyed Finding Her Frontier Home, please write and let me know. Please also visit my website, louisemgougeau-

thor.blogspot.com, *find me on* Facebook at facebook.
com/LouiseMGougeAuthor, or follow me on BookBub
at bookbub.com/profile/louise-m-gouge.

God bless you.
Louise M. Gouge

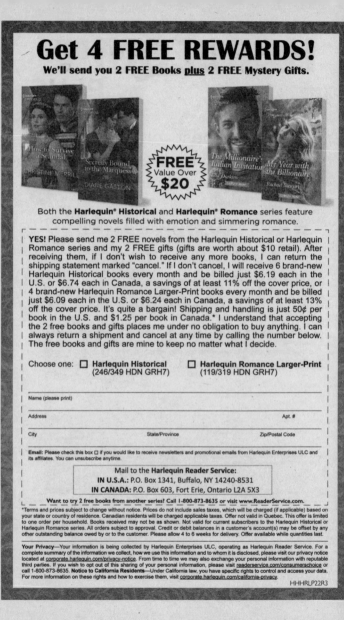

HARLEQUIN
PLUS

Try the best multimedia subscription service for romance readers like you!

Read, Watch and Play.

Experience the easiest way to get the romance content you crave.

Start your **FREE TRIAL** at
www.harlequinplus.com/freetrial.